The *Riverview Murders*

Also by Michael Raleigh

Death in Uptown
A Body in Belmont Harbor
The Maxwell Street Blues
Killer on Argyle Street

The *Riverview* *Murders*

A PAUL WHELAN MYSTERY

Michael Raleigh

St. Martin's Press
New York

Library of Congress Cataloging-in-Publication Data

Raleigh, Michael.
    The Riverview murders / Michael Raleigh.—1st ed.
       p.   cm.
    ISBN 0-312-15641-3
    1. Whelan, Paul (Fictitious character)—Fiction. 2. Private investigators—Illinois—Chicago—Fiction. 3. Chicago (Ill.)—Fiction.   I. Title
PS3568.A4316R58   1997
813'.54—dc21   97-7586
                                                       CIP

First Edition: July 1997

10 9 8 7 6 5 4 3 2 1

*To my adopted clan, the Powells,
and Empress Dorothy.*

The *Riverview*
Murders

Prologue

Chicago, 1946

AT the corner of Clybourn and Western, the sailor shook a smoke out of his pack as he waited for his light to change. Just as it went from red to green, a streetcar pulled in behind him and a rush of people came out both doors, more people than you'd ever imagine a streetcar could hold, a hundred people chest-to-chest on a crowded streetcar on the hottest night of the young summer, and they came out laughing and talking as though it had been no trouble at all. They were going to Riverview, across Western Avenue and into dreamland.

The sailor stepped into the street and glanced behind him at the press of people, men in loose sport shirts and girls in summer dresses, sleeveless dresses, backless dresses. He thought he saw one give him the eye and he wondered if he should drop back for a moment and start up a conversation. Then he strode off ahead of the pack. There would be time enough for that later, after he was finished with his business. It occurred to him that he already had enough women on his hands to satisfy most guys. No, you never had enough. But if things went well tonight, he'd have a roll in his pocket that would choke a horse, and a guy in uniform with money was going to be a tough combination.

Ahead of him he could see that the park was already jammed. Even if you couldn't see the crowd, you could hear them, and the rides, and people hawking things. You could even smell Riverview Park from a block away. When he was a boy, they'd stand around outside their houses and talk about what rides they'd go on if they had the money, and if the wind came in from the west, they could smell Riverview, the smoke and the food smells. Off toward the north end he could see a roller coaster straining up a hill, he could hear the slow clanking sound the train made just before it started down in a rush of screaming. He watched the parachute lift take a group of people to the pinnacle of the ride, then drop them as though punctured. They went into free fall for a few feet, screaming, till the chute opened artificially and they fluttered to the ground.

And off to one side, looming over the park like an alien life-form, he could make out Aladdin's Castle. He could see the huge hollow-eyed face of Aladdin staring from the facade of the fun house. No matter where you went in the great sprawling park, you could still see Aladdin.

If you were supposed to meet somebody at Aladdin's Castle, he could never say he couldn't find the place.

The sailor looked down the row of turnstiles along the white entrance gates and saw a man he planned to avoid tonight. He paid his dime and pushed his way through the white gates and almost ran into a pair of young women. They laughed and one gave him a quick look. When he met her eyes, she smiled. He took a slow puff on his cigarette and smiled back, then caught himself.

First things first.

He knew he was early, so he took his time, sauntering slowly around the whole long, crowded Midway, past the rides, the great Ferris wheel, the fantastic carousel with its carved wooden horses and angels, past the Bobs, the Tilt-o-Whirl, past the freak show and the beer garden. In the light of the fast-setting sun, you could make out the cloud of cigarette and cigar smoke hovering over the drinkers at their crowded tables. As darkness set in and the park's bright lights took over, the smoke hung there like a low blue cloud ceiling, to be dispersed only when the park shut down and the drinkers went home.

Eventually he made it to Aladdin's Castle. He could hear the screams and giggles from the fun-seekers inside, tumbling in the great moving barrel, blasted by jets of air that tugged and billowed at the girls' skirts. He checked his watch and saw that he was almost exactly on time. No matter: the man he was going to meet would make him wait, as he made everybody wait. If you knew that going in, it was less irritating. The sailor shrugged and drew his smokes out of the white shirt. There were only four cigarettes left in the pack: another dead pack of Luckies. Here was evidence that all the world's troubles brought good to someone: The cigarette guys had to be making a mint off all the guys like him who'd picked

2

up the habit in the war. In the Pacific he'd seen hundreds of guys start smoking. People said that war brought no good to anyone, but you couldn't prove it to him.

When he was just reaching the last acrid half inch of his smoke, the other man arrived. The sailor took a couple of steps back so that the wall of the building hid him. The newcomer stood in front of the ticket booth to the fun house and peered up and down the Midway. He was a study in casual fashion: light gray summer slacks and a loose-fitting light green shirt that looked like silk. The sailor would have bet the rent that the shirt was silk. Oxblood shoes—you could see your face in the shine of his shoes. Slicked-back brown hair, newly cut, cut by a pro, and a fresh shave, a straight-razor shave. He didn't even shave himself, this guy.

Ten feet away and you could already smell him: He smelled like money.

As far back as the sailor could remember, he'd associated this man with money, always money. Even when they were kids, he'd always seemed to have more money than anybody else. Never quite enough, though. Always out there dancing on the edge, always scrambling around for a buck. Spent it fast as it came in. But he knew how to spend. The sailor sighed and stepped out from his vantage point. "Chick," he said.

The other man nodded and forced a slight smile. "I thought maybe you weren't coming."

"Nah, you wish. There was never any chance of me not coming." The sailor looked at him with a half smile.

The well-dressed man snorted and extended a hand. "Long time, Ray. You look good. Thought maybe you'd find yourself one of them broads in the kimonos and stay over there."

"Not a chance."

"Well, you look good, anyway."

The sailor shrugged and shook hands. "I'm getting by. Not like you, though. You look like money, Chick. Like always."

"It's just clothes, Ray. I'm a businessman. Guy wants to make money, he's got to look sharp."

The sailor laughed. "Chick, you know what we used to say about you? We used to say you probably put on a suit coat just to take a piss."

The other man took out a small cigarette case from his slacks and pulled out a smoke.

"Want one?" He offered the case to the sailor, who just shook his head.

"No. I want to get down to business. Let's just take care of what we came for, all right?"

"Okay." Chick stepped aside to allow a couple to enter Aladdin's Castle. When he spoke again, he let his voice drop. "You said you wanted to talk about money."

"Yeah."

"You and everybody else. You want to put something on a horse or what? Give you a good horse, Ray."

The other man stared and said nothing.

"What? Not the nags, that's not your style, huh? Baseball?"

"I didn't come here to talk about that. I play cards; I don't bet. I want some money, Chick."

"Can't do yourself any good yet, huh? Well, you'll find something pretty quick. . . ."

"I want my piece of that money."

Chick squinted and made a little shrug.

"Don't play dumb. You know what money. The Kraut."

Chick looked stunned.

"You got it all, Chick. Far as I can tell, nobody ever saw a nickel of that except Chick Landis. You said you'd give me my share. Now I need money and I figure I got some coming."

Chick shook his head. "The Kraut? That's a thousand years ago, Ray. Jesus, that's long gone. It wasn't what we thought. Wasn't that much there."

"You told me some of it would be mine. I never saw a nickel."

"Wasn't nothing to see, I'm tellin' you."

The sailor put his hands on his hips and stared at the other man. He made a sudden movement forward and Chick moved quickly away.

"Take it easy, Ray."

"*Eight grand,* they said it was. That was a lot of money. Shit, it still is. I want my dough, Chick, I want some of that eight grand. I never said nothing about that to nobody, not the cops, not nobody. . . ."

"I know, I know, you're a stand-up guy, Ray. But . . . eight grand? Where'd you hear eight grand?" He grinned and shook his head.

"I don't know how much, but I know it was enough to send *you* running for cover. There's people that would be real happy to know what happened that night. All I want from you is what's mine. That's all I want. I don't want to give you no trouble, but that's what you'll get, Chick, and plenty. Give me my money, Chick. You got money—you *always* got money. I want mine."

"Hold your horses." Chick ran his hand through the slick hair and made an exasperated shake of his head. "All right. I still don't know where you got eight grand, I don't know where that comes from, eight grand, for Chrissakes. This was . . . it was small-time, Ray. But . . . you'll get your dough, I'm good for it."

"How much?"

"A grand." Chick held up his hand. "Come on, Ray. How much would your share be? And there wasn't no eight grand. More like five."

The sailor sighed. "When?"

"Take me a couple days to get it together. I know, I know, you're short. You're down on your luck; you need a little dough. . . ."

"What? I *need* some money? You kidding me? It's *my money.*" A passing man in a green Hawaiian shirt shot them a surprised glance over his shoulder, then looked away quickly.

"I'll have it in a couple days." Unconsciously, he took a half step back.

The soldier said nothing for a moment. He took out his cigarette pack and lit one. Then he took a long slow drag, watching the other man. "What gives, Chick? Why a couple days?"

"Hey, I'm good for it. I got expenses, Ray. I got a saloon and a book, I got suppliers and customers. I take money in, babe, but believe me, I pay money out. Two days and you can have it all. Come on, Ray, how much can you spend in one night?" He brought out a flat wad of new-looking bills in a silver money clip. "I got two hundred on me and you can have it. I'll take the goddam streetcar home and you can go on a toot. Find a broad, have some drinks, live it up. I'll get you the rest Saturday. C'mon Ray, even you can't spend two bills in one night."

"You better have it."

"Oh, I'll have it, kid. And you'll go through it in a month. Then maybe you'll come back and we'll talk business. I'll show you how to make money. I know about money, Ray. You get a couple nickels in your pocket, you're a big shot. You go places, you duke a little here, a little there, throw money at the waiters and the broadies, and then it's all gone. And then you need more. This money you're so hot to get hold of, Ray, it'll be gone like that." He snapped his fingers. "Then you'll be just another working stiff. Me, I'm gonna have a lotta money, and if I play my cards right, it's never gonna run out."

"Just come across with what you owe me."

"Have it your way, Ray. But here, have a little fun." He held out the money to the sailor, but the other man refused to take it.

"I don't want yours, I want mine. You get it, Chick."

"Hey, I'm good for that and a lot more besides. Saturday. You come see me Saturday, at my joint. I'll take care of you. We'll be square, Ray."

The sailor gazed at him calmly, then nodded. "Okay, Saturday it is. I'll be there at noon. And you better have it, Chick. You don't, I'll make you come up with it, right there."

"Yeah, tough guy. Don't worry, I'll have it." He watched the sailor spin round on his heel and walk away. The man called Chick finished his cigarette and tossed the butt away with a carefree movement, pausing to watch it clear a bench and land in the grass.

He took a final look behind him at the departing sailor, then walked away in the other direction, turning at the far corner of Aladdin's Castle.

A few yards away, the sailor stopped and lit another smoke, cupping his hands around the match. He shot a sidelong glance in the direction the other man had gone, shook out the match and let it drop. For a moment, he stood with one hand in his trouser pocket and puffed at his smoke. Then he turned suddenly and retraced his steps, moving faster now.

I know you, Chick, he thought. I knew you'd pull something, I knew you wouldn't have the money. I just wanted to see what kinda story you'd come up with. And, yeah, I'm a tough guy.

At the far corner of Aladdin's Castle, the sailor looked behind him once, then turned in the direction the other man had gone.

"WHATTYA got?" the boy asked.

The older boy hitched up his shirt and revealed the top of a half-pint. Delicately, he lifted up the bottle so that its clear liquid contents showed, as well as the top part of a yellow label.

"Gin!" the first boy said, and his companion grinned, nodding. "Where'd you get gin?"

"My brother. Come on."

"Where? The can?"

"Nah. We can go back here." He nodded in the direction of Aladdin's Castle.

6

"Somebody might see."

"Chickenshit. Cluck-cluck-cluck."

"I'm game if you are."

"Come on, then." The older boy tucked his shirttail around the precious bottle and sauntered toward the rear of Aladdin's Castle. In the faint light, the back of the building was in almost total darkness. The boy almost fell over the body before he saw it. He stopped just short, weaving to reestablish his balance and staring openmouthed at it.

"God Almighty," he muttered, and the other boy came up and looked over his shoulder.

"What is it? Oh. See if . . ." He never bothered to finish the sentence, for questions were unnecessary.

The dead man looked up at them, through them, his mouth agape as were theirs. From the stiff angle of his shoulders, he had attempted to regain his feet, pushing back against the wall before giving in to the wounds in his chest. There appeared to be several, and the white shirt was a mass of clotted blood. His sailor cap hung to the back of his head, pinned between his scalp and the back wall of Aladdin's Castle.

The boys stared without speaking for several seconds and then the smaller boy cupped his hand over his mouth and began running for the rest room.

One

AT the farthest end of the breakwater, where it hooked back toward the beach and the city beyond, two men stood over a third. The third man sat with his back against the thick steel cable and stared sightlessly out over the lake. The larger of the two men wore a thin red windbreaker that just managed to cover the hard bulge around his middle. He went down on one knee and stared into the dead eyes, examined the wound in the chest, no longer bleeding, reached around and found the wallet, fished it out and opened it one-handed.

"Michael Minogue," he said tonelessly. "Name from the old country."

The man behind him shrugged, squinted up into the sun and absently patted his hair back into place as the wind riffled through it. Then he looked down to see his partner touch the corpse's cheek. He'd seen the big man make the odd, tentative gesture before and had heard the explanation twice: "Somebody should always touch a dead man," the big one would say. "Somebody should always touch a dead man."

He peered out over the lake where a big sailboat seemed to be ducking into the stiff north wind, and ran his hand through his hair again. When he looked back, the big man was squinting up at him.

"You through doin' your hair?"

"I wasn't doing my hair. I was waiting for you to get done fucking around. Anything in the wallet?"

The big man smiled to himself and turned his attention back to the corpse. "Yeah. Couple bucks, Social Security card, old lottery tickets. I've seen half a dozen stiffs with lottery tickets on 'em, like they were afraid to let go, maybe there was a mistake and their number's really gonna be good after all." He looked at the dead man again. "Wearin' his watch." He lifted up the dead man's arm and held the watch up for the younger man.

"Ring, too." The big man got to his feet and then looked down at the dead man. "I seen this guy before."

"Where?"

"A saloon. Old guy in a saloon."

A squad car rolled onto the beach and joined the two already waiting. A few feet ahead of the squad cars, almost touching the concrete of the breakwater, sat a gleaming gray Caprice. The big man looked over and saw a white-shirted officer climb out of the car.

"There's the Honorable Michael Shea."

The younger man shrugged, looked at the corpse and then surveyed the end of the breakwater. "Fucking nasty place to die."

His partner looked at him with something like amusement. "No. He liked it. That's his shit over there, he was fishing. This was probably his favorite place."

The big man lit a thin dark cigar and puffed, then shook his head.

He blew smoke out over the lake and didn't look back till the white-uniformed officer was a few feet away. Then he flicked the cigar into the greenish water and hitched his pants up over his stomach.

"Hello, Al." The sergeant smiled and then nodded first at the big man and then at the younger man.

The big one returned the nod. "So how was Florida?"

"Oh, it was fine, Albert. You ought to go down there some time, spend a couple weeks in the Florida Keys. Do you a world of good, although I don't know if the Keys are ready for Albert Bauman."

"They got taverns and dancing girls?"

"Taverns, they got. About a thousand of 'em. And they got girls, all kindsa girls. Don't know if they'd dance for you, though, Al."

Bauman smiled, then turned and gestured with his thumb in the direction of the dead man. "There he is."

The sergeant frowned. "Just an old guy out fishing, huh?"

A younger officer had come up behind the sergeant. "What we got here, Mike?"

"Albert's gonna tell us."

Bauman looked for a moment at the young officer as though daring him to interrupt. Then he turned and looked at the body.

"Gunshot. Just one."

"Through the heart?"

"Nah. Missed the heart, didn't know what the fuck he was doing. Poor fucker died of shock, or loss of blood, one or the other."

"Robbery?" the sergeant asked.

"Uh-uh. Still has money in the wallet, watch, ring. Nothing gone that I can see."

"So what are you thinking?"

"I'm thinking somebody came up to this old guy while he was fishing and killed him. Somebody he knew."

"Why?"

Bauman turned to face his young partner.

"Why somebody he knew?"

The big man pointed to the fishing gear, the white plastic bucket and poles, the small cooler. "His stuff is all over there. He got up and came all the way over here. Least that's what I think."

"So?"

"So he saw this guy coming. You see a stranger coming, you think he might be trouble, you look straight ahead and hope you're wrong. You pretend you're invisible. You see somebody you know, somebody you *know* means trouble for you, you start moving. Maybe I'm wrong, but I think this guy saw trouble comin' and tried to move out of the way. I don't know if he was gonna jump into the water or what. It's not that deep here. But the guy caught him and it was lights-out." Bauman looked around at the concrete surface of the breakwater, then bent over the corpse again and lifted the man's jacket away, using two fingers. He examined the man's fingers and nails, his wrists. "No struggle. Happened fast, or the other guy was just quicker."

"So what do you make, Albert?"

"Fuck if I know. Somebody wanted to waste this guy and he got it done. Who knows why. But I'd bet good money on one thing: I don't think it was, like, coincidence that he caught him out here at the end of the break-water with a fishing pole in his hand. What I think is, we got an organized-type guy here."

He looked again at the dead man and shrugged. "He don't look like somebody you'd think would have enemies."

"Ah, you never know, Al," the sergeant said, taking out a cigarette. "The whole world's nuts."

PAUL Whelan circled the block twice for a parking spot and wound up two blocks away from his destination. Pulling up the collar of his jacket against the wind, he told himself he was having a bad day and began walking south on Broadway.

The dark-haired young woman at the desk looked up and raised her eyebrows in interest as Whelan pushed his way through the door; then she broke into a grin.

"The difficult Mr. Whelan," she said in her musical voice.

"Hello, Pilar. Did anyone ever tell you that you always sound as if you're about to break into song?"

"No. Most people hear my business voice and think I'm a robot. Or they think I've got an attitude. A man yesterday accused me of being a recording."

"You don't sound like any recording I've ever heard. And what's this 'difficult Mr. Whelan' business? Is that what *he* calls me?" Whelan heard the note of surprise in his voice and smiled in an attempt to convince Pilar that he didn't care what her boss called him.

"Sometimes. I believe this was about a bill."

"Lawyers always think other people's bills are unreasonable," Whelan said.

She looked down at her desk blotter and a dimple appeared in one cheek. "No comment," she said. Then she flashed her brown eyes at him and indicated the door behind her with a nod. "He's expecting you."

"Of course. Would I just invite myself over?"

"Sure. You always have before," she said, and started slitting open an envelope with a long silver instrument that looked like a high-class scalpel.

Whelan paused to admire the new door: it was dark, heavy, respectable, and, unlike its predecessor, solid wood. The old door had been thin plywood, hollow between the layers, and an angry man whose wife had come to this office for legal services had put his fist through it. Whelan knocked once and then turned the knob without waiting for permission.

David Hill sat back in the large leather chair like a man fighting gravitational force. He was staring at his ceiling, head pressed back against the chair and one arm dangling over the side. In the dangling hand, he held a piece of paper. Gradually, his gaze came down to earth and his eyes met Whelan's.

"Not exactly obsessed with punctuality, are you, Whelan." It wasn't a question and Whelan didn't bother to answer it. He closed the door behind him and found his way to the visitor's chair.

"Nice door."

"The other fellow was paying for it, so I went first-class."

"You rang, Excellency?"

"Go easy on the smart-ass stuff, Whelan, I'm having a difficult enough day."

"A lawyer having a bad day? This is tragic."

David Hill looked at him for a moment and shook his head. His glasses were on the fancy desk pad, and without them, Hill's face took on an unfinished, somehow unprotected look.

"Sit down. I didn't call you to have you insult me. I have business to send your way. I need an investigator."

"You look like you need medication." Whelan leaned back and fished around inside his jacket for his cigarettes.

Hill ignored the comment and tossed his own tortoiseshell cigarette case and matching lighter on the desk. Whelan gave up the search for his own cigarettes and lit up one of Hill's.

"So what's the situation?"

"One that's right up your alley. I have a client I can't do anything for—an elderly woman trying to find a missing relative. Don't smirk, Whelan. This is different from the previous . . ." Hill let his voice trail off.

"I sure hope so," Whelan said, and allowed himself a small smile as the lawyer momentarily broke off eye contact.

"This one is courtesy of Mr. G. Kenneth Laflin."

"So what can you tell me?"

"The client's name is O'Mara. Margaret O'Mara. She's looking for a brother who may or may not be deceased. I really think we're talking about a street person. She had a hard time bringing herself to talk about the possibility that he's dead, but if he is, I think she is the last remaining member of the family."

"So this is definitely not about money."

Hill waved one hand in the air. "All that she really wants is for some-body to look for her brother."

"So I'm supposed to check this out? Why can't we just go through the Social Security people and the VA and—"

Hill shook his head. "You really do think I'm just jerking your chain. He disappeared, Whelan. He didn't just die. He disappeared, and none of the normal channels are going to help anyone find him."

Whelan ground the cigarette out into Hill's stylish ashtray. "Sorry. This sounds pretty pointless. A street person who disappeared—how long ago?"

"Long," Hill said. "I didn't go into much detail with her." David Hill idly picked up a letter and squinted at it.

Whelan studied the attorney for a moment, decided it wasn't likely that David Hill ever talked to a client without going into detail, and then plunged in anyway. "Okay, a street guy who disappeared a long time ago and is prob-ably buried as John Doe in some public cemetery. Maybe in someplace like Seattle or Galveston. What am I supposed to do with that?"

Hill put down the letter and smiled. "Use your fabled resourcefulness, Whelan. And make some money. You're a businessman, Whelan, albeit not a very sophisticated one. This is a customer for you. Do you want to pursue the case, or should I direct the woman to another operative?"

"You don't have any other 'operative,' and quit talking like a lawyer."

David Hill gave him an amused look. "It's what I went to school for, Whelan. Why can't I use it?"

"Put that way, fair enough. So this lady is going to contact me?"

"You should be getting a call from her. She's a nice old lady, Whelan. I honestly didn't know what else to do for her. I thought if you couldn't help her, you might know somebody who can. A cop, maybe."

"Well, it's not as though I'm real busy. But don't make a habit out of this, all right?"

Hill grinned. "Next one will be the blonde with the Swiss bank ac-count."

"Fair enough."

WHELAN drove back home and parked in front of his house, then ran in to check the mail. If there had been any mail this early—two hours early—he would have been astounded, but he was compelled to check it all the same, and then irritated with himself for his irrational behavior.

She wasn't at his house and there wouldn't be anything in the mail from her when it finally came. There had been no reason whatsoever to run home. But he had no doubt he'd do it again tomorrow. There wouldn't be a card from Sandra tomorrow, either.

He told himself he was handling this badly. It was just a vacation, after all, a ten-day trip to England with her girlfriends from college, planned more than a year in advance—before they'd started going out, she had said. It meant nothing and she would soon be home. That was one way of looking at it; the other was that Sandra McAuliffe, his woman, his first healthy relationship in many years, was off trotting around in London with three other women in their early forties, two of whom were now divorced.

He'd met the three women and he already knew the itinerary: they were going to see Shakespeare, they were going to the best restaurants, they were going to museums, they were going to see castles and ruined abbeys, to shop where the beautiful people shopped, and they might even go out dancing. It was all harmless, and he hated the thought of it, all ten days of it, and harbored the irrational hope that she'd get tired of it all and come home early. She wasn't due for another week.

Several times in the past two days, he'd found himself rehashing their conversations and reinterpreting Sandra's words, her moods. For perhaps a week before she left, she had been vaguely distant, and more than once he'd realized she wasn't listening when he was speaking. He'd ascribed it all to her preoccupation with the trip, but the cold inner voice that delighted in the pronouncement of final sentences and the presentation of bad news told him it had nothing to do with the trip. And the truth of the matter was that Whelan believed the voice.

Two

ON the second floor, just outside his offices—Paul Whelan Investigative Services—Whelan paused and listened at the door of his only neighbor on the floor. A light was on inside A-OK Novelties and he could hear Mr. Nowicki, ostensibly the proprietor, yelling profanities into the phone. Whelan waved at Nowicki's door, mouthed "Good morning," and went into his office.

He popped the lid on his coffee and scanned the first few pages of the *Sun-Times* for good news. There wasn't any. Two people had died in fires, one of them a typical Uptown fire less than three blocks from his office. The first cold snap of the year could be counted on to bring death to a neighborhood like Uptown. Come December and January, Uptown would be among the leaders in two separate categories: deaths by fire and deaths by exposure. When "the Hawk" showed up and brought a windchill that could scour flesh, they found the bodies in doorways every week. And when the big cold air masses came in and wrapped themselves over the town to stay, the street folk froze at the rate of one a day. Sometimes more.

But the weather was only the most obvious enemy of the old ones on the street. A few days earlier, the papers had carried the story of an old man found murdered out on the breakwater at Montrose Beach. It was in all ways a senseless killing, apparently a random act of violence. The man had been shot to death but not robbed. There were no witnesses. All Whelan could remember about the killing was that the man had been in his sixties and a resident at the Empire, a large home for the elderly on Wilson, in the heart of Uptown. Whelan knew the building well: a pinkish monster that sprawled across most of a city block, home to several hundred people, all of them united by age and indigence.

Whelan had consoled himself with the knowledge that, if nothing else, the case would be pushed, officially or otherwise, by a certain ruddy-faced Violent Crimes detective named Bauman. There were dozens of other detective teams that might get the call on this, but if a homicide involved a homeless person or, as in this case, an old street type, Bauman, the truly difficult, the tireless, the obsessive, the very tenacious Albert Bauman, would make it his business.

He looked up at a diffident knock at his door.

"Come in. It's open."

The woman who pushed open his door was in her sixties, perhaps older. She was short, chubby, silver-haired, and disoriented, and the goggle-eyed look she gave Whelan's office said this wasn't quite what she'd expected. One of the lenses in her glasses was measurably thicker than the other, giving her face the faint suggestion of lopsidedness. Eventually, her gray-eyed gaze found its way to Whelan. She stopped just inside the doorway and seemed to be on the verge of panic. People frequently wandered into the run-down little building, some of them looking for businesses or offices long gone and others just operating on a different sort of compass.

"Morning. Can I help you with something?"

"Hello, sir. Are you Mr."—here she consulted a tan envelope and read from it—"Whelan? Are you Mr. Whelan?"

"Uh, yes, ma'am. Come on in and sit down." When the woman just stared in confusion, he came around his desk and made as if to hold the guest chair for her. She folded her free hand atop the one clutching her little black purse and stepped cautiously toward the chair. With a quick glance at Whelan, she allowed herself to drop onto it, then sat looking straight ahead.

Whelan caught himself about to sit at the corner of the desk and realized this would be too close to physical contact for this timid woman. He went back around the desk and took his seat. The woman met his eyes for a moment, seemed to regret the decision instantly, and found an interesting spot on the wall just above Whelan's head.

"You're Mrs. O'Mara."

She seemed to relax at this indication that she'd been expected. "You knew I was coming, then."

"Mr. Hill told me."

She nodded. "He's such a *nice* young man." She spoke with a note of wonder in her voice, and Whelan knew that this was one old Irish lady who'd just met her first and only black attorney.

"Can I get you a glass of water?" He indicated his beloved watercooler, which sat gurgling a few feet from his desk and invested the office with a blue glow.

"No, thanks. I knew some Whelans in the old days. Frank Whelan. And Faith, her name was. His wife."

"I don't think they were any relation."

"But Whelan's an Irish name."

"Yes, ma'am. Now, Mrs. O'Mara. Mr. Hill gave me a general idea of what you wanted done. You want to locate—"

"It's about my brother Joseph."

"Right."

"I already talked to the police. They were nice. They said they couldn't do anything for me. It was all so long ago. . . ." She let her voice trail off and sat there, hands folded on her little purse, head turned to the left. For a moment Whelan wondered if she was about to cry. Then she seemed to catch herself and looked him in the eye. "Mr. Hill said you can find anybody."

"That's a nice thing for him to say," Whelan said. Something Hill would never say to his face, of course, for fear that the price of Whelan's services would go up. But here was a witness that he'd said it. Whelan already had another person's testimony that the bodacious Detective Albert Bauman had ventured a similar opinion.

Hill and Bauman: I have the beginnings of a cult following.

"But it may be an overstatement. No one is foolproof at this sort of thing. There are a lot of things that can affect a missing person's case. For example, a lot depends on whether the person you're looking for . . ." Is dead, Whelan said to himself. To Mrs. O'Mara, he said, "Well, is still, you know, around. Or if this person wants to be missing."

The old woman shook her head. "I don't think Joseph would want to be missing, not from me. I'm his sister."

"It also makes a difference how long the person has been out of communication."

Mrs. O'Mara stared at him this time, blinked once or twice behind her glasses, and looked embarrassed.

"It's been a long time, hasn't it, Mrs. O'Mara?"

"Oh, well . . . you could say it's been a long time."

Bracing himself, Whelan picked a pencil out of his drawer and began fiddling with it. "Uh, how long since you last saw your brother? Approximately."

"Oh, well," she said again, and shrugged, and when Whelan was certain she'd say nothing more specific, Mrs. O'Mara blurted out, "Thirty years."

She said it so fast that it could have been "Thirty years," or "Thirteen years," or, for that matter "Furry ears," but Whelan thought he'd heard correctly.

He nodded slowly, playing with the pencil. Thirty years. "Damn," he said under his breath.

"What did you say, Mr. Whelan?" She stared at him, her thin lips making a little o.

"I . . . I stuck myself with the pencil." He shook his hand as though in pain. Mrs. O'Mara was now giving his office a squinting appraisal.

"Well, let's see what we can determine about your situation, Mrs. O'Mara. Your brother has been missing for thirty years. 19—what, '55, '56? Around there?"

She gave an irritated shake of her head. "He wasn't missing then. I just didn't see him, that's all. That's what you asked me, how long since I saw him. He was down there in Florida with Minogue. They had a tavern. It's been thirty years since I saw him. And I can't tell you exactly when he started to be missing, you see. I only know when I realized he was missing."

"That's an important distinction," Whelan said, and nodded, partly to calm himself down.

I'm going to scream at the top of my lungs and this frail old creature will go into cardiac arrest, and they'll come for me and put me in a cell, and none of it will be my fault. He took a deep breath and started again.

"Let's start at the beginning. What can you tell me?"

"My brother's name was Joseph Owen Colleran and he was born in 1917."

"When was the last time you spoke to him?"

She was already shaking her head. "No, I didn't speak to him, I got a letter from him. I think it was 1959. We always wrote each other letters. He wrote me letters from all over the world. He served in the navy."

"I see. And then what?"

"I wrote him back. I was a great one for the letters. When I was a young girl, I wrote letters to a boy all through the war, you know. He was in the army, the other fellow. He was killed in the war. Just after the Normandy invasion, this was." She looked off at a spot just beyond Whelan's shoulder. A moment later, she collected herself. "Anyhow, I wrote Joe wherever he was, and he answered me."

"So you last heard from Joe when he was in Florida?"

"Yes."

"He wrote you a letter here and . . . then what? He moved?"

"Yes, he did. And so did I; that was the problem. I got married. O'Mara is my married name, and my husband worked for a big accounting firm and they transferred him to New York. My husband passed away in 1973."

"So you lost track of each other at that point."

"Yes," she said, and he would have sworn that she was ashamed.

"And it is possible that he came back here to start a new business."

"I don't think so. But he always wanted to have his own business. That was always his dream, that after the war he'd open a business. Nobody in our family ever had a business. He's always been very smart."

"And what sort of business was he going to start?"

"A nightclub. With music."

"That would take a certain amount of money."

"Oh, there was a bunch of them that was originally going to be in on it, soon as they got home from the war. Joe and a bunch of boys from the old neighborhood. Fritz Pollard and Gerry Costello and Michael Minogue and some others. They all had some money. From the war."

From the *war?* From what, sale of surplus tanks? Poker games with POWs? Whelan looked at Mrs. O'Mara's earnest face and bit his tongue. "I see. And what happened then?"

"Ah, things didn't work out for them here. So Joe decided to try something else. He went away." She looked at him, sniffed, and looked back at the air bubbles rising slowly through the lovely blue contents of the cooler.

"And his other partners, the other men you mentioned?"

She waved this idea off. "Oh, they were gone, a lot of them."

"Dead?"

"Well, for God's sake, of course they weren't dead, not all of them. They were all young men, Mr. Whelan." She pursed her lips and Whelan felt like the slow kid in third grade.

"But you said they were gone."

"They were. They all went their own ways. Joe and Michael went their way. Tommy Moran and Tommy Friesl, they were both killed. Tommy Friesl was a . . . a very nice boy. I don't remember where the other ones went." Her voice trailed off. Whelan decided that Tommy Friesl had meant a little more to her than the others. "All of them left, the other boys. Except for Ray Dudek. He got killed later. It was a terrible shame, a holdup, it was. Such a good-looking boy. They all were just a bunch of good-looking boys."

She clutched her little purse on her lap and looked down, and Whelan's next question caught her off guard. "Mrs. O'Mara, why are you looking for your brother now? What makes you think he's anywhere around here? Somebody gave you information, perhaps? Or are you acting on a hunch?" She stared stubbornly at him, refusing to speak, refusing to move. He met her gaze for a moment and then realized that they were in a staring contest.

I've pissed her off. No, worse than that: she thinks I'm making fun of her. Whelan suppressed a smile, looked away for a moment and then back at the old woman.

"You're misunderstanding me. I am not taking you lightly or trying to talk you out of your search. But something prompted you to begin looking for him now, after the passing of all this time. What was it?"

Slowly Mrs. O'Mara allowed herself to relax slightly. A new look came into her eyes, the look of someone who knows she's been underestimated. She studied Whelan for a moment and then began rustling about with one hand in her battered little purse. After several false starts, she seemed to find what she'd been looking for, a newspaper clipping. She glanced at it and then held it out to Whelan.

He took it and saw there were two separate clippings. He read the first two lines of the top one and realized the story was simply the *Tribune*'s version of the article he remembered from the previous week, recounting the discovery of the body of one Michael Minogue, aged sixty-nine, on the lonely breakwater on Montrose Beach. He read a few more lines and then he made the connection with the name. The second clipping was the death notice from the *Trib*. He nodded, handing the clippings back to her.

"I thought the name sounded familiar when you mentioned it. I saw the same story in the *Sun-Times* when they found him. This was one of your brother's friends. One of the men that he was going to go into business with."

"Yes, Michael Minogue. He was always a nice boy, Michael Minogue. What a terrible thing. There's all kinds of crazy people in the world now. I went to the wake but I didn't know a soul."

Whelan nodded and waited for her to make the connection. When nothing came, he prodded. "I'm still not clear as to what it is about this story. . . . Why did you—"

"They were the best of friends, Mr. Whelan. Like brothers, they were. They left town together, Mr. Whelan. Just the two of them, my brother Joe and Michael Minogue. They were just a couple of young men looking to see another part of the country. They thought they might be able to start a business another place, maybe, after they saw a little bit of the country."

"Do you know where they went?"

"All over the country." She gave him a look of wonder from behind the thick lenses. "Joe sent me postcards from all kinds of places. Texas and Oklahoma and Wyoming and Montana. Alaska, even. They went up there to Alaska, where the Eskimos are."

"Why not? A couple of young guys with no ties to hold them. I can see it."

"That's what I said. And after everything they'd been through, with the war and all. Best years of their lives, they gave up.

"And then they went east. They were in Philadelphia for a while and they went up there to Boston, Massachusetts. Then after that, they went down to Miami. They settled down there for a while, Miami. And they had their tavern there. The Banshee, they called it. Joe came back to see me right after they opened it. He looked like a million dollars, he did. He had on a new suit, new shoes, a nice hat. He always liked his hats. Joe was very smart, Mr. Whelan. I told him he should come back up here and open up a tavern in Chicago. He laughed and he says to me, 'I'll have one in every city in the country, Maggie.' But he just had the one. That was Christmas of 1952. Then he came back in the summer of 1955, for a week. He was with Minogue that time. We had a very nice visit. He took me to the Palmer House and the Drake Hotel for dinner. I never saw him again after that."

"But you wrote him, you said."

"Of course. Of course I wrote him, we always wrote letters. He was a grand letter writer."

"Yes, you mentioned that. Did he ever call you on the phone?"

She nodded and gave him an appraising look.

"Oh, now and then, but he wasn't much for the telephone. And I don't like it myself. We were letter writers. People in those days didn't mind sitting down to write a civilized letter. Anyhow, I got the one letter from him in 1959, but after that . . ." She shook her head and squinted distractedly at the watercooler. "And the tavern was gone. It wasn't there anymore." She shrugged. She looked embarrassed, as though she should have expected this. Whelan watched her for a moment and then her meaning dawned on him, and his opinion of Mrs. O'Mara changed.

"It was gone when? When . . . you went there? It was gone when you went there, you mean?"

She nodded, and Whelan thought he could read a mix of emotions fighting for primacy in her face: embarrassment was still there, and something like hopefulness, and there was just a trace of pride. She had looked for this missing man, this brother of hers; she'd gone off tramping around the country on her own and she was just a little embarrassed by it, by the craziness of it for an old-country woman like herself, but she was proud of what she'd done, as well.

"Yes. I went down there and the tavern was gone. There was a restaurant there—Cuban, it was. A lovely place. They have them down there, you know—Cubans."

"I had heard that."

"Nobody could tell me a thing about my brother. A policeman told me they'd sold the place awhile before and he didn't know where they went."

"Where else did you look, Mrs. O'Mara?"

"I went to Boston. Michael Minogue had a brother there. I couldn't find him, though. There's a lot of Minogues, but I couldn't find the right ones. So I came back here. And I always thought he'd get in touch with me and let me know where he was. Just to know how he was getting along, you know. But he didn't."

She seemed to slump a little, as though acknowledging failure.

"Mrs. O'Mara," he said gently, "have you given any thought to the possibility that your brother is dead?" She sniffed and said nothing, forcing him to go on. "From what you tell me, you had a very close relationship, and he wouldn't have simply stopped communicating. My guess is that he's dead." Whelan stopped himself before saying any more.

Mrs. O'Mara began to nod slowly. She fumbled inside the tiny purse and came up with a small white handkerchief, a handkerchief like the ones his mother always used. He'd seen these little squares of cotton and lace and wondered where they came from—he had yet to come across one in a store.

Mrs. O'Mara did not use the handkerchief but rolled it into a little ball and began to worry it with her fingers. Whelan was about to say something to cover the awkwardness of her pain when she looked up.

"Ah, I know all that, Mr. Whelan. I know he's probably been dead since who knows when. Somebody told me I should go look in the obituaries." She gave him a helpless look. "I wouldn't even know how."

"You couldn't. If you had the actual date—" He'd started to say "of death," then caught himself. "If you knew that Joseph was dead, and when he died, it would be a simple matter of reading microfilm. But if you have no idea of the date, or even, as in your case, whether the person is deceased, you'd just be going through thousands of newspapers and reading thousands of death notices. The papers don't have this stuff in their computers. They go back thirty days, maybe."

She nodded. "I just want to *know*. You know, when I first read about poor Michael Minogue, for a minute I was excited, and then it occurred to me that the poor man was dead and wasn't going to tell me anything about my brother. It's just that maybe Joe's still alive and he's here. You know, if he was anywhere, it would be where Minogue was. Maybe he's still alive. And if he's not, maybe Michael said something to somebody, and I'll know. Once and for all, I'll know, and that'll be the end of it."

"And if you find he's dead?"

"Then maybe I'll know how. And when. And . . ." She waved at the air with the handkerchief. Then she gave him a pained look.

"People do this, don't they, Mr. Whelan? They hire detectives to look for their families? Mr. Hill seemed to think it made sense."

Yes, he thought, they do, but they usually don't expect to pick up a trail that's been cold for thirty years.

Whelan knew what to say here; he'd been here before. There was a whole set of polite, gentle formula responses to a would-be client about to set off on a fool's errand, and it was time to select the proper response for this slightly addled old woman, time to set her straight and send her on her way. A simple matter of pulling the appropriate answer from the list.

"I can ask around, Mrs. O'Mara," he found himself saying.

What am I doing? he asked himself.

"What? You can? Well, that would be grand."

He held up both hands, palms out. "Don't get excited. Don't get hopeful, either." His voice had suddenly taken on a raspy quality he usually reserved for unreasonable creditors.

"And if I don't find anything at all after a couple of days, I won't charge you. Unless I have out-of-pocket expenses."

She frowned. "Is that how you do it? People only pay you if you find something?" She blinked, and Whelan realized he was poised to plummet again in her estimation.

"Uh, not always. But it's how I'm going to do it this time. We can talk money later if we find out that there is something to investigate. So." He leaned forward on his desk and tried his best to look professional. "I'll need a little help, Mrs. O'Mara. Names and addresses of acquaintances, pictures, anything that might give me a leg up."

"I've got pictures. I've got a thousand pictures, Mr. Whelan," she said in an oddly quiet little voice. She rummaged in the tight little handbag and came up with a grayish brown studio portrait of a sharp-featured young man in a black suit. His hair was slicked back and parted just to the left of center, and he showed the camera the lopsided smile of a young man who thinks he's got most, if not all, of the answers.

"Here, look at this one."

She held out a small brownish snapshot of a young man in navy whites, standing at the edge of the curb. A 1940s model car was a few feet behind him, but the street was remarkably free of traffic. A picture from another time—when most people had no car.

"A young guy ready to conquer the world, huh?"

"Yes, that's exactly how he thought of himself."

Whelan studied the photo a moment and nodded. "That's Clybourn Avenue. My grandparents lived over there. In the projects, eventually."

"Ah, everybody wanted to live in the projects once. They were the newest thing. It was a different world then."

"It sure was. But I know this neighborhood. This photograph was taken about two blocks from Riverview, right?"

"Yes. That was taken in front of our building, the corner of Clybourn and Oakley. You could see Riverview from there." A note of melancholy crept into her voice and she looked away.

Then she collected herself and reached back into the purse. "And I have this." She pulled out a photograph of a group of young men at the beach. It was classic 1940s mugging for the camera, with one of the boys even jumping up into the arms of another as if he were a baby. In the background he could see onlookers, a couple of older men, a little knot of smiling young women. A couple of feet behind the young men was a younger boy. As Whelan stared at it, he gradually got the bearings of the picture: North Avenue Beach looking north past the sprawling white beach house built in the shape of an ocean liner. The graceful curving overpass that allowed foot traffic across Lake Shore Drive was years in the future.

Mrs. O'Mara leaned over and made a little pointing gesture with one thin finger. "The one on the far left, that's Joe—and the young boy next to him is Ray Dudek, him that they robbed and killed. The one second from the other end is Michael Minogue."

He looked at her. "Do you know all the others?"

She made a curt nod and recited. "Sure, there's Joe, and Ray, like I said." She hesitated a moment. "And there's Fritz Pollard, Chick Landis, Gerry Costello—and the one jumping up into his arms, you see"—she tapped the photo and looked up to see if he was still paying attention—"that's Tommy Moran. The small boy behind them, that's Casey Pollard, Fritz's little brother. There's Herb Gaynor. Her finger lingered on one grinning face. "And this is Tommy Friesl." She gave Whelan a challenging look and he smiled.

Probably had every detail of the photo memorized, he thought.

"Let me write them down," he said. He pulled over a scratch pad and jotted the names down, asking for confirmation of Landis and Gaynor. "All right. What about these other men? Any idea where I might find any of them?"

"Ah, they're all gone now, dead or moved away. Most of them, anyways. Ray Dudek, I told you about, and you know about Michael, and Tommy Friesl and Tommy Moran died in the war. And that Landis, *that* one, he sells real estate somewheres. Always knew how to make money, that one. I don't know what became of the others. I read the obituaries, Mr. Whelan, and sometimes, you know, I see old names. I know Herb Gaynor was very sick, so I think he's dead. The others . . . I think they're all gone. Except for Chick Landis."

"When was this picture taken?"

"Oh, that was before the war—1940 or 1941, it was."

He nodded and looked at the faces again. There appeared to be a wide range in ages, from midteens to early twenties. For all these boys life was soon to change in many ways, unfathomable, permanent ways.

"Just a few months before the war."

"Yes. All those boys served in the war. Herb Gaynor did, and Fritz Pollard and Michael and Tommy—all of them."

Whelan studied the faces. "Just kids, a couple of these guys. They're just boys. Did they all go in?"

"Oh, they all went and they all went overseas, except that Chick Landis. He spent the whole war in California, he was some kind of clerk or something, God knows what." Mrs. O'Mara's tone left no doubt as to her feeling about Landis. "And Ray Dudek lied about his age but they wouldn't take him yet, he didn't get in till it was almost over. And Casey Pollard wasn't in at all, he was in Korea. 'Police action,' they called it. Casey wasn't old enough for the big war. He was wounded in Korea, the poor boy."

Whelan looked at the picture and waited for the old woman to help him, but he guessed she was pretty well tapped out. This is nuts, he told himself, shaking his head. He sighed and said, "I'll be in touch."

"What are you going to do first, Mr. Whelan?"

"Oh, I'll make some calls and then . . . I'll want to see where Mr. Minogue lived. Talk to his neighbors."

"Oh. Sure," she said, as though it made great sense.

I want to start there, Whelan thought, because I haven't the slightest idea what else to do.

Three

WHELAN knew the calls would be a waste of time but made them anyway, to people he knew at the phone company and the gas company, to the VA, to the assistant manager in Sandra's office at Public Aid, and he found what he'd expected: there was no record of a man in his late sixties named Joseph Colleran.

He didn't bother to drive over to Michael Minogue's hotel, opting instead for the short walk over. The residents of the Empire Hotel lived among society's greatest conveniences: They had both a McDonald's and a Burger King right across the street. On a fair day they could stroll down Wilson to the lakefront, to the park where young Hispanic guys played killer soccer on Sundays, or out to the beach between Montrose and Wilson. This last was apparently what Michael Minogue had done on his final day.

The manager of the hotel was a short graying man with a pained facial expression and bad color. He was on the phone when Whelan entered, and he held up one hand, telling Whelan not to come inside just yet. Whelan nodded and backed out. The hall had once been the lobby of the hotel, and Whelan could just make out the vestigial remains of that lost grandeur: an amazingly high ceiling hung with great chandeliers, replaced now with a pair of ugly lights, each with a dozen or so globes. There were sconces in the wall where imitation torches had been fixed, and a bricked-up, painted-over niche where there had once been a fireplace.

Now the lobby held a handful of chairs and one sofa. There were two men on the sofa, a tiny man whose sharp bony angles stuck out of a shirt two sizes too big for him and a much taller man with an exaggerated slump to his shoulders. The smaller one had contrived to create an almost solid cloud of blue smoke in the lobby and much of it hung directly over his head. His companion didn't seem to notice. Whelan looked at the smoker and crossed the room to sit in one of the chairs across from him.

"Don't sit there," the man said, and caught Whelan in the act of lowering himself onto the chair. He stared at Whelan and puffed on his cigarette.

"Saving it for somebody?"

"It's broken."

"Oh, thanks."

Whelan indicated another chair and the man nodded once. The taller one smiled. Whelan took the new chair and sat down, pulling a brass standing ashtray toward him. He held up the smokes, waited till the old men shook their heads in unison, then lit one.

The old men studied him for a moment as Whelan allowed himself to listen in on the manager's conversation. Someone had done the squinty man wrong. Whelan couldn't follow the whole train of things, but apparently the manager's grievance was with family. He heard the man say, "I trusted you . . . one of the family . . . betrayed my trust . . . living off us since you got married."

"You waitin' to see the Emperor Penguin in there?" The smoker in the lobby leaned slightly to one side to bring himself into Whelan's line of vision. Whelan studied him for a moment and saw amusement in the small dark eyes. Something in the face told him what it had looked like in boyhood, and he had a strong sense that this had been a troublesome little boy, teacher's nightmare, the kid who spent long hours with his nose to the chalkboard and never lacked for amusement.

"The Emperor Penguin? Is that what people call him?"

"Why not? This is the Empire. He's the Emperor Penguin."

The taller man's stooped shoulders quaked with his silent laughter.

"Yeah, I'm waiting to see him. Doesn't sound like I picked the best day, though."

"Don't matter. All his days are like this. He's always whining about something. You tell him you got no heat in your room and he tells you about his corns. You tell him you got roaches the size of rainbow trout in your tub, he ain't impressed. You tell him you got a rat under your bed that's bigger than fucking Lassie and he tells you he needs bypass surgery." The taller man appeared to be going into convulsions at this. The speaker looked to his companion for confirmation, received a shrug, and then looked back to Whelan.

"I'm Dutch Sturdevant," the old man said. He nodded at the other man on the sofa. "This is Pete Koski." Pete Koski touched his hand to his forehead in greeting.

"Paul Whelan." The old man nodded and rooted around in a crushed-looking package of Chesterfields for a fresh one. Whelan waited till he lit it, then asked, "Did you know Mr. Minogue?"

"Sure I knew him. I know everybody on my floor, for Chrissakes. I know everybody's business, too," he said with a raspy laugh. "If I didn't have neighbors to pester, what would I do with myself?" Beside him, Pete Koski affirmed the truth of this with a nod. "No, he was a good guy, Mike. 'Irish,' some of us called him. That was a damn shame what happened to him."

"Do you know much about him? Any family? Things like that?"

The old man nodded. "You're a cop. I thought so at first, then I thought maybe not."

"No, I'm not a cop. I'm just trying to get some information that might lead me to somebody who used to know Mr. Minogue in the old days." One look at Sturdevant told Whelan the old man wasn't buying it. He got up and crossed the room, holding out his wallet to display his license. The two gray heads leaned in together to study the license. Sturdevant pursed his lips and Koski nodded.

"I'm a private investigator. I'm not looking into Mr. Minogue's case, because I assume it's still an open police case."

Sturdevant chewed on that for a moment and then stared at Whelan for a few seconds before speaking. "So who are you investigating?"

"I don't investigate people. I find them. I'm looking for an old friend of Minogue's named Joseph Colleran. They were pretty close in the old days and they left town together back in the fifties, kind of tramped around for fun and then settled in Florida."

"He talked about that. 'Joe,' he said, that's all. Never said the guy's last name." He looked to his companion for confirmation. Pete Koski pursed his lips and shook his long thin head.

"And as far as you know, nobody named Joe Colleran ever came to see him here?"

"Not as far as I know." Sturdevant looked at Koski.

The thin man shook his head. "Can't recall the name."

"Did he have other visitors?"

"Not in a long time. I mean, he had a nephew came to see him once in awhile. Saw 'im yesterday. Guess he's here to clean out Mike's stuff. Said he'd be back today."

"Have you seen cops?"

"Shit yeah, they were here. We had uniforms here and we had the other guys—plainclothes. Homicide?"

"Detectives, you mean? Violent Crimes, they call that department now. Did they question you?"

"Yeah, they asked me this and that, did I know of any enemies he might've had, how well did I know him. Acted like we were all senile already. The one, he talked like you'd talk to a moron. Young guy, this was. Smelled like a French whore. He left my room, the place smelled like the fucking perfume counter at Woolworth's." Old Mr. Koski began shaking again and Sturdevant shot him a glance that mixed tolerance and affection.

"Dark hair, knit shirt, gold chain around his neck?"

"That's him."

"Then the other one was big and heavy, rough-looking, red face, crew cut. Big gut, ugly sport coat, smoked little nasty cigar things."

"You're good. That's him. Looked like Johnny Mize. Remember him?"

"Old Tomato Face. Only from pictures, never saw him play."

"Anyway, the young one asked questions and the fat one just looked around my room like he was bored."

"He wasn't."

"How do you know?"

"I just know."

"Yeah? Maybe so, but he only asked me one question the whole time they were there. Other guy asked all the questions."

"What was the question the big one asked?"

"He asked me if Mike ever acted like he was afraid of anybody. That's all he asked me the whole time."

"That's all he wanted to know. And did he? Mr. Minogue, I mean?"

"No. Why would he be afraid of somebody? He was a nice guy, never had a bad word to say about nobody. He didn't have nothing that nobody would want. No, I never heard him talk about being afraid of anybody. You can ask some of the people on our floor, but I never heard him say anything like that, and me and him, we spent a lot of time together."

"Did he have any trouble that you know of, disputes or arguments with anyone?"

Sturdevant looked amused. *"Disputes?* You mean like over land or money? I don't think so. Seriously, he didn't have no trouble with nobody. I mean, he had words one time with this wino, but it was nothing."

"Tell me."

"It was just this guy, street guy from around here somewheres. I don't know 'im. Just a guy Mike didn't like, I guess. They seemed to know each other, and I think this guy was putting the touch on Mike and Mike told him to get lost."

"Can you describe him?"

"Skinny, like most of us. He wasn't very big. Pale-lookin' guy," Sturdevant said, "sick-lookin' guy." Whelan noted Sturdevant's own pasty skin and hid his amusement. "Wearin' a baseball cap. He was just a street guy, a wino, and Mike didn't like him. I asked him about the guy and he said it was just a guy he didn't like 'cause the guy was always bumming money."

"He knew him from just around here?"

"He didn't say and I didn't ask."

"Did you ever see the man again?"

"I think I saw him one time, sitting on a corner up on Clark Street, at a bus stop. Didn't seem to be bothering nobody that time."

"Anybody else?"

"No. Mike was a good guy, he didn't have no enemies. We spent a lot of time together. Us and Pete here. We liked to watch a ball game together, have a couple beers."

"Where did you drink?"

The old man gave him an amused look. *"Where?* In a room in this joint, pal. My room or his room or Pete's. We couldn't afford to go to a saloon and spend that kinda money. You know, there's some places askin' a buck for a beer, and they hand you a can! Beer in a can for a buck."

"They'll all go to hell, Mr. Sturdevant."

"Great, that's another place I gotta avoid now."

A few feet away, the Emperor Penguin terminated his phone conversation by slamming the phone down. Whelan looked at Sturdevant and raised his eyebrows. "I guess he's ready for his ten o'clock appointment."

31

"Good luck. You need anything, let me know. I'm in room three oh two."

"I'll do that." He handed a card to Sturdevant. "Give me a call if you think of anything else."

At the door to the manager's office, he paused and waited. The manager squinted up at him and indicated a chair with a sharp motion of his hand.

"Come on in. Take a seat."

Whelan dropped a business card on the man's desk and lowered himself onto the guest chair. He waited a moment while the manager studied the card with a confused look.

A gray man, Whelan decided. Gray hair, a gray shirt that had once probably been white, pale, washed-out-looking skin that cried out for fifteen minutes in the sun. A gym rat's complexion: White kids that dreamt of an NBA career looked like this. Gym rats and bartenders and scholars, guys who avoided the light of day and turned into bats at midnight, they all looked like this.

The gray man leaned forward and folded his hands on his desk. "So you're interested in renting at the Empire?"

"I was told I was too young."

The man squinted. "No, I meant for your, uh, loved one. You're not here to rent for your loved one?"

"Nope. I'm here about a resident who was killed recently."

"Oh, yeah, Minogue. Mr. Minogue. That was terrible. Guy tried to rob me once, right outside my house. I was lucky, though. My neighbor came out and the guy took off. But I coulda been killed."

"I'm sure. I was wondering if I could take a look at his apartment."

"I don't know if I'm supposed to do that."

"I'm sorry. I thought you were in charge. Who do I see about this?" He started to get up.

The gray man straightened slightly and gave his office a quick look. "I *am* in charge. It's just . . . I don't get a lot of people dying on me. You know?" He tried to smile but his lips wouldn't take the unfamiliar position. "Maybe you're in luck, though. Mr. Minogue lived in three oh seven. His nephew is up there now, goin' through his stuff. You know, taking care of things."

"Oh, that's right. Mr. Sturdevant was telling me that."

The gray man looked as if he'd bitten into bad meat. "Oh, don't listen to that old fart. He's just a goddamn old busybody. Wouldn't know the truth if he sat on it."

"Really? He told me you were a good guy."

The gray man paused, mouth open. "Aw, you know, he's not so bad. He means well, but you gotta—you can't believe everything he says. Anyhow, why don't you go up and see if this nephew's got any objection to you looking around?"

"I'll do that. Thanks for your time." He bit off the impulse to address the man as Emperor and left the office. The lobby was empty now, no sign of Mr. Sturdevant except for the single plume of smoke where his crushed Chesterfield still burned.

A creaking elevator that hadn't seen soap and water in years took him to the third floor. The doors slid open with an ominous grinding sound and he was assailed by half a dozen odors at once: roach killer, mothballs, mildew, bacon, tobacco, frying food, old plaster. Old people's smells, the smells of age. There were other smells mixed in but he wasn't ready to identify them yet.

A few feet from the elevator, he found 307, the door closed. Whelan waited a moment and thought he could hear faint movement within, then knocked.

"Yeah? Who is it?"

"My name is Paul Whelan. I wonder if I could have a word with you about your uncle."

A silence followed and then Whelan heard footsteps and someone undoing the double lock. The door opened six inches and a thin man with glasses and very little hair stared out at him.

"Yes?"

"You're Mr. Minogue's nephew?"

"He was my great-uncle." The man raised his eyebrows to ask, "What of it?"

"I'm trying to get some information about—"

"You from the building?"

"No, no, I'm—"

"Oh, police."

Whelan waited and the man swung the door open. "I'm sorry. I'm trying to make some sense of his stuff and people keep coming by. The building manager was up here and one of the neighbors was just here and . . . it's hard to get any of it done. And I'd really like to get done with it."

"I know. It's depressing work. Mr. . . . ?"

"Riordan. Ted Riordan."

"Paul Whelan." He held out his hand, and as Riordan took it, he added "I'm not a police officer, though. I'm a private detective."

Riordan nodded. "Building security, right?"

"No. I'm working for someone who knew your uncle. My client is interested in finding a family member and thought that since your uncle knew the missing man, he might have said something to someone."

"Nice timing, huh? I mean, why did they hire you now?"

"Apparently these folks all lost track of one another. The person who hired me didn't know Mr. Minogue had returned to Chicago until this story appeared in the news."

"Oh, we're talking about the *real* old days. Before he went down to Florida, right?"

"Right."

"Your client wants to find somebody from those days?"

"Yes."

Riordan blinked and looked as though he was fighting to look serious. "That's crazy. But I guess it's no crazier than anything else, is it?"

"I've been asked to do more bizarre things than find an old friend for somebody."

Riordan nodded once and then looked around at the room behind him. "Well . . ." He indicated the little room. "Come on in. I'm not sure how I can help, but it sure couldn't hurt. Sit down anywhere—there's a lot of chairs. It's about all he had, chairs. That and a black-and-white TV. Not much of a life, was it?"

Whelan shrugged. "Not much space, not many possessions, but I've known people to be happier with less."

"Well, he always seemed happy enough. As long as he could fish, he was happy. He liked to go down there to the lake and sit on the breakwater and fish. I guess he knew all the other old-timers down there and they'd chat, maybe pass a bottle of wine around sometimes. Still, you'd think a man who worked hard all his life would have a little more to show for it. Doesn't seem fair."

"No, sometimes it doesn't, although, if he was happy, then maybe it was fair enough."

Riordan shrugged and sat down on the edge of a chair and Whelan found one directly across from him. "I guess, but if he was happy, you sure couldn't prove it from what he had. Couple bucks in a drawer, a wallet full of old lottery tickets. Old lottery tickets and holy cards. Look at his place, look at what he had. And then somebody goes and kills him. They didn't even get anything, the cops told me. Still had his money and his watch. Somebody spooked 'em, I guess. Well, what can I do for you, Mr. Whelan?"

"Well, for starters, can you tell me if your uncle was still in touch with a man named Joe Colleran?"

"I don't know who he was in touch with, to be honest with you. I didn't see him all that much. I don't think I know that name, though."

"I think Joe Colleran was with him in Florida."

"Oh. Oh, maybe that's the guy he was partners with down there. Jeez, I wouldn't know that for sure. That was like, oh, has to be twenty years ago. That's really goin' back."

"How long had your uncle been back up here?"

"I don't know, maybe ten years, something like that."

"Do you know who his friends were?"

Riordan winced. "Jesus, I don't know. I . . . we didn't talk about that much. See, he was my grandmother's brother, but half the time he was living down south or some other place. And she's long gone now. My parents are dead, too. So I kind of inherited Uncle Michael. I looked in on him sometimes, but just for a cup of coffee, like that. He mentioned people sometimes. I heard him talk about maybe half a dozen other old guys, but just first names." He looked embarrassed.

"That's more than I have right now."

"Okay, I know he talked to a couple of neighbor guys on this floor. A guy named Pete and another guy named Dutch. Dutch lives right down the hall."

"I met them."

"Okay. And then I heard him talk about this old black guy he went fishing with all the time down by the beach there. Where they found him. This guy's name was Franklin."

"Any idea where I can find him?"

"No. I guess he must live in the neighborhood somewhere, but where, I don't know."

"Who else?"

"Couple of guys at a tavern he liked. It's not around here. Over by the ballpark. On Southport, I think."

"Got a name for it?"

Riordan shook his head. "I know it's a liquor store, the old-fashioned kind, with a saloon attached. I never went there, so I can't tell you much about it. I don't drink myself."

Whelan thought for a moment and then said, "Crown? Was that it, Crown Liquors?"

"I don't know. Coulda been. Is it near a movie theater?"

"Sure. Right up the street from the Music Box."

"That's it, then. I know one guy's name from the tavern was Archie. I think the other guy's name was Fred."

"Well, thanks. Is that about it?"

"Yeah. Not much, is it?" Riordan squinted at him and seemed to be struggling with another question.

"It's not bad. You gave me some names, I've got his fishing partner and his favorite saloon. Not a bad start. Well, thanks. And I'm sorry about your uncle." He hesitated, then said, "I think you've got one more question. What is it?"

Riordan shrugged. "I don't know squat about private detectives, but here's what I'm thinking. I'm thinking somebody kills my uncle and this guy comes to his apartment before I've even had time to take care of his stuff and asks about some other person that my uncle knew. I'm thinking you're not here about that at all."

"Makes sense. But it's not true. I never knew your uncle. His name appeared in the paper and a person who used to know him thought maybe a good investigator might be able to retrace some of your uncle's steps, run down some of the people he hung out with, maybe come up with her missing relative. That's all there is to it. If my client had known that your uncle was here, I would have been here just the same, only I would have been talking to him instead of you."

Riordan stared at him for a moment. "Maybe you'll find out something else." He nodded toward the sofa, as though his uncle were dozing on it. "About the old man."

"Wouldn't surprise me."

"Then what?"

"Then I'll let somebody know."

"Like who, me? If I give you my number, will—"

"Like a cop I know at Area Six who I think is already on this. He's good at what he does, better than anybody I can think of. If I find something, I'll let him know, and he'll handle it. Believe me, if I could pick a cop to work on a problem of mine, it would be this guy."

Riordan looked around the room for a moment, then nodded. He held out his hand and smiled. "Fair enough. And if you need any information, you call me. Anytime." He reached into his back pocket and came up with a wallet, stuck two fingers into it, and handed Whelan a business card.

It read "T.C. Riordan, Certified Public Accountant."

"Thanks."

Whelan tucked the card away in his pocket and left the dead man's room. Behind him, the door to Michael Minogue's room clicked shut, and Whelan heard matching clicks farther down the hall. One, he was sure, came from the door to 302.

Four

DOWN at the lake, he parked in the big lot where kids came to practice driving and teenagers came to get lucky. He got out and made the short walk to the beach. The breakwater was empty. A man had been shot to death—it would take awhile for the old fishermen to start putting their lines in again.

Fifty yards or so to the south, the lakefront made a long sweep back toward the shore, like a thumb meeting a finger, and created a little harbor. At the very end of the hook, Whelan saw a single figure fishing. He had several lines in, and he looked over his shoulder several times as Whelan approached and then half-turned when Whelan was a few feet away.

"Are you Franklin?"

The fisherman made a shrug and his eyes studied Whelan's. Whelan scrambled down the rocks and sat a couple of feet away.

Up close, the man was bigger than he'd looked, Whelan's height and much heavier. He sat with one hand holding a pole and the other flat against the rock. It was one of the biggest hands Whelan had ever seen.

Whelan held up a card. "This is who I am." He held the card out and the big hand took it. The fisherman studied it for a moment and then looked at Whelan from the corner of his eye.

"Now I know who you are. What you want with me?"

Whelan realized how far his original notion had been from reality: this old fisherman hadn't moved from the breakwater because he was afraid. He was looking in the eyes of a man who'd seen it all and decided there wasn't much he was afraid of.

"I want to ask you some questions. But probably not the kind you expect."

"I don't expect nothing. Except to be left alone." The big head turned to study his lines again.

Whelan hunched his shoulders against the stiff wind off the water. "Well, I'll leave you alone as soon as I can. I'm freezing to death here."

Franklin quickly scanned Whelan's lightweight ski vest and made an amused shake of his head. "Come out here dressed like that, you deserve to freeze to death. Leave the world a smarter place," he muttered, looking back at his lines.

"Nice to meet you, too. I want to ask you about Michael Minogue's friends."

Franklin studied him with new interest. "What for? Think one of them know who killed him?"

"No. I'm not looking for his killer. So you think his friends would know who killed Mike?"

"Maybe."

"Did you talk to the police about it?"

"I talked to 'em. They ast me some things, I told 'em what I thought. Now, what is it you want?"

"I'm trying to find somebody Michael Minogue used to know."

Franklin gave him an amused look and then glanced at his lines. "Mister, you late."

"I've always been a step too slow. This fellow is somebody he grew up with, an old friend I think Michael traveled with. This man's name was Joe. Joe Colleran. That do anything for you?"

Franklin held Whelan's gaze for a moment, then looked back at the water. "I heard the name. That was his old partner. They ran a saloon together someplace down south."

"And you never met him?"

"No. And Michael talked about him like somebody he never saw anymore. Like he's dead." Franklin squinted at him. "I think this man's dead, mister."

"That's kind of what I think, too." He climbed to his feet and brushed off his pants. "Catching anything?"

"Only just got here. I got all day to catch fish. Why you looking for this man?"

"His sister hired me. It's what I do."

Franklin nodded, frowned at one of his lines, picked up the pole, reeled in his hook, and recast it, tossing the line in a fine gentle arc that ended in a silver splash thirty yards out.

"Cops seem to know anything?"

Franklin shook his head.

"How about you?"

"I don't know. Maybe he did, though."

"Did what? Knew the killer?"

"Maybe. He acted like he knew somebody was lookin' for him."

"Did he talk about it?"

"Naw. Just acted jumpy. I saw him lookin' around when we were fishing. Wouldn't say what was wrong and I didn't want to push it."

"Did he ever actually say he was afraid?"

"Just acted kinda jumpy. That's all. He'd sit out there on the breakwater and be lookin' up and down the beach like he thought somebody was watchin' us. Things bothered him that you wouldn't normally notice."

"Such as?"

"Like this one day, it seemed like Mike couldn't stop watching this one fella. Told me there wasn't nothing wrong, but he be looking over his shoulder at this man till the man went away."

"You got a look at him?"

"Well, we was all the way out at the end of the breakwater, and this man was back there on the shore, by the sidewalk there. You can't make out faces that far."

"Young man?"

"Couldn't tell. Didn't look old. Looked maybe fifty."

"You're pretty sure this man wasn't as old as Michael?"

"Oh, no. I could see this man still had dark hair. He mighta been fifty-five, even sixty, but he wasn't nowhere near our age."

"Do you remember anything else about the man?"

The old man thought for a moment and then nodded. "Had a bent kinda walk."

"Like he was injured?"

"Like he was injured a long time ago and learned to live with it. He moved pretty fast when he walked away."

"Anything else?"

"Dressed shabby."

"Like somebody living on the street?"

"Yeah. And look like he was wearing some kinda windbreaker, no coat. A little bitty jacket out here on a cold day."

"What color?"

Franklin thought for a moment. "Blue. Had on a baseball cap, too. Couldn't say what kind. Just wasn't Sox or Cubs. It was red."

"When was this?"

"About a month ago. Maybe less."

"And that's the only time you saw him?"

"Only time *I* saw him. That's all I can tell you."

Whelan watched the wind whip the green water to a thick froth. Overhead a pair of gulls circled and whined at one another. "I was afraid I wouldn't find you. I thought maybe you'd just find some other part of the lake to fish."

Franklin looked at his lines. "I don't know about sitting out there and putting my lines in where Michael got killed. Have to think on that some. But I ain't about to start fishin' on the South Side, if that's what you mean."

"You pretty sure nobody's going to bother you?"

The older man gave Whelan a long look. "What's that old thing, that good-luck thing? 'May you outlive your enemies'? I outlived the only ones I know about."

"Maybe there's a new one out here. Maybe he picks people at random."

Franklin shrugged and squinted out at his bobber. "He come for me, I be here. I'm too old to let crazy people scare me. He come for me, I'll take him with me." He held Whelan's card out in his thick fingers.

Whelan shook his head. "No. Keep it in case you see something I should know about." He got to his feet. "Well, thanks. See you, Franklin. And watch your back door."

"Good luck, man," Franklin said without turning.

THIS time there was mail, an audaciously high bill from the electric company and a solicitation from De Paul University, his alma mater. He tossed the mail on his couch and told himself there might be something in tomorrow's mail—after all, he'd get mail both at home and at the office. The prospect of dinner beckoned, but a quick scan of the contents of his refrigerator told him dinner would best be found somewhere else.

I have no dinner, I have no girl.

Slamming the door to the house, he went out in search of dinner and a new attitude.

He was still a block away when he saw the new sign. In truth, he could have seen it from Evanston. He thought he'd probably be able to see it from the space shuttle. It was bold, gaudy, oversized, and in poor taste; it used enough bulbs to light up the North Side and its message flickered constantly, maddeningly, like some fiendish attempt to induce petit mal seizures in the population. It was ugly and inappropriate. It said HOUSE OF ZEUS.

After the blinding light of the sign, the interior of the House of Zeus was dark, cavelike. Whelan thought he could make out other life-forms, but he paused just inside the door to allow his eyes to adjust. Gradually, he could see again. There were half a dozen diners, if you included the guy sleeping in the back booth. There was always someone in a state of reduced consciousness at the House of Zeus.

At the counter, a dapper-looking man seemed to be talking to the owners, Rashid and Gus, who were both smiling. A few feet away, a taller man squinted around at the bloody murals adorning the walls. He wore a wrinkled black trench coat, his hair was pulled back in a ponytail, and he appeared to be carrying a camera bag.

Rashid looked at Whelan and grinned, showing Whelan all his teeth at once. Rashid's smile had given Whelan the unshakable notion that Iranian people had two to three times as many teeth as other people.

"Hello, my friend the detective." He waved and beamed exaggerated happiness at Whelan, and the dapper man turned to look at him. The man was short, middle-aged, and trim-looking, a man for health clubs and tennis courts. He wore a tapered blue shirt open at the collar and a dark sport coat. His silver hair was styled so tightly, it looked painted on. In his left hand he held a leatherbound notebook, and in his right, an expensive-looking pen.

"This man," Rashid said, "is typical customer of House of Zeus. He is officer of private detectives."

The dapper man frowned. "Your typical customer is a detective?"

"There is no typical customer at the House of Zeus," Whelan said. "There's no typical day at the House of Zeus. There's no typical anything here. Hello, boys."

Rashid flashed teeth again and Gus shot him an uncharacteristic smile.

Smiles from Gus were rare and hard-earned, and Whelan wondered if this dapper man was from the Illinois Lottery office.

"This fine gentleman is great and famous journalist from *Chicago Sun-Times* newspaper."

Oh God, Whelan thought, the newspapers. Jail can't be far away, boys. To the dapper man, he extended a hand. "Paul Whelan."

The other man took Whelan's hand in a tight grip meant to show manliness and a stout heart and said, "Kermit Noyes" in a voice that showed how tickled he was to be Kermit Noyes.

"Oh," Whelan said. He looked from Rashid to Gus and said, "This is your big chance, boys. A famous restaurant reviewer at the House of Zeus."

Somewhere the Gods are laughing, he thought.

Rashid nodded at Noyes. "My father was journalist in Iran. Very brave man. He spoke out against crimes of Shah. He was political prisoner."

"I thought he was an engineer," Whelan said.

"Yes, yes, engineer, but before, he was journalist, like this man."

"And before that, cleaner of streets!" Gus said, then burst out laughing.

"And yours? Your father was cleaner of toilets." Rashid's hand groped the countertop for a weapon.

"I will put *you* in toilet." Gus took a step toward his cousin.

Mr. Noyes blinked in alarm, then looked at Whelan. "Are we going to have trouble here?"

"No, but I'd get my food order in early."

The cousins stared at each other for a moment and breathed heavily, but the danger had clearly passed. Rashid was the first to collect himself.

"We have distinguished guest. You, too, Detective Whelan."

"Do you want to wait on Mr. Whelan?" Kermit Noyes asked.

"Oh, uh, yes, sure." Rashid feigned interest in Whelan's direction.

"I'm in no hurry, Rashid."

"Oh. Good."

"Go ahead, then, Mr. Abazi, you were talking about your California days."

Rashid shot Whelan a guilty look and cleared his throat before launching into the interrupted narrative. Whelan was soon sorry he'd missed the beginning, for the California part of Rashid's story was a roaring wonder of a tale, a fanciful stew of Mark Twain, Jack London, and Bret

Harte, featuring two hardworking and indomitable immigrants fighting poverty, the corruption of local politicians, and the prejudice of all the one thousand and one ethnic groups living in the Golden State, just to obtain a toehold in American society. And when the heartless government of the state of California closed them down on "one little technicality," these two dreamy-eyed capitalists moved back to Chicago, where they met with even more resistance, more petty corruption, more prejudice, and a brief brush with the American legal system. In Rashid's expurgated version of events, the boys had overcome the forces of evil by hiring the greatest legal mind in America. It was not mentioned that the legal mind belonged to another cousin, Reza, or that they'd overcome evil at least in part by paying people off.

When Rashid was finished, Whelan felt like clapping. He was fighting to keep a straight face when he realized that the restaurant reviewer was looking at him. He quickly trained his gaze on the overhead menu.

"Quite a place, Mr. Whelan."

"Yes, it is. I like to think there isn't another one anywhere like it. At least not in our solar system."

Kermit Noyes had apparently lost interest in him. He was squinting around at the improbable murals, in which ancient Persians and Medes in shiny armor slaughtered Greeks. "God, is this gory! Hey, Wally, how about that wall there?"

Cigarette in mouth, the photographer jettisoned his dark raincoat and shrugged. "If that's what you want."

"I thought, me at that table with a couple of plates of food in front of me and that picture of the temple behind me."

The photographer shrugged and Kermit Noyes looked at Whelan again. "So what do you recommend?" Rashid and Gus hovered nearby, cutting and chopping onions and tomatoes, and pretended not to be listening.

"Oh, it's all interesting. I thought when you guys did a review, you didn't introduce yourselves until you were leaving, if then."

Kermit Noyes smiled. "This isn't a straight review. This is a feature. It's part of my ongoing series on ethnic Chicago." He frowned when it occurred to him that Whelan wasn't aware of the series. "I'm covering the entire spectrum of restaurants in the metropolitan area."

"Good luck."

Noyes shot an uneasy look at the two Iranians and leaned closer to Whelan. "Listen, what kind of place is this, exactly?"

"It's pretty much what you see. A Greek restaurant run by Persians."

"That doesn't make any sense."

"What does sense have to do with it? This is Chicago. I've eaten in a Chinese restaurant with a Greek cook and a Mexican restaurant run by an Irishman. You think this is weird, you should have eaten at their other place: the world's first and last Persian A & W."

"That's nuts."

"Go with it. It'll look good in your series. As far as ordering food here, for starters, I'd recommend what they do best."

"The gyros, probably, huh?"

"No. They won't admit it, but what they do best is their own cooking. Try the shalimar kabob or one of the other Persian things. I think you'll like it. I know I—"

Kermit Noyes's patronizing smile stopped him. "I've eaten dozens of Persian specialties in other restaurants, so I'm quite familiar with them."

"Well, that's what I'd recommend. And if you come here again"— Noyes raised his eyebrows, exuding smugness from his every pore, and Whelan was powerless against the wave of irritation that crested and engulfed him—"try the ham and cheese." He winked at the boys, who beamed at him like proud fathers. In all his long, harrowing association with Gus and Rashid, there had always been a ham sandwich on the menu, and he had never known anyone to order it.

"The ham and cheese? Huh. Well, okay. Thanks."

"And I'll have the shalimar kabob, guys, with a large root beer."

"Coming right up, Detective." Rashid leaned over and raised a conspiratorial eyebrow. "You see the sign?"

"Rashid, planes coming in to O'Hare see the sign."

"You like him?"

Whelan considered for a moment. "It is a thing of great beauty. It shows . . . it shows passion. That's what I like most about it."

"Cost a lot of money." Rashid's eyes bulged with the enormity of the expense.

"Lot of bulbs, Rashid. Lot of everything."

"Good for business, though. This sign, it tells the people, House of Zeus is here!"

"I think it tells them a lot more than that, Rashid."

Rashid nodded and gave Whelan a little pat on the shoulder. "You are special customer."

"Thanks, but tonight"—Whelan nodded toward the self-absorbed journalist—"that guy right there is your special customer."

Rashid winked. "I know how to speak to this kind of people. I know how to handle him, this one. I will take care of him."

"Oh, I know you will, Rashid."

Whelan's food was ready in a few minutes, and he found himself a spot at a small table in a far corner, from which he could watch the high jinks of the other patrons. The guy at the back table still hadn't moved, but the other diners seemed captivated by the presence of the photographer and what was obviously a very important little man. Kermit Noyes played to the crowd. He waved his arms and gesticulated, sighed and shook his head, posed with his hands on his hips and gave Wally the Photographer his instructions in a voice that would have been audible to the crowd at a Blackhawks game.

Whelan ate his shalimar kabob, which had a nice bite to it tonight. He no longer felt guilty about recommending the ham and cheese: if anyone deserved an evening in the leaden company of a piece of salt-soaked meat from the early Cretaceous, it was Mr. Kermit Noyes. Whelan finished his dinner, waved to the boys, and left, pausing only to take a pulse on the guy in the back booth. It wasn't great, but it was a pulse. Whelan glanced at the remnants of the guy's meal: When he came out of his stupor, he could finish his fries.

Outside, the sign still bathed Broadway in the glare of a midday sun and Whelan decided to go back to work.

Five

THE sky was still the color of a robin's egg, but the sun had dropped off the edge of the table and the night had lost ten degrees. A loose line of people, young couples mostly, made their way toward the Music Box for some sort of festival of foreign animation.

He parked on Waveland and sat in the car for a moment. The radio was tuned to a jazz show on a small suburban station. The signal was weak and the disc jockey spoke in a voice only dogs could hear, but he was spinning very old vinyl, Bunny Berrigan, Duke Ellington, Benny Goodman, powered by the maniac drumming of Gene Krupa. His parents' music, and the music of the young men on the beach in Mrs. O'Mara's picture. Somewhere in a box in his closet, Whelan had a picture very much like it, of another group of young people on a beach just before their world had gone nova.

In the photo were his parents. A number of the young faces in that photo had not come back from World War II, and his father had come close to being one of them. His wounds had earned him a stateside assignment for the duration of the war. Whelan even had a picture of his father like the one the old woman had of her brother: a cocky young buck in navy whites, prepared to conquer the Pacific.

As he climbed out of the Jet, Whelan wondered how many of the people in his parents' photograph were gone now. Probably half, he thought. Probably half, maybe a little more. Not quite the casualty rate of Mrs. O'Mara's little group. And at least four of Mrs. O'Mara's young men had died violent deaths, two in the war, two more murdered. One missing and—Whelan presumed—dead. A lot for one picture.

Crown Liquors was a serious tavern: no one looked up when Whelan

47

pulled open the door. There were a dozen or so patrons lining the rec-
tangular bar, not including the middle-aged couple arguing in the front
window. A little cirrus cloud of cigarette smoke hung just over the heads
of the drinkers, like some alien life-form about to suck out their minds.
In the back of the long room, four young Latino men played pool and
mocked one another's skills. They were the only customers Whelan's side
of fifty.

A tall white-haired man held court over it all. He was easily six three
and big-boned, and his short-sleeved sport shirt displayed enormous fore-
arms. He nodded to Whelan and interrupted a three-way conversation,
the apparent subject of which was Babe Ruth's bat.

The bartender turned his attention to Whelan.

"What'll it be?"

Whelan scanned the handwritten signs on the walls announcing the
bar's various specials. An Italian lager could be had for half a buck and
any of a number of American whiskeys were going at fire-sale prices.
Then his eyes fell on a sign proclaiming that a shot of Courvoisier was
going for seventy-five cents and a "jumbo" could be had for ninety.

"Nobody's ever offered me French cognac for under a buck. I'll have
one of your jumbos."

The bartender nodded and came up with a hefty shot glass and poured
an ounce and a half of cognac.

"Water back," Whelan said, and the man nodded and filled a small
glass. "One for yourself?"

The old man smiled. "Give it up twenty years ago."

"What did it take?"

"My old lady sayin' she was taking the Greyhound back to Memphis."

"That would do it for me."

The barman shrugged. "You have twelve kids by a woman, you develop an attachment." He winked again and took a single from the pile
of bills Whelan put on the bar.

When the bartender gave him his change, Whelan held out a business
card. The bartender grinned. "Last one of you I saw was looking for me."

"I'm looking for someone who was a friend of a former customer of
yours. Michael Minogue was the customer."

The bartender grew serious. "Wasn't that a damn shame. Probably kids,
probably some damn drug addict. Those are the ones that go out looking
for old men. I'd like to see one of those little pricks jump me."

Whelan looked at the old man's big hands and wide shoulders and decided not to bet against the bartender. "I'm trying to track down a fellow who grew up with Mr. Minogue, a fellow named Joe Colleran."

"Don't ring no bells for me."

"I don't think he ever drank here. Is there a man named Archie who comes in here? Or a guy named Fred?"

The bartender looked down the bar and nodded. "Down there. See that short fella there at the bend in the bar? That's Archie. Fred's in the can."

"Would you do me a favor and ask him if he'd mind talking to me? I'll buy him a drink. Fred, too."

The bartender shuffled the length of the bar, spoke for a moment with the man at the far end and returned a moment later.

"Says come on down."

Whelan grabbed his drink and moved to a stool next to the old man. Archie looked straight ahead of him until Whelan was seated. Up close, Archie was pushing seventy and losing mass as he did. He was swimming in a blue work shirt and work pants meant for a tight end. He had a remarkably big head and gray eyes magnified by a pair of Woodrow Wilson-like bi-focals, so that he gave the impression of great intelligence. Baggy clothes or not, he was clean, meticulously so: close-shaved, nails clipped, and the scant strands of white hair left to him were combed straight back. He looked Whelan up and down and was smart enough not to start the conversation.

"My name's Whelan and I'm looking for a man named Joe Colleran. I understand he was an old friend of Michael Minogue and I was wondering if I could talk to you about him."

"About this Colleran or about Michael?" Archie spoke precisely, like a man used to considering his words.

"Either."

"I only knew the one."

The bartender set a bottle of Hamm's in front of Archie and another at the vacant spot to Archie's right. Whelan waited as the old man wiped the mouth of the bottle and then carefully poured half of it down the side of his tilted glass. Then he held it up and saluted Whelan.

"Slainte," he said, and took a sip.

"Slainte," Whelan said, taking a sip of his shot.

Archie looked at him and nodded. "I knew you were another Irishman. Anyhow, I still don't know this man you're looking for."

"I didn't really think you would. I was wondering if Michael Minogue ever talked about the old days and the guys he grew up with. This Joe Colleran would be one of them. As far as I know, they roamed around the country and even ran a tavern together down in Florida for a while."

Archie nodded. "Sure he talked about those times. Old men will talk about anything, son, and he was no different, except that he didn't do it as much. He was more interested in talking about the events of the day. But he talked about the tavern he had. And he mentioned his partner."

A man emerged from the rest room just the other side of the pool table. He was a tall, angular man with a long jaw and a high, hard 1940s-style pompadour that looked as though it could withstand small arms fire. He was resplendent in a baggy red bowling shirt that read PAT'S SHAMROCK INN across the back in peacock blue lettering. The tall man took his seat beside Archie and picked up his new bottle of Hamm's. Archie turned to him and jerked a thumb in Whelan's direction.

"Fella wants to know about old Mike and a friend of his." Fred nodded as though this made all the sense in the world. "The beer was on him."

Fred saluted Whelan with the Hamm's.

"What can you tell me, Archie?"

"Not much. To tell you the truth, he never called the man by name, just 'my partner.' He didn't call him Joe. At least not to my recollection."

"Did he mention any of the people from the old days?"

"Talked about this fellow in real estate a couple times. Don't remember the name, but I got the impression Mike wasn't overly fond of this guy. Said he was the kinda guy that always landed on his feet."

Real estate. Whelan thought back to his conversation with Mrs. O'Mara. "Landis, maybe? Chick Landis?"

"That's the name. Yeah. I guess this guy Landis, he was in and out of trouble and never spent a day in jail. From what Michael said, I guess they were all in some sort of trouble once, the whole lot of them. Kind of a wild bunch, it sounded like."

"Did he ever tell you what kind of trouble?"

Archie sucked at the tiny remains of his Lucky, blew out smoke and ground the butt in the little tin ashtray. "Nope, but I can tell you it was genuine, honest-to-God trouble."

"How do you know that?"

Archie gave him a sardonic look over the top of the Woodrow Wilson glasses. "It was serious enough for them all to leave town for a while till it cooled down. He told me once that he was one of the few people in the world that could say the war saved his ass. That's how he said it, too—'saved my ass.' Now you can ask around and you'll hear a lot of different stories, but you won't find a whole lotta guys that enjoyed World War Two."

"He's the first I heard of."

"Well, that's what he said. Got themselves mixed up in God knows what and had to find a hole to crawl into. Little while after that, we declared war on the Japanese and these boys had an excuse to stay out of town for a while." Archie paused but seemed to be recollecting something, and Whelan gave him time.

"You shouldn't be surprised if he didn't talk much about this man you're looking for. You see, I think it really bothered him to talk about the past. He didn't like it. It was a lot of stuff that he didn't want to remember. One night, he was in here and he was really upset because he saw this young kid who apparently looked just like one of those fellows from the old days. Just a young guy in a crowd, somebody who didn't know Mike from Adam. But a spitting image, he said, and it made him remember things he didn't want to remember. You know how that is. . . ." Archie paused, squinted at Whelan, and smiled. "No, you don't. You're not really old enough yet to know about that."

"Did he ever tell you he was afraid of anybody now?"

Archie looked at Whelan for a moment as if surprised by the question. "No, he didn't. But he did ask once if anyone had come in looking for him. You remember that, Chuck?"

The big bartender raised his eyebrows.

"Do you remember when Michael asked if anyone had been in looking for him?"

"Yep. That wasn't no more than a month ago, seems to me."

"What did he say?" Whelan asked.

"He said a guy had been following him on the street. Wanted to know if this guy come in here asking about him."

"That sounds like someone who knew him."

"Never said," the bartender muttered.

"Anybody asking about him would know him."

"Not necessarily," Archie said in the voice of one who lives for arguments.

"And did this man ever come in?"

The big bartender shook his head, then moved away to serve a customer who had just come in.

"What did Michael say about this man?" Whelan asked.

Archie pursed his lips. "He just said this guy had been following him around, watching him. Mike said he saw the guy down at the lake when he was fishing and then again on the L platform when he was waiting for a train."

"Did he say what the guy looked like?"

"Like somebody who lives on the street. Kind of dark, you know, they get that windburned look from exposure to all the elements. Not an old man, though. He thought this fellow was younger. I think that's why it spooked him a little. He was a feisty guy, Mike was, but this was a younger man. Middle-aged guy, from what he said."

"Clothes? Did he describe the man's clothes?"

"Dark jacket of some kind, like a windbreaker. And a baseball cap—red baseball cap. And this one time, he said the guy was wearin' a long, heavy wool coat, even though it was like eighty-five degrees out." Archie shook his head. "You know, he came all the way here, on the El and the Addison bus, to drink in a decent place where nobody would bother him. That neighborhood he lived in, I wouldn't give you two cents for it."

Whelan looked at Fred. "Any of this ring a bell for you, Fred?

"Yeah, he told me about this guy he thought was followin' him. But I never saw the guy."

"Well, thanks for the tip, and the conversation."

"Don't mention it," Archie said, and then leaned closer to Whelan. "This guy that just come in, I think he's been watching you."

Whelan turned casually and his heart sank. The new customer was a figure out of the world of nightmare, a hulking red-faced man in a salmon-colored sport coat, who leaned one thick elbow on the bar and studied Whelan the way a hawk watches its dinner. Whelan returned the stare, telling himself that Death or Fate probably looked something like this. The man down the bar grinned.

Nothing is ever simple, Whelan told himself.

"What's up, Snoopy?" the newcomer said across half a dozen stools.

"Albert Bauman. Gee, this is pleasant. What a surprise to find you in a saloon."

"Oh, you know me, Whelan. I like to visit all the spots of local color. Pull up a stool."

"Excuse me, guys," Whelan said, and moved down to sit next to Bauman. "This is business."

The bartender came over and smiled, tossing a coaster on the bar, then poured a new shot into Bauman's oversized shot glass from the bottle he'd been working on. "You gonna drink with this fella?"

Whelan looked at Bauman's shot and beer. "Against my better judgment."

Whelan sat down and busied himself for a moment lighting a cigarette, aware that Bauman never took his eyes from him. He nodded toward his money on the bar when the man set up his drink, then indicated Bauman. "And one for him, if he's ready."

Bauman grunted, "I'm fine," and continued to stare at Whelan.

The barman patted Bauman on the arm and moved back down to the far end.

Whelan sighed and looked at Bauman. The other man raised his thick dark eyebrows and gave Whelan a loopy smile, but Whelan was fairly certain he wasn't drunk.

"Imagine *my* surprise, Whelan. I come into one of my many hideouts, Crown Liquors, for one quick one before I head home, and here's the famous detective Paul Whelan buttonholing the locals."

"Name a tavern I could go in without running into you."

"Gay joint at Halsted and Cornelia. No, wait a minute, I been there, too."

"I just stopped in for a drink."

Bauman nodded, took a sip of his bourbon, washed it down with his beer and then began fishing in the pocket of his plaid jacket for a smoke. After an irritable moment plumbing the depths of his inner pockets, Bauman came up with a badly wounded pack of the evil little cigars that he smoked, then located one that wasn't broken. Whelan watched him light up and spew smoke out into the air, and waited for the conversation to enter stage two.

"So now we both lied to each other. Now what, Snoopy?"

"You tell me. I still think maybe we both came into the same tavern for a shot."

"No, you don't. All the gin mills in this town, including a bunch that I know you like, and you walk into one I never seen you in before. Although"—and here he scanned the noisy little crowd at the bar and the raucous pool players—"I can see Paul Whelan in a joint like this. Anyhow, we both come into the same joint on the same night, and neither one of us believes in coincidences. So why are you here?"

"See those guys down there? Tall one's Fred, the other guy, looks like an owl, that's Archie."

A tiny but malevolent light came into Bauman's eyes. He ran his big hand over his brush cut and sniffed.

Whelan smiled. "Let me guess: those are the guys *you're* here to see."

"Could be. This is the part I don't like, Whelan. Where I got to tell you you're crossing that line again."

"I don't think so. Not this time."

"Yeah, you are. This is about that old guy we found down at Montrose Beach, right?"

"Not exactly."

"What the hell does that mean, 'Not exactly'? It either is or it isn't."

Whelan drank some of his cognac. His second shot and the sun hadn't fully set yet: trouble coming. He sighed. "What I'm doing has nothing to do with your investigation. I *am* working on something, but not that. I'm looking for somebody who was a friend of his. This guy's sister's been looking for him for years, and when this Michael Minogue's story hit the paper, she hired me to help her. Basically, Minogue was the last person to know the whereabouts of this woman's brother and she thinks there has to be somebody who knew this Minogue and also knew her brother."

"Why didn't she just pick up a phone and call Minogue?"

"She never knew he was here. He apparently left town in the early fifties with her brother. For a while they ran a tavern together in Miami. She lost track of both of them, never heard from her brother again after about the mid-fifties, thought she had a shot at finding out something about him."

Bauman blew out smoke and grinned through the little cloud between them. "Sounds like another one of your 'special cases' there, Whelan. Hope your client's throwing fistfuls of money at you. Or tossing something else your way."

"She's about sixty-eight years old and she's not going to toss anything at me but lint from her purse. Anyway, somebody referred her to me, and no, she doesn't have money and she doesn't have a clue, either. She's a simple old Irish lady who can't figure out what happened to her little brother and why the big bad world swallowed him up. And there really isn't anyplace to send her, so I thought I'd poke around a bit, see if I turned up anybody who knew her brother. The major problem I'm running into is that her brother doesn't seem to have left any kind of trail and this old guy Minogue didn't have much of a family. I've really got nowhere to start."

"He had a nephew."

"I met him. I got nothing from him but where the old man drank and who he drank with. Same thing he gave you, apparently."

Something changed in Bauman's face. For a moment he looked around at the tavern, then he turned to Whelan again. "Nah, he didn't send me no place. I come here 'cause I know these guys."

A look of something like fatigue came into Bauman's eyes and a sudden thought struck Whelan. "And Minogue—you knew Michael Minogue."

"Ah, you know how it is. Yeah, I knew him but I didn't know anything about him. I knew him to say hello to. I'd come in here sometimes on Sunday nights and he'd be there watching the tube, him and these other guys. Never bothered nobody. I drank across the bar from him on Sunday nights, Whelan, and now I'm investigating his murder. It's a helluva world."

"So you haven't talked to Archie and Fred yet."

"No. They give you anything?"

"Not about the guy I want to find, no. Like I said, he doesn't seem to have left any trail."

Bauman cocked an eyebrow at Whelan and smiled. "You said not about the guy *you're* looking for. So what else you get?"

"Not much."

"Give."

"Archie said Michael Minogue thought somebody might be following him."

"Like who?"

"He didn't seem to know. He said Minogue asked if a guy had been in asking for him."

Bauman put his elbow on the bar and cupped his fleshy chin in his hand. "Description."

"Sounded like a street guy to me. Windburned, poorly dressed—windbreaker and a baseball cap, a red baseball cap."

"That's it?"

"Yeah."

"And did he? Did this guy come in asking for him?"

"No. But this guy with the baseball cap—it's not the first time I heard him mentioned. I talked to one of Minogue's fishing partners and he said the same thing. And he actually saw the guy."

"Same description, you didn't help him out?"

"No, this was before I talked to Archie. He said he saw a guy watching them, a guy in a dark blue windbreaker and a red baseball cap. Not young, but not as old as Minogue. Fifties, maybe."

"So who's the fisherman?"

"A black guy named Franklin. I found him down there not far from where it happened."

"Not bad, Whelan. You're saving me all kinds of work. What say you wait here while I slide on down the bar and have a chat with the boys?"

"Fine with me. By the way, where'd you ditch Landini?"

"We don't sleep together, Whelan. He's on his own time, he's got women to chase, cologne to buy, that kinda stuff. Me, I'm a simple guy. Stay here. I'll be back in a minute."

Whelan watched Bauman move down the bar. The material of the sport coat was stretched so tightly across the detective's back that the lines in the plaid were curved in the middle. Archie blinked his wise eyes in Bauman's direction and then looked away. Fred glanced up, saw Bauman bearing down on him, and looked like a sailor watching a squall line. Bauman set down his shot and beer, then came up with his badge and showed it around.

Archie stared behind his magnifiers and Fred looked as if he'd found a worm in his drink, but in a moment, their body language showed that Bauman had them both calmed down. He signaled for the bartender, called him Chuck, and ordered a round of drinks, including another jumbo shot for himself.

Whelan had watched Bauman work dozens of times, but this was a new persona. The two old men watched Bauman wordlessly for a moment and then all three exploded in laughter. Whatever he'd said had left Archie and Fred shaking their heads and chuckling as Bauman wiped his eyes. They talked for several minutes and then Bauman broke up his audience again. A moment later, he lifted his beefy form from the stool between them, patted each of the old men on the back, and waved.

He smiled at Whelan as he set his empty shot glass down.

"I'll have another when you're in the neighborhood, Chuck. And take care of my pal here," Bauman said with a nod in Whelan's direction.

The barman was on top of him before the sentence had cleared the air, pouring a shot and grinning and asking Whelan if he wanted one.

"No thanks. Not yet."

"Come on, Whelan. You used to be such a good time."

"All right." He took a sip of his shot and studied Bauman. "I thought I'd seen all your moves, Bauman."

"Ah, they're okay. That little Archie is a sharp old fucker. Now Fred there, he wouldn't notice a bus in the men's john, but he's good people."

"You looked like one of the boys there."

"You gotta know when you can't be a cop. I tell fucking Landini this all the time, but he don't get it yet. Thinks he's gotta sound like fucking Rommel on the march no matter who he's talking to." He drained the jumbo shot, took a sip of beer and belched. "So. Do yourself any good?"

"Not as far as I can see. Neither of them knew anything about this Joe Colleran."

"What do you do now?"

"I think I'm pretty much finished. Now comes the part I don't like. I have to tell this old lady there's no trace of her brother."

"Could be worse, Whelan. You could be tellin' her he's dead."

"I think he is. I've pretty much thought that from the beginning." Whelan took a sip of his beer, which had by now gone to room temperature. He'd talked to four of Michael Minogue's friends and a relative and not one could remember Minogue mentioning Joe Colleran by name.

That probably meant two things: the first was the obvious, that Colleran was dead and had been for some time. The second was vaguely troubling: a man who avoided talking about an old friend and business partner, living or dead, had a reason. He thought about the photograph Mrs. O'Mara had given him, of the happy group of pre–World War II kids on the beach at North Avenue—and decided he needed to know more about them. At least one of them was still alive and there had to be others. No, he told himself, he wasn't finished with this one, not entirely. He took a sip of the lukewarm beer and noticed Bauman staring at him, grinning.

"Know what I think, Whelan? I think you're blowin' me smoke, that's what I think. I don't think you're finished at all."

Whelan looked at him calmly. Sometimes you spook me, Bauman. Aloud he said, "That's news to me, Bauman. And I don't care what you think."

Bauman shrugged and turned back to his beer. "Besides, you hurt my feelings. You never asked me how I made out."

"Okay. How'd you do?"

Bauman beamed at him. "I did good, Whelan. I did real good—but I didn't get anything from these guys. I didn't even ask them anything, actually. I knew you had it covered already. So I did okay, but not with them. With *you,* Whelan." He sniffed, rubbed his nose, finished his drink and left the bar with a wave to the bartender and a cheery "See ya, Whelan."

What the hell did I give you? he wondered.

Six

MORNING broke sunny and chilly and the new day made the usual false promises not to be like the one before. Whelan made himself toast and coffee and listened to the radio, then decided to walk to work. He stopped at the Subway Donut Shop for a quick cup of coffee. Steam coated the windows, and the long counters that faced Broadway were lined with patrons drinking coffee, eating biscuits and gravy, or smoking. There were times when it seemed that all the world's smokers collected in the Subway—to pool their efforts and turn the air gray. Whelan grabbed a cup of coffee to go, scanned the faces, looking for Tom Cheney or one of the other old men he liked to talk to, then left.

He opened the door to his office and all the breath was sucked out of him into the airless room. He opened the windows onto Lawrence and felt perhaps a two-degree change. During his absence, a large fly had apparently invaded the office, checked out the entertainment and food prospects and then died on his desk.

"I don't blame you," he said to the dead fly and brushed it into his wastebasket with a business card. He drank a quick cup of water from his cooler, listened to the comforting gurgle of the air bubbles in the lovely glass tank, and laid Mrs. O'Mara's beach photo on the desk. For several minutes he thought about what he'd learned the previous day and wondered anew what it was that he'd given Bauman. Finally, against his better judgment, he put through a call. Predictably, Bauman was out and Whelan was glad: too early to go begging. Ten seconds after he put the phone down, it rang.

"Paul Whelan."

He heard a snort and then the voice said, "That supposed to impress a client? You sound like you're under sedation."

"Morning, Shelley. That was my preoccupied voice. I'm trying to sound busy and distracted."

"*Lose* that one, baby. You got a nice sexy voice. Don't sound like you just got off the toilet."

"Thanks for the professional advice."

"Hey, you never know when you're gonna be hired to handle phones. Anyway, you had a caller yesterday afternoon, called twice. A Mrs. . . ."

"Margaret O'Mara?"

"Yeah. She get hold of you?"

"No. What did she want?"

"I didn't take the calls. I took the day off. Lydia was working."

"Oh Lord."

"Yeah. Anyhow, this is her note, in her own unique prose. And I quote: 'For: Paul Whelan. From: Mrs. Margaret O'Mara. Message: Have you made any progress yet?' Then she adds a whaddyacallit at the bottom."

"A postscript? P.S.?"

"There you go. It says, 'Caller gave off real intense vibes, rich peasant voice, many-layered life experience. France, Burgundy, Prussia.' Then she's got the word *Goths*. Question mark after *Goths*. Maybe she wasn't sure of the spelling."

"God Almighty. What does the other one say?"

"It says, and again I quote, 'Mrs. Margaret O'Mara, second message. See previous comments.' And then in, like, smaller letters, she writes 'Kingdom of the Franks.' "

Whelan sighed. "Thanks. I think I'm going to be out of the office most of the morning. . . ."

"So what else is new?"

"So if she calls again, tell her she'll hear from me sometime today."

"Okay. Later, Sweetie."

Whelan sipped his coffee and thought for a moment, then reached behind him and grabbed the phone book. There were a number of Pollards listed, but neither Fritz nor Casey appeared. With the name Gaynor, he was a little luckier: a Herbert Gaynor was listed in the 4100 block of Addison and another on the 2300 block of School. Chick Landis would be even easier to find. Landis had paid a few extra bucks and gotten Landis Realty listed in block letters. The office was on the 3600 block of Marshfield. Just below it, Charles Landis was listed on North Oakley. Whelan wrote down both addresses.

Judging from the listings posted in its windows, Landis Realty was a prosperous concern and it appeared to be spreading. It currently occupied a pair of storefronts in a squat yellow brick building and was threatening, according to a building permit in the window of a third storefront, to spread to an adjacent building.

The current quarters were crowded enough to justify the move, and busy enough to justify Landis's apparent confidence in his enterprise. Whelan pulled open the door and saw the signs of progress: busy salespeople. Two were speaking with clients in the office, the others were on the phone with clients. At the far end of the room, a trio of typists hammered away at their keyboards.

The oldest of the three, an animated-looking woman in her fifties, turned from her screen and gave Whelan a half smile.

"Can we help you, sir?"

She had large, startling brown eyes with a hint of humor in them. At eighteen, this one had been dangerous.

"I think I want to see that man." Whelan nodded in the direction of the inner office. Through the window, he could see a fleshy gray-haired man in a tan suit addressing his speaker phone.

"He's busy at the moment. Is he expecting you?"

"No one is ever expecting me." He handed her a card and watched her eyebrows rise.

"One moment, please," she said, and got up from her chair. She entered the man's office and dropped Whelan's card in front of him. He frowned at it, looked up at her and apparently missed something from the speaker phone. He gave the woman an irritated look, which she met with the same half smile she'd shown Whelan. The man made a helpless gesture, curled his lip at Whelan, barked something at the speaker phone and snapped at his secretary.

Oh, I like this fella already, Whelan thought.

The secretary emerged from the office and raised her eyebrow again. "Wait till he's off the phone. He doesn't really want to see you."

"Can't remember the last time anybody did."

"Perhaps you ought to get a straight job, then."

"Nope. Then I'd have a boss. Maybe one like that."

"You've got a point."

"Charming guy?"

"I can handle him," she said, gazing at the address on a letterhead.

"I believe it."

She shot him a sly smile and went back to her keyboard. Whelan took his eye off her and saw that the man in the office was waving him in impatiently.

"Paul Whelan, Mr. Landis."

"Yeah. Sit down." Landis made a stiff-armed gesture of minimal politeness and Whelan slid onto the visitor's chair in front of Landis's desk. The desk was almost bare, a startling contrast with the walls of the little office, which sported two dozen framed photographs, most of them showing Landis shaking hands with politicians and retired ballplayers and posing with teams of little boys wearing the name LANDIS REALTY on their Little League uniforms.

"You seem to know a lot of people."

"I'm active in the community," Landis recited. "You got a responsibility to the people that enable you to become successful. I wanna give something back."

"Right," Whelan said, and reminded himself that he'd always wanted to kill someone who said "I want to give something back."

"So . . . what can I do for you, Mr. Whelan? I assume you're not looking for a house or a building." Landis pursed his lips and did his best to show his utter indifference. Whelan found himself admiring the tan suit, cut so well that it almost concealed the protruding gut beneath it. But it would take more than a tailor to cover what this man had created in a lifetime of eating. Landis still had all his hair, much of it still dark, but the rest of him wasn't wearing nearly so well. His nose had broadened and was shot with burst capillaries, and the skin beneath his eyes was dark. The eyes were close-set and heavy-lidded, giving Landis a wary look.

"I'm trying to track down some people, and your name came up."

"What do you mean, it 'came up'? Who from?" Landis tried on a smile. "Maybe we got friends in common," he offered, but his eyes said it wasn't likely.

"Margaret O'Mara hired me," he said, and Landis was already pursing his lips and shaking his head. "Margaret Colleran, you'd know her as."

"Maggie Colleran?" Landis blew air out and reached for the pack of Camels on the desk. Whelan took the opportunity to light up one of his own.

"Maggie Colleran—boy, you're goin' way back there. Way back." He gave Whelan a sidelong look. "So what's she need a detective for? Why did she hire you?"

"Basically to find out what ever became of her brother Joe."

Landis frowned and the confusion seemed genuine this time. "Her brother? God, I don't know what to tell you there, Mr. Whelan. I never had much to do with her brother. Oh boy, I can't even remember the last time I heard his name. He left town a long time ago. I heard a few things back in—oh, gotta be the fifties. He was roamin' around like, you know, one of the beatniks. Him and, uh, another guy."

"Michael Minogue."

"Yeah." Landis watched Whelan for a moment, then added, "He just died. Somebody killed him, actually."

"I know."

Something flickered in the close-set eyes, but Landis just shrugged. "Fucked-up world, ain't it?"

"In many ways. I wonder if there's anything you heard about Joe Colleran over the years, anything that sticks in your mind. I'm basically trying to trace a guy no one has seen in thirty years, so anything you can give me . . ."

Landis was shaking his head before Whelan could finish. "I can't tell you a thing about Joe. We weren't . . . we were in the same group, you see, but we weren't as close as some other people. I had my friends, he had his. Couldn't tell you what happened to him. Tell you what I think, if you want the honest truth: I think he's dead."

"Do you know anyone who might know something?"

"God, I don't even know who's left from those days. I woulda said Michael Minogue 'cause, like I said, they went roaming around . . . but now *he's* gone. I didn't even know he was back in Chicago until . . ." He shrugged. "Anyway, I lost track of these guys; they were down there in Florida for, like, years."

"Right."

"That's where I'd like to be. You can sell anything, any kinda property in Florida right now, that's where it's at." He chuckled and swept an arm in a gesture meant to include his vast empire. "Not that I'm complaining, you understand."

"Course not."

"So you got my name from Maggie?"

"Yes. She gave me a couple of names and you were the first one I was able to track down. She also mentioned Herb Gaynor."

"Herb." Landis nodded, feverishly processing this last card of Whelan's. "Herb Gaynor," he said. "What's he doing now?"

"I don't know. I haven't talked to him. And you haven't heard from him?"

"Nah. Boy, these names. You're really taking me back." Landis puffed at his cigarette and tried to look like a man reminiscing. "Like I said, Mr. Whelan, I don't see any of those folks. I keep busy here and I've my other interests. To be honest with you, I'm trying to give myself a break these days. I'm only working about two-thirds time now and pretty soon I'll cut that down to maybe two mornings a week. I'm gonna turn the business over to my son." He nodded toward the window. Whelan followed his gaze and saw that he was indicating a good-looking young man in a blue suit. He could see the resemblance, though Landis's son was a little younger than Whelan would have expected.

"Maybe you can tell me a little about this fellow, though," Whelan said.

"Like what?"

"I've gotten the impression that at one time or another this man Colleran and maybe Minogue and some other people from their crowd were in trouble."

"What kind of trouble?" Landis furrowed his brow and looked interested.

"I was hoping you could tell me. I mean, maybe I'm looking for a guy that's going to be hard to find because he spent most of his time on the run."

Landis tilted his head to one side and nodded. "Makes sense. Maybe that's why they left town together?"

"Not exactly. I think this would have been before the war. I think this problem, whatever it was, may have made these guys pretty eager to serve their country. I think this happened in 1940 or '41."

Landis opened his mouth and then shut it immediately. "I never heard of anything back then, and I think I would have."

"I think you would have, too. I got the impression you were involved. Doesn't ring any bells, huh?"

Landis gave him a wide-eyed look. "Me? I never got into any kinda trouble, nothing more than any kid in those days. . . ."

"This apparently involved all or most of the guys in your group. And

Michael Minogue told people you were involved in whatever happened."

Landis passed a hand over his face and let his gaze wander over to the photos on his far wall. After a moment, he shook his head.

"There just wasn't nothing like that. Nothing I can recall, and if there was, it didn't involve me. And as far as everybody running down to enlist, well, you got to understand how we all felt back then. Yeah, guys went down right away to sign up but . . . I know *I* wasn't in a hurry to go overseas, Mr. Whelan. You see, I was already doing something the other guys all envied: I was making money. I was the one guy who always had a buck in his pocket."

"What were you doing?"

"Oh, I had a bunch of different things going. I've always been able to make money. I had a job downtown in a big store. Remember the Fair? I worked there. And I had a little book on the side. Parlay cards—you've played the parlay cards, right?"

"Sure. Never won."

Landis grinned. "You're not supposed to." He jabbed his chest with a thumb. "I'm supposed to win. Anyhow, I had a connection and I was selling the cards, and it brought in a good buck. So, no, I wasn't in a big hurry to leave it all, even though we all wanted to do right by our country. So this thing you're talking about—it didn't have anything to do with me. And I don't know who else you can ask. I just don't know who's around anymore."

"So you're really not in touch with any of the people from the old days?" He made a show of putting away his cigarettes and zipping up his vest.

"Nah. I haven't heard from anybody from the old neighborhood in years. And, listen, I hung around with a lot of people in those days, different groups. I didn't like to stay in one place too long. I guess what I'm saying is, I wasn't all that close to these fellas you're asking about."

Whelan nodded and then pulled the brown envelope from his pocket. Still looking at Landis, he drew the photograph from the envelope and laid it on Landis's desk.

"So you wouldn't know where I could find *any* of these people?"

Landis eyed the photograph and blinked. His gaze went rapidly from the picture to Whelan and back to the picture. He reached down for one last smile and came up short.

"Whoa, that's an oldie but goodie. That goes way back. Way back. I don't even know if I remember all these names."

Whelan said nothing and Landis scrambled to fill the silence.

"But there's me, and there's Joe Colleran right there. And . . ." He paused and shot Whelan a little smile. "It all comes back to you. There's Mike Minogue. Tall one's Fritz Pollard, there's little Casey—Casey Pollard. Herb Gaynor." Landis looked up and Whelan made it clear that he was in no hurry. "Tommy Moran, Tommy Friesl. Gerry Costello. Couple other guys from those days. And the babes, of course." He nodded and let his eyes linger for a moment. He grinned at Whelan, one old buddy to another now. "You can't tell from the old pictures—you can't tell nothing with these old bathing suits but lemme tell you, a couple of these were hot numbers, these broads. There's Maggie right there. She was something, Maggie was. Lot of personality, good sense of humor. Nice figure, too. There were better-looking girls in our crowd but she always had guys around her."

Landis had his attention now. Whelan leaned over and pretended to be admiring the women. There were three of them in a little group off to one side, far enough so that he'd assumed they were merely onlookers. He studied the faces and found the smiling, confident younger version of Mrs. O'Mara, light-years from the slightly dithering old woman who'd been in his office.

"Who are the other women?"

"The tall one, that's Betty Henke. The one in the middle, *that's* Ellen Gillette." Landis grinned at him. *"She* was really something: big brown eyes, a body like Marilyn Monroe, and a smile that would light up a room. She married this guy with the long face, Herb Gaynor. What a waste." He pointed to Gaynor's face in the photo. "Never seen it to fail: there's always a good-looking dame that takes up with a guy that don't have much going for him. I think they just want to settle down so bad . . ." He grinned at Whelan and shrugged. "Ah, we had some good times. And then the war happened. The war came and everybody had to grow up real fast."

"That's what my father always said."

"He was in the service?"

"Navy."

"I was in the Air Corps."

"See action?"

"No, never saw any action." Landis took another look at the photograph and shook his head. "Different world, different world back then."

"And you don't have any idea where any of these people are?"

Landis chuckled. "Hey, if you know where Maggie Colleran is, you're way ahead of me. No, Mr. Whelan, I really couldn't tell you. . . ."

"You haven't seen Herb Gaynor, then?"

"Hearing his name from you is the first clue I got that he's still alive. Last I heard, he was on his last legs."

"Gerry Costello?"

Landis shrugged. "He was a kinda spooky guy. Don't have any idea where he is."

"What about Casey Pollard, or Fritz?"

Landis met his gaze for a moment, then put on a look of distaste. "You never know when you're a kid how your friends are gonna turn out. I wouldn't wanta know either of them now. Casey, he was a drunk. He was out on the street—he was a bum, Mr. Whelan. You know what I'm sayin'? A bum. And Fritz, well, I suppose you could say he turned out better: he's in, uh, *precious metals.*" Landis grinned. "He was a junk dealer, last I heard. You throw out your old muffler, Fritz might be the guy to come along and pick it up for you." Landis laughed again. "You know, you're in your car and you're in a hurry to get somewhere and the guy ahead of you is in an old truck full of junk going eight miles an hour 'cause he's afraid his truck's gonna fall apart before he makes the next light. *That's* Fritz Pollard, Mr. Whelan. That's how he makes his living. He picks up your garbage and he hauls it to a junkyard and they give him five bucks and he buys, I don't know, he buys a bottle of Thunderbird." Landis leaned forward, putting both hands on his desk. "I don't know guys like that anymore, Mr. Whelan. I'm a businessman."

He handed Whelan the photograph and said, "I'm sorry I couldn't be more help."

"No, you've been very generous with your time."

"Don't mention it."

Whelan got up, nodded once more, and left. In his car, Whelan stretched, turned the key in the ignition. He pulled away from the curb and tried to sort out what Landis had given him. First, Landis had said enough to convince him that he'd been involved in whatever sent them all running to the recruiting station back then. There was one more thing as well, Whelan decided, a bonus: not from anything Landis had said, but from what he hadn't.

"All right," Whelan said to himself, and hit the buttons on his radio till he found something with a lot of horns.

Back in the office, Whelan called Mrs. O'Mara and she answered on the third ring. Whelan almost laughed aloud at the change in his client. On her own turf, Mrs. O'Mara was transformed: Her voice was brisk, sure of itself. This was the voice that got rid of salespeople and made certain that wrong numbers got it right the next time.

"Paul Whelan, Mrs. O'Mara."

"Oh, Mr. Whelan. Have you found out anything yet?"

"No, ma'am. It usually takes more than one day."

"Oh, it does. Well . . ."

"But I'm glad you called. I was wondering if I could drop by for a few minutes this afternoon."

"To my *house?*" She didn't exactly sound irritated, but it was obviously an odd notion. "Well, it's a mess but . . . you can come over, Mr. Whelan."

"Say around one o'clock."

"All right, Mr. Whelan. I'll give you some tea."

"That'll be great. Where am I going?"

"I'm at nineteen forty-eight West Wellington."

"I'll see you then."

Next, Whelan pulled out the Yellow Pages and looked under "Metals" and "Scrap Metals" and found nothing. Under "Recycling," he found a few obvious junkyards and the directive "See also Junk Dealers."

Of course, he told himself. You want to find junk, look under "Junk."

Under "Junk Dealers" he found three columns of listings for dealers scattered all over the city and Cicero; many were on the South Side, and if you knew the city, you could picture them. Most were in vacant lots in run-down areas, a couple were on Maxwell Street and several more right around the corner from Maxwell along Halsted, and at least half a dozen were clustered along the Chicago River. Some of the dealers presented themselves as "recyclers" or "hauling services" and many claimed to specialize: in aluminum, brass and copper, auto parts or steel, glass and plastics. But a couple of honest souls just advertised themselves as "junk dealers" and one declared his interest in "all types of junk."

He called half a dozen of them, asking if they knew Fritz Pollard or did business with a dealer or hauler named Fritz. One knew a Fritz who brought in aluminum cans in a small pickup, but the Fritz in question was apparently black. Dealer number seven occupied a large area along the river and sounded like serious junk; Whelan decided this one was worth a visit.

He sped north on Ashland to the bridge at Webster where the river passed a couple of big junkyards, one for scrap metal and the other a haven for deceased tires, and slowed down for a moment to admire the great pyramid of black rubber in the tire yard. As you drove along the river, you passed a number of great heaps of the city's detritus, little mountains of tin cans and scrap iron. He'd even seen a hill made up of crushed, discarded automobiles, but nothing that was quite the urban folk art of this dark wonder of bald tires. Carefully inserted atop one another so as to interlock and prevent the whole business from coming undone in a strong wind, the tires formed a curious herringbone pattern that ran unbroken around the perfect pyramid of used rubber.

In a more logically constructed city, Whelan thought, there would be a single street that followed the river, but not here, and it was just as well. It wouldn't be the safest street and it might offend the town's more delicate noses. But it would be a very interesting street: it would take a person through quiet tree-lined neighborhoods where boathouses stood in place of garages, past vast boatyards, little forests of masts where people with money stored their yachts for eight months of the year, past housing projects, past vacant lots overrun by weeds up to a man's chin, past railroad yards and abandoned sidings, past discarded automobiles, slag heaps and little mountain ranges of assorted junk and scrap metal.

There was a population as well: groups of small children scrambling around the banks, homeless people carving out small campsites in the old railroad yards, wild dogs on a constant search for food, feral cats with scrawny bodies and bad attitudes, and the rats. Big, sleek, well-fed rats inhabited the banks of the Chicago River, the meandering brown stream that had been the big town's birth mother. And if you were patient and stared long enough as the water went by, you might see a fish. It might be a fish out of your darkest nightmare but more than likely it would be a catfish, a fat brown catfish. Whelan shuddered at what a bottom-feeder like a catfish would be munching on during the course of a day.

Whelan navigated his roundabout way through traffic and the tree-lined streets of the Lincoln Park neighborhood, eventually ducking into Kingsbury Street, a long, narrow alleyway that ran along the river behind factories and vacant lots and the huge Finkl steel foundry. The scrap yard occupied a flat piece of land along the river between Cortland and North Avenue and marked itself with hills of scrap metal, a yellowish cloud of dust, and the constant growl of engines, dozens of engines, a hundred engines.

So this is where they all come, Whelan thought.

There were ten thousand of these trucks in the city, and they always seemed to be headed north, always loaded down with far more than they should be allowed to carry, always traveling at approximately eight miles per hour and frequently leaving bits and pieces of their load on the street behind them, and Whelan had never known exactly where they were all going. Like termites scuttering back to the nest to give goodies to the Grand High Termite, these rickety trucks on antique engines and bald tires were coming here, to the edge of the world.

Whelan realized he'd come in with the rest of the convoy and now was in a long line of them. He pulled off to one side, parking the Jet next to the remains of a plywood wall and hoping no one would mistake his car for scrap.

Belching smoke and gas fumes, the trucks moved in an ellipse around a small shack on high wooden stilts. One by one, they pulled onto a steel platform, waited while they were weighed, and a moment later a woman's arm came out the shack window and handed the driver what looked like a check. The trucks then pulled out of the long line and unloaded their odd piles of steel, tin, and copper where a couple of men in blue work uniforms and hard hats directed them. Both wore surgical masks.

From the hundred truckloads, a new mound of scrap metal grew at the side of the road, fifty feet high and a hundred feet around, made up of wire and pipe, metal scraps and rusted sheet metal, old boilers, bathtubs, refrigerators, washing machines and stoves of a dozen types and representing several generations of technology: once the hottest items on the block, they were all just scrap here.

A pair of heavy machines on ten-foot tires roared and growled and worked at the mound; a bulldozer pushed and dug at the mound to compact it while a backhoe scooped great mouthfuls of scrap from the far side and fed it into a high steel structure that resembled a garbage disposal gone mad. At the far end of this structure, fifty yards away, new mountains were being formed of shredded steel that glistened in the warm afternoon sun.

Above it all, a yellowish cloud had formed, a cloud that seemed half smoke and dust, half noise, and threatened to suck away all the blue in the sky. Whelan winced at the constant roar of the engines and the grinding, cracking sounds of scrap steel being ground and crushed into heaps. There was nothing to breathe, no escape from the sun, and the acrid things that hung in the air made it seem ten degrees hotter. Every other place in Chicago, it was a crisp sunny morning in early fall. Here it was whatever season was native to the underworld.

Whelan waited beside the platform for a couple of minutes but no one got out of the trucks, and he was running out of time. He went back toward his car and then, as an afterthought, approached one of the men in the hard hats.

Up close, the man looked to be Mexican, and his dark eyes showed puzzlement over the surgical mask. He looked past Whelan and shouted over the roar of the bulldozer.

"Watch the trucks!"

Whelan moved a few feet away from the traffic and came closer.

"Noisy place."

The eyes crinkled in what Whelan presumed was a smile and the man nodded.

"All the time, noisy."

"These drivers come in every day?"

"Every day. Some guys two times every day."

"Do you sell steel to the foundry over here?"

"No. It goes other places—Michigan, Indiana, sometimes Canada."

"Do you know the drivers?"

The man shrugged.

"I'm looking for an older man, a guy—"

"White guy, black guy, Mexican guy, what kind?"

"White guy. Older. Named Fritz."

The man squinted against the acrid air and nodded. "Blue truck."

Whelan looked around. "Here?"

"No. Not now. He was here already. He come real early. Maybe nine, nine-thirty. Blue truck. He's tall and skinny, right?"

The man in the photo had been a couple of inches taller than any of his friends. "Right."

The man squinted and waved a truck into the long oval line, then looked back at Whelan.

"What you want him for, this guy? He owe you money?"

"No." Whelan produced a business card and handed it to the man. "I'm trying to find a guy he used to know, a long time ago. I just need to ask him some questions."

The man studied the card for a while, then handed it back to Whelan. "He maybe come back late. Four o'clock, four-thirty." He shrugged. "Sometime he come back, sometime no. Come back and pull your car out of the way. You see him. Blue truck, say FRITZ on the side. He don't come back, you try nine o'clock tomorrow. Every day he come."

"Thanks a lot."

The man shrugged and moved a step away, beckoning a dusty red truck to close up ranks and get in line.

Seven

WHELAN went back to his car, squinting against the smoky air and trying not to breathe till he got inside. He started the car, glanced at the dashboard clock, and saw that he had less than a half-hour for lunch. He shook his head. Not enough time. A proper lunch didn't have to be expensive or fancy or exotic, but you had to do it right, and that meant taking the time to enjoy it. Sure, you could eat lunch in a half hour, in twenty minutes, even fifteen. All over America, they made schoolkids eat their lunches in twenty and then wondered why the kids were half-crazy the rest of the day. Whelan understood why.

The hell with it, he said.

Mrs. O'Mara had found herself a place in the old neighborhood. Usually it happened that a group of people who grew up together spread out later in life, separated sometimes by attitude or income, and frequently by geography. Whelan could name half a dozen of his friends from boyhood who now lived in the suburbs, and one was out in Oregon and another in Wisconsin. But once in awhile, you came across a group of people who happened to stay rooted to the old neighborhood no matter how many changes it had seen. In poor neighborhoods, this was the rule rather than the exception. For whatever reason, Margaret O'Mara's house was no more than four or five blocks from the spot where someone had taken a picture of her brother in uniform, and whether she knew it or not, Chick Landis was her neighbor. And if the Herb Gaynor on School Street proved to be the one she'd known, then all three were within a mile of one another.

You could see Hamlin Park from Mrs. O'Mara's front stairs. A small park, just one city block in area, it had been the hub of Whelan's childhood—the closest thing to a real park with a field house and swimming pool. Just a couple blocks west of the park was Clybourn Avenue and the Lathrop Homes housing project. And, up until Labor Day of 1967, when it closed forever, the great mad spectacle of Riverview Park.

He half-expected the door to open before he reached it. Instead, he was greeted by a note taped to the little diamond-shaped window in the center.

It was written in the language that Whelan recognized as incipient panic.

Mr. Whelan.
   I am not here. Am at shop. Sorry. Please come over to shop. 2012 W. Belmont. I am there.

Mrs. M. O'Mara.

"The shop" proved to be a small storefront on Belmont, approximately in the center of Antiques Row, a long strip of Belmont dotted with a mixture of genuine antique stores and a few junk shops. Mrs. O'Mara's was called the Tea Rose, and apart from the elegance of its name, it was apparent that she owned one of the junk shops. Whelan sat in his car for a moment and studied the shop. The casual customer might not be able to tell what kind of shop it was: her window display featured a great deal of semiworthless glassware and crockery alongside a wonderful hand-carved oak table. Some of it was marked, some bore no tags, and Whelan wondered whether Mrs. O'Mara knew the junk from the antiques. Whelan had been inside every antiques shop on the North Side, frequently in the company of Sandra, who loved old things and was knowledgeable about a great many. He preferred the junk shops because you never had any notion of what you might find, and his great love was the Queen Mary of junk shops, the great, sprawling, smelly, smoky, raucous Sunday-morning circus that was Maxwell Street.

A little cluster of bells on a leather belt made Christmas noise when he opened the door and two people gave him quick looks. One was a tall dark-haired man in glasses and a worn bomber jacket. He frowned briefly in Whelan's direction and went back to his business, peering at a heavy wooden picture frame with the intensity of a hawk at breakfast. The other was Margaret O'Mara. She was standing a few feet behind the hawklike man and working at her chin with her chubby fingers. When she saw Whelan, she blinked, glanced at the dark-haired man and gave Whelan an apologetic smile.

"Oh, Mr. Whelan. I'm sorry . . . we're just—this will take five minutes, five minutes."

"That's fine, Mrs. O'Mara. I'll just have a look around."

"Let me know if you see anything you like," she said in a voice that had gone instinctively back to business mode. She looked slightly embarrassed, then turned back to the dark-haired man, still tugging at her chin.

"Twenty on the frame," the man said in a monotone. She hesitated and he gave her a quick squinting look, as though trying to get a fix on her.

"Twenty? I was asking thirty. All right." She made a little shrug and took two steps forward to keep up as the man moved on.

He picked up a small porcelain basin with faint tracings of gold leaf around the edges. After a moment, he shrugged and said, "Twenty-five on the planter."

Mrs. O'Mara moved a step closer. "I thought thirty-five because it looks English."

He cut her off with a quick shake of his head. "Nah. It's Hull. It's American. Twenty-five?"

"All right," she said quickly.

The dark-haired man put it on a countertop next to the mirror. Next he did his hawklike assessment of a standing lamp, made a little grimace, and walked on. The standing lamp had apparently done something to displease him. He moved on and picked up a small mirror, holding the reflecting surface up to the light, then turning it over to examine the back.

"I can do thirty on this." He held the mirror up for her examination.

"All right," Mrs. O'Mara said with a little sigh, and Whelan wished he didn't have to watch her being steamrolled.

The man nodded and placed the mirror with the other items he'd bid on. As the man walked back, Whelan saw him glance quickly at an ornate wooden armchair. The man picked up a milk-glass vase, held it up and said, "Ten on the vase?"

"Oh, I guess that's okay." The man had paused in front of a pair of painted ceramic figures and Mrs. O'Mara seemed to relax a little. He looked at the bottom of one figure, then picked up and examined the second. He made a little shake of his head as though calculating, stood perfectly motionless for a moment, then said, "Fifty on the figures. I could do fifty."

"Oh dear. I think I'm asking ninety for the pair."

"A hundred, you've got marked here." He flashed his teeth at her in a friendly grin, but his eyes hadn't gotten the message yet.

"A hundred. Well, I can take ninety."

"Nah. I mean, maybe I can do sixty-five. It's what they're worth, really."

"Occupied Japan, they are."

"Who's gonna give you ninety?"

"I don't know. Maybe the man that gave me a hundred for the last pair. He collects Occupied Japan figures, you see."

The man blinked twice, shrugged, said, "Seventy."

Mrs. O'Mara said, "No thank you," and the man wore the surprised look Whelan had seen in fighters who underestimate their opponents.

"All right, ninety for the pair."

"Ah, that's wonderful."

"Well, I guess that's it for now." His eyes made a sly sweep of the room and his gaze rested on the chair. "Still got that great chair, huh?"

"Yes."

"What are you asking again?"

"One fifty."

He looked directly at the chair now. "Beautiful chair. You came down a little, I think."

"A little."

"Need to come down just a little bit more. One fifty is a lot to ask. . . ." His eyes made a little survey of the room and it was obvious that he really meant, Nobody's going to pay one fifty for anything in a junk shop.

"Ah, well." Mrs. O'Mara made a self-deprecating shrug, then smiled. "Can I offer you a cup of tea, Mr. Logan?"

The question seemed to puzzle Logan, till he realized she'd just ended their session. "Uh, no thanks. Let me pay you what I owe you here. One seventy-five, right?"

"Right."

He pulled out a checkbook and made hasty, scratchy sounds, then tore the check out with a short, sharp motion. Mrs. O'Mara beamed at his check and then went over to put it inside her ancient-looking brass cash register. The man wrapped the ceramic pieces in newspaper and then made several trips outside to pack his purchases in his car. When he was finished, he waved an airy good-bye to Mrs. O'Mara and left with the walk of a man late for many appointments.

When he was gone, Mrs. O'Mara looked at Whelan. "I'm so sorry to keep you waiting. I forgot about this appointment."

"It's all right. It was fun to watch. Nice work."

She pursed her lips in an effort to keep from smiling. "Oh, sometimes you make a dollar or two." She let the smile out of its cage. "The frame cost me a dollar. That milk-glass vase, I found at Amvets. It cost a quarter."

Whelan nodded. "You didn't get that chair for pocket change, did you?"

"It was mine—when I was married to O'Mara. We bought it at a resale store in New York. That fellow is going to buy it, I think. You just have to be patient with these things."

"He's a dealer?"

"No, he's sort of a finder. He sells to dealers."

"A picker?"

She gave him a surprised little smile. "Yes, that's what we call them. He's a good one. He sells to the best dealers, so I know I can hold for my price now and then. He'll buy that chair at one twenty-five and sell it to a dealer for two hundred, and some poor soul will buy it from a beautiful shop somewhere for four fifty. It's crazy." She shook her head. "He can't figure out how much I know, you see. Poor man, he sees I've got a little junk shop and thinks I don't know the worth of things." She made a clucking sound and then looked at Whelan with raised eyebrows, looking light-years away from the dithering old woman who'd come to his office.

"A cup of tea, Mr. Whelan?"

"That'd be fine." She nodded and went into her back room, and Whelan browsed while she made clinking and stirring noises from her back room. She emerged a couple of minutes later carrying a tray with cups, saucers, cream, sugar, and a porcelain teapot. She also had a little plate of what appeared to be sugar cookies.

The elegant little tray came to rest on a small round table in front of Whelan. "Grab yourself a chair, Mr. Whelan."

Whelan looked at the delicately made antique chairs, most of them cane- or rush-bottomed, and made a shrug of helplessness.

"Take one of those nice cane chairs, Mr. Whelan. They're just chairs, they were made to sit in."

He pulled the strongest-looking chair over and perched on the edge of it. She handed him his cup and saucer, then lowered herself onto a great fat armchair near the window, effortlessly holding her cup and saucer. Whelan sipped at his tea and burned his lip. Across from him, Mrs. O'Mara drank hers and nodded in satisfaction. She reminded him of a house cat sunning itself.

"Have a cookie. Is your tea all right, Mr. Whelan?"

"It's fine." He reached for a cookie, hoping it would take his mind off his burning lips.

"This is Irish breakfast tea. Maybe it's not what you're used to. You're probably used to Lipton's."

"Uh, no. Actually, the tea I usually drink is what they give you in a Vietnamese restaurant."

"Do they have Vietnamese restaurants now?"

"They have every kind under the sun, Mrs. O'Mara, and I eat in them all."

She squinted at him slightly, and he wondered what he'd done wrong this time.

"You're not married, Mr. Whelan?"

"No."

"Do you have . . ." Mrs. O'Mara caught herself in the act of saying "a girlfriend" and gave him a stricken look. She suddenly found the depths of her teacup vitally interesting, as though reading her fortune in the leaves.

He shifted slightly in his chair and felt himself blushing slightly for the first time in years. "I, uh, I have someone I see, but we never—we haven't, you know, talked about getting married."

I'm babbling. She has me babbling now.

"Oh. Well, that's good."

Whelan was about to ask why but caught himself. A man could be lost in conversation with this woman, he thought, tossed this way and that upon the rocky shoals of her mind and destroyed.

"Mrs. O'Mara, there are a couple of things you mentioned yesterday that I'd like to ask about, just to clarify them in my mind." She nodded and looked into the bottom of her teacup and he pushed on.

"First, I don't want to pry into old things that are better left alone, but . . . from what I've been able to learn, something happened just before the war broke out."

"Pearl Harbor, you mean?"

"No, Mrs. O'Mara. Something happened in your group, among those young guys in the picture. Something happened and they all joined the armed forces, and from what I've found out, they were happy to. Michael Minogue talked about it to some of his friends. He gave them the impression that he was glad to get into the army. I think something happened in 1941, and soon after that your brother and every one of his friends was in the service."

"Everybody was in the service—it was a war."

"I understand. But I think your young men were in a little more of a hurry to get into the fight than other people. They were in trouble, Mrs. O'Mara. I need to know what kind."

She sat motionless and expressionless, her rigid pose announcing her unwillingness to cooperate.

"I don't mean to pry, but you hired me to do this, to ask questions. . . ."

"Well, I didn't know you'd be asking *these* questions."

"I ask all kinds of questions, Mrs. O'Mara, of everyone. And I keep at it till I get something. It's not a scientific method but it works. Was your brother in trouble back then, Mrs. O'Mara?"

"Some of them that he hung around with, *they* were in trouble. Not Joe. He wouldn't do anything like that."

"Like what, exactly?"

"Anything that would get him into trouble," she snapped, and her eyes dared him to try and get more out of her.

"Fine. His friends were in trouble and he was . . . just a bystander?"

Her shoulders seemed to soften a little. "I think Joe was worried for a while. He thought he was in trouble, but it was mostly his friends, Mike Minogue and Fritz, and Chick Landis. And whatever they did, they all had to get out quick and they did. And poor Joe, he just went along with 'em. He was a good friend, Joe was. Loyal to his friends."

"What did they *do,* Mrs. O'Mara?"

"I'm sure I don't know. It had something to do with money. I think somebody took some money." By the time she got to the end of it, her voice was barely audible.

"Whose money?"

"Well, I'm sure I don't know."

He sighed. "Yes, ma'am. And all these young guys, they all left town at about the same time?"

"All the ones that were old enough, the grown ones. The young ones, I don't think knew anything about it. Casey Pollard and Ray Dudek—they were just . . . they were younger than the others."

"And then what?"

"Oh, we heard things—you know how it is. We heard this and that, we heard somebody was looking for them. . . ."

"The police, you mean?"

"I most certainly do not." She impaled him for a moment on her gaze and went on. "We heard someone was after them because of . . . this money." She sighed. "People do crazy things about money."

"But you don't think Joe had anything to do with whatever it was."

"I just said I didn't."

"What about"—Tread softly here, Whelan. "The other boys in the group, they all knew what was going on. Am I right?"

"I don't think Tommy Friesl knew much about it," she said almost before the question was out. "Tommy didn't have anything to do with any of these shenanigans, especially if they had to do with that Chick Landis. Tommy didn't like Chick. I don't know if anybody did, really."

"So why was he part of the group?"

"He knew people. And he always had money. And liquor. Even when none of us was old enough to drink, Chick had liquor. He was carrying a flask when he was fifteen years old, Mr. Whelan." She punctuated this information with a sharp nod, clearly sending Mr. Chick Landis to hell on the next flight, at least in her mind's eye. "Tommy never liked him. In one of his letters, he told me Chick caused the whole thing."

"But he didn't tell you what it was?" Whelan asked, hoping he was hiding his exasperation.

"No. He just said that Landis was the cause of all the, you know, the trouble."

The trouble. To Whelan's grandmother, "the Trouble" had meant something more significant, the Easter Rising and the Irish civil war, the Black and Tans. God only knew what it meant to Mrs. O'Mara.

"And then, you know, the letters stopped coming and he was gone. I wrote him all through the war, sometimes I wrote him a letter every day, all through the war. And then he was gone. France, they buried him in. He's buried in France."

She said the last four words very softly, not fully resigned to it yet after all these years. He found himself wondering how long she'd had to wait for O'Mara to come along and take her mind off her young soldier.

"I'm really sorry to be digging around like this."

"Oh, no, it's all right. You're just doing your job, like you said." She composed her features and sipped at her tea, and Whelan could see the visible effort of will involved. Once more he reminded himself to take her a little more seriously.

"I know it must seem strange, my asking about all these things that may or may not have anything to do with Joe, but I have to do it. Trying to find someone who hasn't been seen in many years is a tall order. I have to look at everything, no matter how odd it may seem, even to me."

"I understand," she said, but there was grave doubt in her voice.

"I was wondering if there was someone else that he was close to back then, somebody other than the guys in that picture. Someone he might have gotten in touch with—friends, acquaintances, distant relatives."

"Nobody."

"How about a girl?"

"Oh, Joe wasn't really much of a ladies' man. Not like some of the other boys—Michael Minogue and Tommy Moran, they were the best-looking boys. Ray Dudek was very handsome, but he . . . he was younger. The only girl Joe ever went out with back then was Betty Henke, and that never amounted to anything."

He remembered Landis naming the three young women in the photo, including the young Maggie Colleran.

"A friend of yours?"

"Oh sure. We were in school together. She married a Swede."

"Is she still . . ." He caught himself about to say "alive," and switched to "in town?"

"I don't know, Mr. Whelan. I haven't seen or heard from her in . . . oh, it must be twenty years. We used to go out together to parties and the movies, things like that. I remember we had a party on VJ-day, all of us, over at Johnny Van Horn's on Roscoe. That was a big hall with a bar and a dance floor and—"

"I remember it. My parents took me to a couple of family parties there. A wedding, too, one time."

"You grew up around here?"

"When I was very small, we lived about four blocks from here. On Clybourn."

Mrs. O'Mara blinked slowly and seemed to look at him with new interest. "Anyhow, she was at that party. She got engaged a few months after that. She was a very nice girl, Betty, but Joe wasn't interested in getting married just then and Betty wanted a family. So she married this fellow. He was a Swede, I think. Maybe a Norwegian. I get them all confused."

"I think it confuses them, too. So you're not in touch with her."

"No, but you can look her up in the book. Torgeson, her name is now. Her husband had some kind of strange name like Larry. It wasn't Larry, though."

"Lars?"

"I don't know." She seemed irritated. "Maybe that was it. Lars. The names people give their children."

"I think it's common over there."

"I never heard of any Lars in the Bible."

"The Swedes don't care. And what about the rest of them, Mrs. O'Mara—what happened to the boys when they came back?"

"Well, nothing. I never heard any more about the trouble, whatever it was. The ones that came back, most of them settled down, went back to work. That's when they were going to start their business, Joe and Mike Minogue. But it never happened."

"Do you know why?"

"Oh, a lot of things. See, they wanted to open a tavern. There's good money to be made in a tavern. But you need a liquor license for that, and they couldn't get one, at least not here."

"Did he say why? I assume he had enough money."

Mrs. O'Mara gave him a look that meant, You are a mooncalf, and then said, "You had to know somebody to get one, Mr. Whelan. That part never changes. You have to know somebody. And you have to know people to pass all the inspections. Joe knew a few people but there were other tavern owners around the neighborhood that didn't want any competition. They would have made it hard for a couple of boys starting a new one. So they just did this and that for a while, and saved their money. Then they just left town."

"It's still that way to some extent, Mrs. O'Mara, and the number of liquor licenses is strictly limited. Now somebody has to give one up for a new place to get one."

Something was missing: more than likely, she was leaving something out, whether intentionally or because it was painful to her. He sipped at his tea and waited for a moment, conscious of Mrs. O'Mara watching him.

"Mrs. O'Mara," he began, pretending to study the delicate floral pattern in her china, "I don't know for sure, but if it was my dream to open a tavern and I'd just come back from years in the service, I think it would take a little more to start me thinking about leaving town. And if you proved to me that I just flat out couldn't open a tavern, for whatever reason"—now he met her eyes—"I'd find another kind of business to open. I wouldn't leave town over that. I think the thing that drove these kids into the army in 1941 is the same thing that eventually drove your brother and Michael Minogue out of town for good."

"No." She stared at him for a moment. "That was all finished, that trouble. And Joe didn't *want* to open another business, he wanted to be a saloon owner. It was what he'd always wanted, a tavern, his own tavern." Her face reddened and she stiffened slightly in the big chair. There was nothing else in her face to indicate her change in mood, but he'd gotten to her.

"He was a young man; he was a bachelor with a dollar in his pocket and he could go where he pleased. He had no wife—I already told you he didn't have any girlfriends, not really. He tried to start seeing Betty Henke again, but she was already seeing this"—she waved a hand irritably—"this Norwegian, and I think that's when he realized he had to get serious about settling down or she was gonna marry this other boy. And he wasn't interested in marrying her. And then that terrible . . . thing happened to Ray Dudek. It was a bad time for all of us."

It looked to Whelan as though she would go on, but she was slightly out of breath, and she stopped suddenly and picked up her tea. She did not look at him as she sipped at it.

"Mrs. O'Mara, I'm just trying to make certain that whatever these young guys did back then didn't continue to dog your brother." She set down her tea and said nothing. "And Ray Dudek is the man who was killed, you told me."

She nodded and seemed reluctant to add anything, then simply said, "In a holdup." He gave her a long silence and she filled it. "They stabbed him for his wallet. They didn't have to kill him, not for the few dollars he had. Just back from overseas, he wasn't even out of the service yet. He was in his white uniform. In Riverview, it happened, Mr. Whelan. The poor boy went to Riverview in his uniform and somebody killed him for his wallet. People are crazy, Mr. Whelan."

"Did the police ever charge anyone?"

"No. They never caught them. Everybody said it was kids. Some of the boys said maybe it was a fight."

"A fight?"

"Ray was always fighting. He had a terrible temper and he was pretty tough, he came from a very tough home. Not a good home at all. Joe thought Ray just got into a fight and the ones that killed him just took his wallet because it was there."

Whelan sat back onto the fat sofa and let it play in his mind: he could see it happening. A quick-tempered guy, good with his hands, running into somebody that said something about the uniform, maybe. Words exchanged, a couple of quick punches thrown, and the other guy pulls out a knife when he realizes he's picked one with the wrong sailor. He shook his head.

"What a place for a murder—Riverview."

"We used to go there at least once a week before the war, a bunch of us girls. Like a big party, it was. We would meet there and go on the rides. The big roller coasters and the Ferris wheel and the tunnel of love—only they called it the Mill on the Floss. We loved the rides. Do you remember Riverview, Mr. Whelan?"

"Sure. Actually, I'm haunted by it. I've never come across another place like it."

"It was a grand place. Like a dreamworld, it was. The rides and the sideshow and the little monkeys that drove those tiny cars. And sometimes we'd try to get a beer in the beer garden but they wouldn't always serve us. Even when we didn't have money, we'd go. You could always afford to get into Riverview, it only cost a nickel then."

Whelan was about to make a light remark when the change in her tone stopped him cold.

"I never went there after that. I don't think any of us did. They found him behind Aladdin's Castle. June of 1946, it was. The end of June. It was a Thursday, all the rides were two cents or five cents." Mrs. O'Mara looked past Whelan and her eyes lost their focus. "I never went there after that," she repeated, and this time she shuddered.

"And soon after that, your brother left town with Michael Minogue."

"Yes."

"Was your brother very close to Ray Dudek?"

"The younger ones all liked Joe, Mr. Whelan. He was kind of a big brother to them, he took them places and bought them things, taught them how to play ball, things like that. He liked Ray Dudek. They weren't close, but I know he was upset about Ray's killing. He said he'd always worried that Ray Dudek would have trouble in life."

"What did he mean by that?"

"Oh, just his temper, like I said. And Ray took chances and lived wild. He was a great one for taking chances. He said taking chances made life interesting."

"He told you that?"

"He told Joe. We didn't—he was younger. I didn't have much to say to Ray. He was a nice boy, though."

Whelan couldn't see any other angles to push. He set down his cup and saucer and got to his feet.

"You're leaving already, Mr. Whelan?"

He wanted to laugh. A moment ago, the old lady had probably been thinking of tossing him out on his ear for impugning her brother, and now she didn't want to lose his company. No, he thought, not *his* company—any company.

"I have to, but I'll probably stop by again as questions occur to me. For the moment, you're my only real source of information on Joe. I will be trying to look up a couple of the people from the old days, though."

"Good God, you found some of them?"

"Yes. Chick Landis, and I've got an address—"

Mrs. O'Mara wrinkled her nose at the mention of Landis. "And what did he say? Landis?"

"Not much, I'm afraid. And I've got an address for a Herb Gaynor, though I don't know if it's the right one."

"Herb Gaynor," she repeated. She blinked at Whelan. "I thought he was dead," she said in a flat voice.

"Might not be the right one, like I said. But I'll get back to you if I turn up anything."

"Thank you, Mr. Whelan. And I appreciate what you're doing for me."

"Don't thank me till I've done something. And thanks for the tea."

"Oh, that. Well, you're welcome to it. Anytime."

She showed him to the door and waited outside till he pulled out, and it occurred to him that she wanted a better look at his car.

He sighed. Maybe she'll think it's the automotive equivalent of sensible shoes.

Whelan hit the horn and she waved again and he drove away. He was almost relieved to be out of her little window into the past, and now he understood what it was that bothered him even as it fascinated him. It was his past as well, and the places, the street names and the events were the ones he could still hear his family talking about at dinners and parties thirty years ago. His grandparents had lived in the projects a stone's throw from Mrs. O'Mara's front stairs, his aunts and uncles on both sides had lived around here. He thought of his mother's fat, rain-warped photo album somewhere on a shelf in a closet of his home. The album was stuffed with hundreds of old black-and-whites relating the youth of his parents and their circle. He made a mental note to look for the beach picture of his parents and their friends. The beach in the picture might even have been North Avenue Beach.

It suddenly struck him like a blow that there was actually a chance that some of his relatives, perhaps his parents, had known some of the people in Mrs. O'Mara's photo, although Whelan's own photo predated Mrs. O'Mara's by a few years.

At the first light, Whelan lit a cigarette. At times, he was obsessed with the past, and Mrs. O'Mara's photograph fascinated him, as did the harsh fates awaiting so many of the people in it. In two days of carrying the picture around, he had succeeded only in generating more questions. He knew he was going to have trouble letting go of this one till he'd learned what had caused the whole bunch to scatter.

Now, as he drove up Damen, he forced himself to concentrate on what he'd learned from his morning's work. He wondered what the old woman had made of his conversation with Chick Landis. Whelan was certain she would have noticed the same thing that Whelan had, not what Landis had said but what he'd carefully omitted.

Whelan could see Landis looking at the photograph, he heard the nervous pause after Joe Colleran's name, and he could hear Landis ticking off the names, all the names but one. All but the most dramatic of them all, the one murdered as a young man. Landis hadn't mentioned Ray Dudek.

Eight

ON his way back from Mrs. O'Mara's, he stopped at Man-Jo-Vin's for a late lunch and ordered what he considered the house special, a greasy double cheeseburger and onion rings. The cheeseburger passed all the various tests for a great cheeseburger: it dripped grease and melted cheese, and pieces of relish and onion dropped onto his napkin from it. You could somehow taste the grill and most of the two thousand–odd things that had been cooked on its much-scraped surface.

He put the burger down and wondered what Sandra was doing in England. In his mind's eye, he saw her taking in the sights, the British Museum, the castles, the pubs, Piccadilly Circus. With her friends, or had she run into a Brit with a charming accent and winning ways? She'd told him once, to his surprise and consternation, that other men still called her and asked her out. Up to that point, he hadn't given much thought to the competition.

A woman had once told him that a man in a relationship that's getting serious has trouble imagining the existence of other men, and Whelan now guessed she was right. He thought of Sandra across "the pond" and now seemed to recall an acquaintance whose girlfriend/fianceé of ten years had gone to Europe, met a Frenchman and never come back.

Well, that proved nothing except that you couldn't trust the French.

He sat at the window counter, took a couple of bites and then put the burger down, distracted. For several minutes he watched the traffic and forced himself to think about Mrs. O'Mara's case. So far, this one wasn't turning out like any he could remember. He seemed to be learning about a dozen different things, and none of it was what he'd hired on for. None of it or all of it, he told himself. It was beginning to remind him of one of those children's coloring puzzles, where you colored in all the numbered spaces and nothing seemed to be happening—till you saw that the spots left uncolored were forming a picture.

In the case he had before him, Joe Colleran was the blank spot in the center of the drawing; things around him were beginning to take color and shape, but not the missing man. The more Whelan thought about that, the more he realized what it probably meant.

BACK in his office, he picked up a pile of unpromising mail from the floor and dropped it again when it contained no postcard. He crossed the room and opened his windows.

The first call was a quick one to the Herb Gaynor on Addison, who turned out to be a man in his thirties who knew none of the people Whelan mentioned. The second was an older man and, by the sound of his wheezing voice and deep cough, a sick man. Whelan mentioned Mrs. O'Mara by her maiden name, and the man grew more animated. When Whelan explained the reason for his call, the man began to sound confused.

"I haven't seen Maggie in . . . thirty years, it's got to be. Maybe more. And Joe's dead."

"How do you know that if she doesn't?"

He heard the man's slow, labored breathing. "That's what I heard."

"Can I talk to you for a few minutes? I won't stay long—I've got a couple of other calls to make this afternoon."

The man wheezed and cleared his throat and when he spoke again, he was panting. "Maybe when my wife's here. She's not home," he said in the tone of one accustomed to relying on other people.

"This'll take a few minutes at most."

The man breathed into the phone and Whelan asked, "When will your wife be home?"

"Three o'clock, three-thirty. She's shopping with my son."

"I'll come by around then.

"Arright," the man said. He breathed into the phone for a moment and then repeated, "Arright," and hung up the phone. Whelan heard the phone drop off the receiver and he thought he heard the old man mutter something. Then Herb Gaynor slammed the phone down, and this time it stayed.

Whelan swung by the Sulzer Library, where he fed microfilm into a machine and found himself back in the postwar world of 1946. As he sped through the *Chicago Tribune* for June of 1946, he ignored the ads and tried not to dwell on the sports stories—the real players had come back from World War II, and the great Joe Louis had won his long-anticipated rematch with Billy Conn—and then Whelan found what he'd come for— in the *Chicago Tribune* for June 28, 1946.

The story ran on page two, in the first column, under a small headline that read HOMECOMING SAILOR SLAIN IN RIVERVIEW. Whelan scanned the article, then read it twice more. It confirmed the general outline of the story Mrs. O'Mara had given him: that a returning sailor had been stabbed to death in Riverview Park, with robbery as the apparent motive. The article identified the dead man as "S1C. Raymond Dudek of 3132 N. Oakley," then went on to say that Dudek had seen duty on several ships and had recently returned from a tour of duty that included "mopping-up" operations in the Philippines and six months in the occupation force in Japan. Dudek had been currently assigned to Great Lakes Naval Base and was due to be discharged in December. There were believed to be no witnesses and the exact time of death was uncertain, according to a police spokesman. Whelan looked long and hard at the name of the police sergeant and smiled, for the man quoted was Sgt. Walter Meehan.

"The great Walter Meehan," Whelan said aloud.

On his way out, Whelan found a phone and called Meehan without having to look up the number. Four rings later, a serene voice, a cultured voice, the voice of Arthur Godfrey reading Scripture, answered.

"Hello."

"Walter? Paul Whelan."

"Well, hello, Paul. Good to hear from you. Are you calling to see if I'm still alive?"

"No, I've always assumed that you'd outlive me. I need some information."

"I'm afraid you've caught me at a poor time. I'm going out shopping with herself."

"Wouldn't want to get in the way of that."

"Would tomorrow do? I'm free tomorrow. We can have lunch!"

"One of my favorite things, lunch."

"I remember. Say one o'clock?"

"I'll be there."

Whelan hung up the phone and smiled to himself. Just the sound of Walter Meehan's voice brought reassurance that there was yet order in the universe. He had no idea whether Meehan would remember this case from the hundreds he'd investigated, but it was worth a shot and, after all, the prospect of lunch with his mentor and personal hero was better than a sharp stick in the eye.

TIME had done no favors for the Gaynors' house: it needed a fresh coat of paint and a couple of new boards in the front staircase, and the whole neighborhood would benefit if somebody stripped the ugly tar-paper facade. Whelan remembered when false brick facades of various types had been the fashion, just after the war. This one was a study in ugliness and it was beginning to peel off in places. The Gaynor house didn't really stand out, though—this was a neighborhood in need of an infusion of cash or jobs. Many of the old frame houses lining both sides of the street needed work, as did half a dozen or so men sitting on porches. A trio of them sat in sleeveless T-shirts on the porch next to the Gaynors' and stared at Whelan as he got out of his car. The three men shared the same flat faces, reddish hair, and beer bellies threatening to burst free and go rampaging through the neighborhood.

Before he could knock, the door swung halfway open and a man in his late thirties wedged himself in the opening. A bit under six feet tall, he had blondish hair beginning to show gray, a flat nose and hazel eyes. He tilted his head to one side, as though Whelan had just said something hard to swallow, and either the pose or the facial expression reminded Whelan of someone he knew.

"Can I help you?" the man said in a monotone.

"My name is Paul Whelan. I'm here to see Mr. Gaynor."

"I'm Mr. Gaynor," the man said, and the trace of amusement showed in his eyes.

"Then it's your father I'm here to see."

He nodded. "You're the one who called earlier, right?"

"Right. Paul Whelan." He held out one of his business cards.

The man studied the card and frowned at Whelan. "A detective? For what? I mean, can you tell me why you need to see my dad? He's pretty sick. He has emphysema."

"I'm looking for someone that your father knew in the old days. I'm not going to stay long."

"Let the man in, Dan," a woman's voice said with a touch of exasperation. The man in the doorway closed his heavy eyelids in the briefest show of resignation and stepped back to let Whelan pass.

"I was just asking a question, Mom. Come on in," he said, and stepped aside to allow Whelan inside.

A handsome older woman of medium height leaned her head out of the kitchen and studied Whelan with undisguised interest. She had dark silver hair, small, regular features and large brown eyes that gave her an air that mixed inquisitiveness with shrewdness. Whelan could see that, like the older women of his youth, she fought off her wrinkles with nightly applications of cream that never quite left her skin. At a distance, she could pass for fifty and was probably proud of it. In her hands she held a plastic grocery back that sagged with the weight of several cans.

"Hello. I'm Paul Whelan."

She smiled and came out of the kitchen, hand extended. "I'm Mrs. Gaynor. Come in, sir." She carried herself with a stiff elegance and seemed to glide slowly toward him, like a model, except that she wasn't tall enough. She flashed her son a look that she'd probably been giving him all his life and nodded toward the living room.

"Are you a police officer or a reporter or—what?"

"I'm a private detective."

"Oh. We've never met one of those." She blinked and gave Whelan a puzzled look. "And you were asking about Joe Colleran?"

"That's right. His family hired me to find him."

Her eyes widened. She blinked several times and looked distressed.

"I was told that your husband knew Mr. Colleran and—"

"Well, of course he did. So did I. We all grew up together. But Joe's . . . dead. He's dead ten years now, at least."

Whelan nodded and tried not to look shocked. "It's quite possible, ma'am, but—"

"You say you're working for his *family?* I didn't think he had any except his sister."

"That's who hired me."

Now she smiled. "Maggie? You know Maggie Colleran."

"Yes. It's Maggie O'Mara now. She's doing well."

"This is the first time I've heard her name in years. She moved to New York years ago. We were great friends in the old days, we went to grade school together—St. Bonaventure's."

Whelan smiled. "I went there for about four years."

"Really? Well, what do you know. And Maggie . . . you know, she moved away and she just . . ." Mrs. Gaynor waved one hand in the air in a gesture of helplessness. "She fell off the end of the earth! We never heard from her again. My goodness, this is hard to believe. Well. Where does she live? I'm sorry, this is like Twenty Questions. You came to see Herb, and he's in there, Mr. Whelan, but he might be dozing. I don't know what he'll be able to tell you, though."

"I'd like to talk to him all the same."

"Go ahead in, then. I'll be with you in just a second."

"Thank you, ma'am."

Whelan paused at the arched doorway to the living room and squinted into the semidarkness of the room. In spite of the closed blinds, he could see that the room was a masterwork of clutter, a salute to bygone notions of decorating: a piece of furniture every few inches, and no blank walls. Several of the bigger pieces—the sofa and an antique platform rocker—were covered with thick plastic gone cloudy with age, and though there were at least four lights in the room, only one was on, a small table lamp with an elegant fringed shade. At the base of the lamp lay a pair of bifocals. The lamp gave off a pale yellowish light that barely encompassed the man in the dark armchair beside it. Anyone could have seen that he was a very sick man, a dying man. He didn't appear to be awake. Whelan took a couple of hesitant steps in and then stopped. A moment later, the woman came out of her kitchen.

"Nice house," Whelan said.

The woman looked around at her crowded house and shook her head. "It's always so crammed with things. Clutter, a lot of clutter. I always wanted to get a bigger place. But we never really needed one." She watched her husband for a moment and then walked over to him and put one hand on his shoulder.

"Herb? Herb. The man is here to see you, Mr. Whelan."

"I'm really sorry to be bothering you. I promise I won't stay long."

She looked at Whelan and frowned. "Don't be silly. You have your work to do. Herb takes his nap every day but he doesn't mind talking, and it sounds like you have interesting information. We haven't heard Maggie Colleran's name in twenty years. He needs to ask about Joe Colleran, Herb."

The man in the chair stirred as though seeking a more comfortable position, then opened his eyes. He stared at Whelan for several seconds and then pulled himself upright in the chair.

"Joe Colleran," the man repeated through his throatful of gravel.

"Sit down, Mr. Whelan," Mrs. Gaynor said. "Here." She pulled a straight-backed chair close to Herb Gaynor's easy chair and pointed to it.

Born to command, Whelan thought. "Thanks, ma'am."

"Can I get you a cup of coffee?"

"No thanks, I'm fine."

She nodded and left the room.

He lowered himself onto the chair and looked at Gaynor.

"Maggie Colleran's here? In Chicago?"

"Yes. She lives here."

"We thought she was long gone. What do you know?" His voice dropped and Whelan thought he was talking more to himself than to anyone else. He nodded slowly and fixed Whelan with a long stare. "Now . . . you want to talk about Joe Colleran?"

"Yes. Maggie lost touch with him years ago and she's trying to see if anyone knows anything about him."

The older man shook his head once, then reached over to his side table for his smokes and lit up in what seemed like slow motion.

Of course: emphysema and he still smokes.

Whelan used the time to pull out his own and look around for an ashtray. He found one on a table across the room and returned to his chair.

Herb puffed on his Camel for a moment and seemed lost in thought. Then he looked at Whelan.

"What was it you wanted to know about Joe Colleran?"

"First of all, have you had any contact at all with him in recent years?"

The question seemed to take Gaynor by surprise. He frowned and his breath caught in a long low rumble, a sick man's cough, and Whelan found himself looking at his own cigarette. When he looked up again, Gaynor was shaking his head.

"Far as I know, Joe's dead. Car accident, I think."

"What? A car accident? Do you know when?"

"Oh, no, I sure don't. Long time ago, though. How long would you say, Ellen?"

Whelan was surprised to see Mrs. Gaynor standing a couple of feet behind his chair, watching her husband. He hadn't noticed her returning to the room. Her eyes were very animated and he got a glimpse of the youthful good looks Chick Landis had spoken of.

"I was telling Mr. Whelan when he came in, I think it's been ten years or something like that."

The man nodded. "Ten years at least. More, maybe."

"Where did it happen?"

"Oh, downtown someplace."

"We didn't even know he was back. He was in the South for a while," Mrs. Gaynor added.

Herb Gaynor nodded. "He got hit by a car. Some kid, they thought it was."

Whelan considered this for a moment. "How did you hear?"

Gaynor looked at his wife. "Who was it that told us? Did you read that in those obituaries?"

The woman came several steps farther into the room and made a little gesture of uncertainty. "I read the obituaries." She seemed embarrassed about it. "When you're older and you start to lose some of your friends—you know, people you haven't seen in a long time—it's the only way to find out sometimes. But I don't think we saw an obituary, or we would have gone to the funeral. We heard about it later. But I can't think of who might have told us." She looked at her husband. He shook his head weakly.

"Could it have been Michael Minogue?"

Mrs. Gaynor shook her head slowly. "Poor Michael. You heard about what happened to him?"

"Yes."

She was silent for a moment and seemed to be turning this over in her mind. "Well, you know, it could have been. They were great friends. Partners in a tavern in Florida. Do you think it was Michael, Herb?"

Herb Gaynor coughed and raised one hand in a gesture of uncertainty. "Coulda been."

She seemed to notice the cigarette for the first time and gave him a well-practiced look of irritation. "You don't need that, Herb."

He gave her an equally ritualized wave of dismissal and took a puff of his cigarette.

"Do you remember when this was?" Whelan asked.

Mrs. Gaynor gave him a stricken look. "You mean the actual year? Oh, no, I don't, I just know it was ten years ago at least. I'm sorry."

"Do you remember the time of year?"

"Fall. I remember it was fall."

Whelan pondered her words and realized that he was disappointed. He'd told himself all along that there was no chance for this man still to be alive, but one little compartment of his mind had hoped to bring good news to Mrs. O'Mara. Now the best he could do would be to find someone who could tell her something about Joe's passing. If Mrs. O'Mara was living in New York and unaware of her brother's passing, then perhaps friends had handled the arrangements. Perhaps Michael Minogue.

"Do you know anyone who went to the funeral?"

"No. I never heard about it."

The younger Gaynor stepped into the room. He had a cigarette in one hand and a mug in the other and a look of curiosity on his face. When he saw Whelan looking at him, he stopped short and held up the hand with the cigarette.

"I'm sorry. I was just wandering."

"It's not private, and it's your house. Come on in."

Dan Gaynor set down his cup and allowed himself to flop into a battered armchair.

"Well, if you're certain about Joe Colleran, I guess my work is just about done. Can you think of anyone I might talk to who was in touch with Joe Colleran before he died?"

Herb Gaynor made the slightest shrug of one shoulder, and Whelan was convinced it was the maximum movement he was capable of. "Can't think of anybody," he croaked. "All of 'em dead now."

"Oh, they're not *all* dead," his wife countered. "A lot of them, though. Surprising how many. And poor Michael. Murdered, Mr. Whelan. That poor man. What a terrible way to go. You think about all the things a person survives—he fought in World War Two, he was wounded, he traveled all over the country, he survived all of that, and then some . . . some nut kills him."

"How did you hear?"

"It was in the paper. It was in both papers, we get them both." She looked off in the direction of the darkened windows and Whelan wished he hadn't done so much to remind them of death. To change the subject, he pulled out Mrs. O'Mara's envelope.

"I have an old photo you might be interested in. I think you're both in it."

"All *right,*" Dan Gaynor said from across the room. His father didn't look as though he'd heard, but his mother craned forward with a look of interest.

"I'm in it? What picture would that be, I wonder?"

Whelan held it out and she took it, holding it carefully by the edges. She moved back a couple of steps and lowered herself gingerly into a wooden armchair with a little pained gasp.

"Arthritis in both hips," she said to Whelan, and made a little shrug. "Oh, my Lord, look at that. There they all are." Her eyes grew wide as she scanned the old photo. As she studied it, he studied her and noted, besides the youthful skin, the untouched but graceful hair and long eyelashes. Her nails were perfect, done in a darkish pink and flawless, her skirt unwrinkled, her blouse crisp and spotless. The older women he'd seen this well put together were usually in far grander surroundings—in huge mansions along the lakefront and climbing out of limos on Michigan Boulevard.

She stared at the picture for more than a minute without saying anything more, then shot a quick look at Whelan and at her son. "This is North Avenue Beach. Oh God, this must be back in 1940 or somewheres around there. Herb? We're in the picture, Herb; it's that whole group." There was a dreamy, preoccupied note in her voice. Then she looked at her husband and frowned. "Put your glasses on, Herb, if you want to see anything," she said, and the dreamy tone flew away.

Herb Gaynor was almost but not quite galvanized by his wife's hectoring voice. He struggled to get upright, felt around on the side table for his glasses, then managed to get them on. Slowly, he reached out and took the photo from his wife's outstretched hand. His skin was dark, mottled with liver spots and sagging, his arm bony compared to hers. For a moment he held the picture out almost at arm's length. It shook slightly.

After a moment, he gave a short nod. "Nineteen thirty-nine. Maybe '40. Just before the war, anyhow. Yeah. Huh. They're all there. Got a dozen of these."

He held it out for his wife and removed the glasses. Mrs. Gaynor took the picture back and gazed at it with obvious fascination.

"Oh, we don't have this one. We have lots of pictures from this time, but we don't have this one." She shook her head slowly. "There we all are. Some of the boys in this picture were dead within a very short time of this." She tapped the picture with a nail. "A couple of them never came back from the war."

"That's what I understand."

She gave him a puzzled look, then nodded. "Maggie. If you've talked to Maggie, you know about that."

"Can I see?" Her son leaned forward slightly.

She handed him the picture and for a moment he scanned it.

"Okay, I see Dad. Do I know any of these other—where are you, Mom?"

"Oh, who cares?"

"I do. Where are you? Oh, okay, here. The babes, huh?" He shot Whelan a quick smile and looked back at the photo. "Hey, Mom, you were a hot number. Look at you in that suit."

"Oh, stop," Mrs. Gaynor said, waving him off. She shook her head and blushed slightly. "Ridiculous old bathing suits. *Now* the girls at the beach are hot stuff."

"These other two aren't bad, either."

"The one in the dark bathing suit is Maggie Colleran. The tall one is Betty Henke. She's way out in the suburbs now, I don't even know which one anymore. They were both great girls."

Dan Gaynor handed the photo back and got up. "I've got to go." He nodded to Whelan. "Nice to meet you."

"Same here."

Mrs. Gaynor gave him her cheek and told him to have a nice time.

He shrugged. "I don't expect to. You don't go to these for fun." He said, "Bye, Dad," and left the room.

Mrs. Gaynor flashed Whelan a look of mother's pride. "He's going to a fund-raiser for the Democratic party. He's thinking about going into politics. He knows a lot of people in the party, and these affairs are good for his career."

"Pretty impressive," Whelan said. Mrs. Gaynor nodded and glanced at the photo again.

"I was wondering if you knew where any of the people in that photo are?"

"Oh, no. We don't hear from anybody now. And some of them are dead, you know."

"I know. I'm told that Fritz Pollard is still around, and—"

"Who told you that?" she asked, interested.

"Chick Landis."

"Chick Landis," she repeated in a dead voice.

"He seems to provoke the same reaction in everybody."

She turned her head and made a face. "I never liked that man."

"Who's that? Landis?" her husband croaked. "Watch your wallet with that one."

She shot him a quick look, then faced Whelan. "He caused more than his share of trouble for people. I wouldn't accept anything he said."

"What kind of trouble? Did he cause you trouble?"

She made a little waving motion with one hand. "No, no, just . . . people who knew him. He was kind of a gangster. At least he knew gangsters. That was the kind of man he was. What did he tell you about Fritz Pollard?"

"Not much. Just that he's still around, hauling scrap metal and things like that. I got the impression Landis hadn't seen him in a long time, and I take it that you haven't."

"No, like I said, we don't see anybody from the old days."

"How about his brother, Casey? Have you ever heard anything about him?"

"Oh, I'm afraid he's dead, too, Mr. Whelan. Long time ago. Poor boy. Haven't heard his name in years. Casey Pollard, he's talking about, Herb."

Herb Gaynor cleared his throat with apparent difficulty. "We heard he was dead. He was a drinker. Dead now. Good thing, too." Gaynor gave Whelan the look that goes along with a father's sermonizng. "He was no damn good, mister."

Mrs. Gaynor shot her husband an embarrassed look. "Oh, Herb, that's not fair."

"Like Landis?" Whelan asked.

"No, not like Landis. Landis is a crook, always been a crook. Small-time, thinking he was big-time. I had to kick his ass for him a couple times in the old days. But that Casey Pollard, he was trouble. He was no good. Always in trouble with the cops, always. Turned out to be a bum, too. Living on the streets like a bum. Good place for 'im."

"Herb. Stop."

Gaynor tried to lean forward in his chair, the better to ignore his wife. "She didn't know 'em the way I did." He tilted his head toward her. "She don't know."

"Well, I did too know them, at least—"

He waved her off and looked at Whelan. "The both of 'em were no good. Especially the young one. Little shit that he was."

"Well, Herb, he came from a very bad home. And Fritz was always nice. He was always very pleasant to me."

"Nah, he was a con artist, too. The both of 'em—you couldn't trust 'em far as you could throw 'em, and Casey was dangerous." He fixed Whelan with a knowing stare. "Goddamn jailbird, that little shit. He did time for robbery, armed robbery." The prospect of malicious gossip seemed to have worked a miraculous cure on Herb Gaynor. Maybe if you gave him the chance to dish up enough dirt on the old gang, his emphysema would disappear forever.

"How about Gerry Costello?"

Mrs. Gaynor pursed her lips and shook her head. She looked at Herb, who now wore a blank look, as though he'd just about run out of gas.

"Oh, God knows, Mr. Whelan. I'd be surprised if he was still alive."

"He was sick?"

"Well . . . I mean mentally. Maybe physically, too, but Gerry Costello just wasn't all there, you see. I think his war . . . his war experience was a very terrible thing for him, more than for most, I mean. He was wounded and he was captured by the Germans and God knows what else. When he came back, he just wasn't all there. I remember seeing him a couple of times after the war, once at a big party at a church hall, but he just sort of dropped out after that. I heard once that he was a recluse, staying in his house all the time. I haven't heard his name mentioned in twenty years, so I don't even know if he's still alive."

Whelan nodded and got to his feet, then decided to toss out one more question, pointless though it might be.

"There seems to have been some trouble just before the war, something that made a few of these men want to leave town in a hurry. Would you know anything about that?"

They were shaking their heads before he was finished. Herb Gaynor opened his mouth for a pronouncement, but his wife got there first.

"That was Chick Landis," Ellen Gaynor said. "It had nothing to do with Herb. He was never in any trouble. He was a working man already when Landis and those others were still punks."

"I didn't think it had anything at all to do with your husband. Do you have any idea what it was all about, this thing with Landis?"

"Oh, I wouldn't have any idea." She looked at her husband, who said nothing.

"But you knew it involved Landis as soon as I mentioned it." He smiled and she gave him a stricken look. "What was it?"

"I . . . I just know he was in trouble."

Whelan kept his eyes on her but was conscious that her husband was staring at him. He decided to push a little. Leaning forward, he said, "Mrs. Gaynor, let me ask you something else. . . ."

"She don't know about any of that."

Whelan looked back at Herb Gaynor. The sick man seemed to be trying to get up. He grabbed at the arms of his chair with clawlike motions. His eyes were shining—whether with emotion or with the effort of getting up, Whelan was unsure.

"You wanna know about that time? Awright, I'll tell you. He robbed somebody. He was a thief, Landis. He always had a scheme for making money or . . . or just takin' it. He robbed somebody, that's what he did. Somebody you didn't screw around with, understand?"

"I think so, but I'm not sure. Do you know who it was?"

Gaynor shrugged but had to look away. "I dunno. Some Kraut, that's all I know."

"Well, that's a start. Let me ask about one other thing. A name that keeps coming up from those days is Ray Dudek."

Whelan watched their reaction: She shut her eyes, he looked off in the direction of the window and made a little shrug.

"I know he was a friend of yours—he's in that picture, too."

"Of course. Poor boy. He was killed in a robbery."

"And was he involved in . . . in this thing Landis put together?"

"He was just a boy before the war," she said, hands flat in her lap.

"Oughta ask Landis," her husband said. One side of his body was shaking, and in his eyes Whelan caught just a flash of what a young Herb Gaynor had looked like angry.

"That would mean talking to him again, Mr. Gaynor, and that's not a prospect I relish."

Gaynor relaxed with visible difficulty and nodded. His wife gave Whelan a half smile, and he was decided to leave before he upset them even more. He waited as Mrs. Gaynor struggled out of the chair and then walked with her into the hall. At the door, he thanked Mrs. Gaynor for her time. "I hope this wasn't too much of a strain for your husband."

"Oh, he's stronger than he looks. He has good days and bad days, you know. He just has very hard feelings for Chick Landis. Landis was a hateful man." She reached back inside and came up with her old-fashioned manners. "But it was very interesting to talk to you, and it was delightful to see that picture of all those old faces. Please, Mr. Whelan, give my number to Maggie. I'd love to talk to her sometime. Tell her to give me a ring someday if, you know, if she feels like it."

"I'll do that." He shook hands with her and left.

In his car he summoned up the image of Chick Landis, conceited and gone to fat and in the money. He thought of the celebrities on Landis's wall and what he'd just heard, and shook his head.

Just who did you rob?

ON his way back to the land of dead refrigerators and bald tires, he stopped at a Vienna place on Clybourn and grabbed a cup of coffee. He leaned against a window counter and looked up Clybourn, once the main thoroughfare in a crowded blue-collar neighborhood. Up the street he saw the projects where half his relatives had lived—in a simpler time when moving into the projects meant running water year-round and no rats. In the distance, a white concrete overpass loomed like a futuristic bridge over the old street. The overpass had not been there when Whelan was a child. Beyond it, he knew, were Area Six Police Headquarters and De Vry Institute of Technology and a shopping center, but none of them had been there during his boyhood, either. In those days, you drove up Clybourn and you could see the park, you could see the two-hundred-foot steel skeleton of the Para-chutes and the tops of the roller coasters and the haze from the food tents and the thousands of smokers. And you could see the dark silhouette of Aladdin's Castle. From this hot dog stand, you might have seen Aladdin's giant face peering out at the world.

Nine

AT 4:20 he was sitting in his car with the windows rolled up against the fumes, sipping the bad coffee and watching the endless procession of all the junk trucks in the world.

Whelan would have sworn that none of the trucks he'd seen this morning had gone home, that they'd been moving around like this all day in a long noisy ellipse, eating one another's exhaust and making the sounds a truck makes just before it gives up the ghost. Many of them had the names of the owners printed on the doors or the sides of the bed, and most of them hinted at the wishful thinking or grandiose notions of the owners: *Brownlee* IRON HAULING AND SALVAGE; TOM'S SHEET METALS; R & K HAULING; P. SANDERS SCRAP AND SHEET METAL; R & S SALVAGE. The Mexican in the surgical mask was still there, idly motioning trucks over to dump their loads and move on. His eyes showed dark above the surgical mask, dark and tired and irritated.

The orangish haze overhead had nearly solidified and Whelan wasn't sure he could handle the noise for much longer.

He saw the blue pickup about the same time he finished the coffee. A thin white man and a short young Hispanic sat in the swaying cab. The truck was laying down its own dark cloud of exhaust. Rust had taken large bites out of the wheel wells and along the doors, and the load of scrap made the whole body of the truck wiggle and shake. On the side of the door, someone had printed FRITZ'S SALVAGE badly in white paint.

He waited till the blue pickup joined the little dance around the shack and then got out and headed for the spot where the truck would have to stop and be weighed. When the pickup eased onto the scale platform, Whelan slid around to the driver's side. He found himself looking into a gaunt dark face of hollows and beard stubble, with close-set brown eyes, intense brown eyes.

"Fritz?"

"What?"

"I need to talk to you after you drop off your load. I'll wait over by the Mexican guy there."

The eyes widened but before the driver could protest, Whelan walked away. A moment later, the blue pickup pulled over to the growing pile of scrap and the two men got out to unload. Their haul seemed to comprise a pile of badly damaged pipe, a few pieces of sheet metal, scraps of aluminum siding and a partial coil of copper wire. Watching them pile their take onto the growing mountain of scrap, Whelan wondered if they'd be physically able to handle some of the bathtubs and heavy appliances carted in by some of the other haulers.

When they finished, Whelan stood by the open door on the driver's side. Fritz Pollard was taller than Whelan had guessed but walked with a slight stoop. He was winded and his dark blue shirt was sweat-stained, and the little Latino man was soaked through. If this was a typical day in Fritz Pollard's life, Whelan didn't envy him.

"I'm Paul Whelan, Mr. Pollard." He held out his business card and Pollard took it with the look of a man who has seen only trouble from people with business cards.

"Detective? What you want with me?" His young companion climbed into the truck and pretended to see nothing.

"I need information. I've been hired by Margaret Colleran, whom you knew a long time ago. She's trying to find out what happened to her brother Joe."

Pollard was shaking his head before Whelan finished the sentence. "I don't know nothing about that. Can't tell you a thing. Now let me—"

"Maybe there's something you've heard that would be helpful."

"Mister, I don't know nothing about what happened to Joe Colleran, 'cept that he's dead." Pollard spoke in a curious monotone, as though detached from the conversation, and if Whelan hadn't seen the eyes, he'd have thought Pollard was bored.

"Do you know that for certain?"

"I'm just saying what I heard."

"Who told you?"

"I don't remember. Now—"

"Just give me a minute. . . ."

"Hey, move the truck. Hey, *blue!*" the Mexican was yelling. "Hey, move it or you gonna lose it." He laughed and waved Pollard's truck out.

"Where can we go to talk?" Whelan asked.

"I already told you—I don't know nothing. Now get the hell out of my way." Pollard caught Whelan with his long wiry arm and pulled him away from the cab of the truck, digging his long nails into Whelan's shirt. The movement and the strength behind it took Whelan by surprise, and by the time he had his balance, Pollard was clambering into the truck with surprising agility.

"Never underestimate an old man with muscles," his father had once laughingly told him.

Next time, I'll listen, Pa.

Pollard slammed the door shut and glared at him, then gunned his engine and pulled at the wheel. Whelan stood rubbing the scratches under his shirt and watched Pollard's truck grind its way out past the unending line of trucks bringing in new loads.

He lit a cigarette and walked slowly back to his car. Then he took out his small spiral notebook and jotted down the address written on Fritz Pollard's truck. It was an address on Elston Avenue, near the river. He didn't relish the notion of visiting Fritz Pollard there but consoled himself with the fact that Fritz wouldn't enjoy it much, either.

BACK at the office, he brought out his phone book and a pair of old suburban directories he'd picked up when one of the other tenants in the building had tossed them out. There were several Gerald Costellos listed but only one on the North Side—on Clark. Whelan squinted at the address: Andersonville, home of several of his favorite Swedish eateries. Things were looking up: if any of these Gerald Costellos was his man, it would be this one. An older man wouldn't move to the South Side after spending most of his life as a North Sider. It would be like a German pensioner moving to France: within the realm of possibility but not likely.

Though they appeared on the map to be part of the same whole, it was perfectly understood by all Chicagoans that the North Side and the South Side were actually two separate places, sharing the city name and at least certain aspects of a common language but little else. The South Siders had their own attitudes on social issues, their own baseball team, their own unique pronunciation of basic English words, their own system of numbering the streets, indeed, their own name for certain streets that ran the width of the big town: on the North Side, you drove down Pulaski. On the South Side, it was Crawford. Certain kinds of social change took longer on the South Side, particularly if they involved race.

On the other hand, South Siders were less likely to fall victim to the senseless economic swindling that passed for business on the North Side, so that just about everything cost less once you got past the Loop.

It was still possible for the mail carrier to be punched out because he stopped into the wrong South Side bar for a drink of water on a hot day, and pockets of the South Side still waited optimistically for the repeal of the Civil Rights Act. On the other hand, Whelan admitted a soft spot for certain of the South Side's contributions to Chicago culture: the archaeological treasures of the Oriental Institute, the great James T. Farrell, and the Dove Bar, widely considered the perfect ice cream bar. He called the North Side Gerald Costello and heard the phone lifted on the third ring. After a heartbeat's pause, a man spoke tentatively into the phone.

"Hello?" It was a high-pitched voice, and the tone could indicate the querulousness of a man protective of his privacy or the confusion of one unused to human contact.

"Mr. Costello?"

"Who's this?"

"Mr. Costello, my name is Paul Whelan. I'm doing some work for Margaret Colleran. Maggie Colleran, from the old neighborhood."

Whelan waited through a long pause, heard the man on the other end mutter, "Maggie Colleran," and then Costello said, "I don't see any of 'em anymore."

"That's okay. If I could just ask you a few questions, it would be very helpful. . . ."

"I told you, I ain't seen none of 'em in years. I don't need this."

Before Whelan could try another tack, the phone call ended with a loud crash that popped his eardrum.

Pretty smooth there, Whelan, he thought.

He had a little more luck with the second task: a Lars Torgeson was listed as living in Arlington Heights. He dialed the number and a woman answered. Sometimes you could tell many things about a person by the way he answered the phone. Anybody could tell that Gerry Costello was uncomfortable with phone calls, and anybody could tell that the woman on the other end loved her phone. In case of a fire, she might run to rouse her husband from his nap, but it was more likely she'd try to save the phone. She didn't so much say "Hello" as sing it. It didn't much matter to her whether the caller was her best friend or a guy selling magazines, she was delighted to hear from anybody. He recognized the type; his mother had been this way, a chattery, cheery little Irishwoman living with the silent, moody type.

"Mrs. Torgeson?"

"Uh, yes. Who's calling?"

"My name is Paul Whelan and I'm a private investigator."

He decided to play just one card and see how she reacted.

"A private investigator? Oh. Really? And what is it that you—what can I do for you, Mr.—did you say your name was Wheeling?" A note of suspicion colored the musical notes now.

"Whelan. It is very complicated to explain, but I'm working for a woman named Margaret O'Mara, whom you knew as Maggie Colleran. That is, if you are the former Betty Henke—how am I doing so far?"

"Maggie? Maggie Colleran? Oh, good God! What a name from out of nowhere." She burst into laughter, and he could tell she was holding the phone away from her to be polite. It made a nice picture: the tall, angular girl from the 1940 photograph, now gone gray, throwing her head back and laughing unabashedly at the name of an old friend.

"Now how—what are you doing for Maggie, exactly? First tell me, is she all right?"

"She's fine. She's, uh, she's a widow, and she's here in Chicago. She's currently—"

"She's back here? Oh, what do you know! She was gone for years. She married a man from New York—oh, she's a widow, you said. The poor thing."

"I can put you in touch with her if you like. I've also been in touch with another of your friends from the old days."

"Ellen Gaynor, you mean? Is that who?"

"Yes."

"You certainly cover some ground!" She laughed again.

Her good humor was infectious, and he let her pump him for information about Maggie Colleran for several minutes before he returned to business.

"What I'm trying to do for her, Mrs. Torgeson, is find out something about her brother Joe."

"Oh dear. Oh, God help her, the poor thing. She probably—does she know?"

"What?"

"That he's dead." She spoke gently, quietly. "She doesn't, does she?"

"No, ma'am, she doesn't, although I have a feeling that she suspects it. She just lost touch completely. How did you hear?"

"An old friend of ours named Michael Minogue." She paused after Minogue's name.

"I know about his death, Mrs. Torgeson."

"Anyhow. He wanted to get in touch with her and I didn't know how to. I used the number I had for her in New York and she had moved, and I didn't know how to contact her."

"Did Mr. Minogue tell you how Joe died?"

"He was in an accident, a car accident."

"In Chicago?"

"Yes, they were back here by then. Michael took care of everything because there was no family here. Then he left again, poor man. I don't know where he went."

Whelan swore under his breath and tried to ignore the heaviness that was growing in his stomach.

"You didn't know any of this and now you have to break it to her."

"Uh, no, actually, I had already heard some of it, but . . . not with enough detail to convince me. Now I'm convinced. Do you, uh, remember the date? The year, maybe?"

"No. It was eight or nine years ago, though. Maybe ten, but that's about as close as I can come."

"Well, thanks."

"Oh, I wish I could tell you something else that would make her feel better. I know he—this sounds terrible, but it's the only positive thing I can think of—he died instantly. That's what the police said. He was never in any pain."

"That's something. Thanks."

"Mr. Whelan, you have my number. Give it to Maggie and tell her to give me a call. Or ask her if I can have hers, and you can give it to me."

"I'll do both. I'm sure she'll want to talk to you. Maybe you and Maggie and Mrs. Gaynor can all get together."

"Oh, I don't know about that. Ellen isn't much for socializing anymore. I've talked to her a couple of times over the years and, well, she always says the right polite things, but she's not really interested in getting together."

"Why is that?"

"Her husband. I don't know if you've met him, but he's a very unpleasant man and he doesn't like her seeing her old friends. He cut her off from everybody when they got married. Such a nasty man."

"He did seem to have a few rough edges."

"He's just one big rough edge, Mr. Whelan. Actually, he's an old bastard. Excuse my French. He was an old man at the age of twenty-two. A nasty, suspicious, bad-tempered old man."

"Right now, he's a pretty sick man."

She made a little snort that was anything but ladylike. "Mr. Whelan, he's been sick for*ever.*"

"Well, thanks for everything," Whelan said.

"I didn't do anything. And tell Maggie to call me."

"I will."

Now he was certain, now it was over, confirmed by not one but two sources. Whelan sat at his desk and looked around the room. Then he swore softly to himself. He'd been here before, more than once. There was nothing surprising about it: if you looked for people who'd disappeared from life, you weren't always going to enjoy what you found. Still, there was an emptiness, an anticlimax to this one that bothered him. He pulled over the notepad and stared at Mrs. O'Mara's number. This was his next call, should be, but he wasn't going to make it just yet. He reminded himself that Mrs. O'Mara was a big girl, smarter than the dotty persona she stepped into so frequently, that Mrs. O'Mara probably had a pretty good idea that her brother was dead. Still, he needed to bring her more than that, he needed to be able to tell her something solid. Her brother was dead and in the ten or so years since his passing, he seemed to have dropped from people's memories.

You ought to be able to tell them something, he told himself.

He looked out his window at the traffic on Lawrence and argued that he'd learn something about Joe Colleran if he could just find out what happened to Michael Minogue. If he waited long enough, Bauman would give him table scraps.

Sorry, chubby, I don't have the time.

IF you stood at the corner of Wilson and Sheridan long enough, you'd experience the local color, whether from the halfway house patients chatting to unseen companions or the street punks trying to give the world the evil eye. Homegrown blacks and Appalachian whites, Asian immigrants, Russian Jews, American Indians from a hundred different tribes, Latinos from a dozen countries, bag ladies with shopping carts, and the men and women who lived in doorways, they all passed through this intersection where the People's Church met Burger King and McDonald's.

On a gaily painted bench at the bus stop, a bit of the local color was in evidence. A little man in a red jacket perched at the very end of the bench with his legs crossed and bopped to the music from the transistor radio in his hand. Oblivious to public opinion, the little man swung his free foot and smiled at the traffic.

A heavyset Latin kid frowned at him and the little man leaned forward suddenly as if about to pounce. The kid kept on walking, shaking his head.

Whelan sat down at the free end of the bench. "Easy there, Dempsey. He's out of your weight class."

Dutch Sturdevant looked surprised and then broke into a grin, and the nasty little boy showed himself again. "Hey, kiddo. You come to back me up if I get into a street beef?"

"When was the last time you got into a street beef, Dutch?"

"Fuck, Lincoln was President. Last time I got laid, too, I think."

"So you come out here and frighten the neighborhood, huh?"

"Ah, I like to get some fresh air. I stay in that joint"—he indicated the Empire Hotel with a nod—"I'll go nuts. Whole place is fulla old people, kid. Ain't my kinda place. I gotta be outside or I'll crack up." He shot Whelan a quick glance to see if perhaps his audience thought he'd cracked up already.

Whelan just smiled and said, "I don't spend too much time inside, either."

"I got that impression. So what's up, or you just wanna share my bench?"

"I was just wandering through the neighborhood and I thought I'd wander up here in your direction."

Sturdevant nodded. "Doing yourself any good looking for that guy?"

"No. I'm finished looking for him." For a moment, his own words startled him, and then he realized it was true. "He's dead," he admitted.

"You tell his people? His sister, you said it was."

"Not yet."

"That'll be a bitch."

"Yeah, so I'd like to have *something* to tell her. I'm trying to get a handle on how he died."

"Got anything so far?"

"Nope. I think it would help me if I could piece together a little bit more about Mike Minogue. If I could retrace Minogue's steps, I'd be closer to finding out something more about Joe Colleran."

"How'd he die, this guy?"

"Car accident. I'm putting together a theory about something that happened a long time ago, something Mike Minogue was probably involved in. I wanted to run some names by you."

"Shoot."

"Ray Dudek."

"Nope."

"How about Chick Landis?"

Sturdevant's face brightened. "Yeah, Mike called him a 'hoor.' The guy was in the paper, you know, the neighborhood one. He was shaking hands with some asshole from the Park District and Mike shows me the paper and says, 'I knew this hoor in the old neighborhood. I woulda thought he'd be in jail by now.' "

"Did he tell you anything about Landis?"

"Just that he thought the guy was a thief. He said the guy got a bunch of them in some kinda trouble but he didn't say what kind. You think this is that thing that happened in the old neighborhood, before the war?"

"Yeah, I do. Did he express any fear of this man?"

"Nah, it was more like he was irritated. He laughed a little bit about the picture—you know, a couple of fat political guys in ugly suits shaking hands and mugging for the camera. You had to see it, I guess."

"I've seen a thousand like it. And the guys in them always think they're hot shit. How about Fritz Pollard?"

"Don't mean nothin' to me."

Whelan thought for a moment. "Ever see a blue junk truck around here?"

This seemed to tickle Dutch Sturdevant. "I seen a thousand junk trucks around here. Never noticed if one of 'em was blue."

"So notice now. If you see a blue one, especially if it says FRITZ'S SALVAGE on the door, give me a call."

"Can do."

"One more thing. The man you said Michael Minogue had words with on the street—the street guy in the windbreaker and baseball cap, remember?"

"Yeah."

"Have you seen him since?"

"I don't think so."

"If you do, I'd like to hear about it."

"Why? You think he knows something about . . . you know, about Mike?"

Whelan got up. "Yeah, I do. So I'd like to hear."

"I see this guy, I'll be on top of him like flies on shit."

"You've got a poetic streak, Dutch."

"I always thought so."

Whelan waved, moving off, and the old man nodded and went back to the big-band music.

A chill wind had come up from the lake and announced a change in the season. The colder air had the smell of the icy water, the bite of the north, the promise of worse to come. Soon the clouds would join together and hang lower and stay that way till May.

He waved at Gus inside the House of Zeus and thought briefly of stopping for a cup of coffee, but the boys tended to make one big pot at lunchtime and let it stew and thicken till you could chew it.

In front of the Walgreen's Whelan threaded his way through a tight little knot of Vietnamese people, a family, eight or nine of them, all in tennis shoes. The oldest woman carried a plastic grocery bag and barked at the rest of them, making angry little gestures as she talked. Her wrath seemed in some way directed at Walgreen's, and the two youngest members of the clan, a pair of pretty and Americanized girls, giggled unrestrainedly at Grandma's anger.

Directly ahead of them, a half-naked man stood blocking the sidewalk and talking to the sky. At least it seemed that his remarks were directed up there. He turned a sunburnt face up to the sky and squinted and pointed with his index finger, muttering and nodding at his own observations. His dusty T-shirt was tucked away in the waistband of his pants, he'd lost his shoes somewhere, and he was weaving.

The Vietnamese family noticed him now, and the whole troupe came to a momentary halt as they studied the situation. Grandma wasn't impressed, though. She had seen worse, probably people with guns running through the street outside her home, and she barked something, then pushed on around the bearded man, shaking her head all the time. Her family went around him on both sides and he never gave them a look, intent on his conversation with the heavens.

From the corner of his eye, Whelan caught a stealthy movement and saw three kids, baseball caps sideways, sidling along the shaded wall of the Walgreen's. One of the boys was black but the two bigger ones were white. They pointed at the bearded man and snickered, and it was clear that the biggest of the three was going to have some fun with the man. He hitched up his pants and moved till he was standing directly behind the bearded man. When he was close, he grabbed his nose and rolled his eyes, and the other two went into convulsions. Then he bent his knees sharply into the back of the bearded man's legs and the man staggered forward. He turned, slightly off balance, and it was clear from the look in his eyes that he'd seen this routine before.

"Leave him alone," Whelan said.

The kid blinked and looked around in confusion, then saw Whelan. "Who're you, my old man?"

"I wouldn't admit to it if I was. Leave him alone."

"I ain't doin' shit. Am I, bro?" He took a step toward the man, holding out his hand as if to shake, and the man took another step backward.

The kid was turning to grin at his friends when Whelan caught his arm. "You're not big enough to do this kind of shit on the street."

The kid spun free and faced Whelan, his face red and hard.

"Don't fuckin' touch me, man, or I'll—"

The kid never finished his speech. He never saw the apparition in red that burst into the scene and actually was unaware of the newest development till he was already airborne. Whelan hadn't seen Bauman coming, either, but he saw the big cop put a shoulder and 230 pounds into the skinny kid's back. The boy left his feet with a deep grunt and struck a lightpole.

For a moment he lay motionless, then rolled over on his back and made sucking noises as he tried to get air back into his lungs.

Whelan turned to the other two kids and shrugged. "He's dead. You have to avenge him." The bigger kid blinked and began to back away and the little black kid looked about ready to give up his lunch.

Bauman knelt over the stricken boy and held out his shield. The boy stared at it and made goggle eyes.

"What's your name?"

"Can't breathe."

"I don't give a shit. Breathe later. What's your name?"

"Jerry. Jerry Oleski."

Bauman sniffed. "Dog-shit name. Where do you live?"

"Montrose and Ashland."

"In what, a cave?" Before the kid could respond, Bauman said, "Go back there. Now. Go real fast. I see you here again, I'll make you wish you were born in a fucking foreign country."

The kid made a whimpering sound. "I'm hurt."

"Nobody cares."

"I think you broke my ribs."

"No, next time. Next time you get the ribs."

The boy stared for a moment, gasping, and then began crawling slowly to his feet. His companions were already long gone.

Bauman stood up and turned his back on the kid, then growled at the little crowd that had assembled.

"You got nothing to do? Get outta here. What, nobody's gotta go to work? Move! *You.*" He pointed at a little man in sandals, a Slavic-looking little man with an unruly fringe of dark hair around an otherwise-bald head. "Move it."

The little man tugged at one of his stray locks and smiled shyly. "Not speak English," he muttered, still smiling at Bauman.

"What?" Bauman took a couple of steps and started to give the little man the Chicago version of the evil eye.

"Not speak English, mister," the little man repeated. He tried on another, slightly toothier smile and blushed slightly. Bauman started to say something, then seemed to wilt in the face of the little man's diffident good humor. He broke off eye contact and put his hands on his hips, then had to turn away completely and Whelan saw that Bauman was fighting to keep from laughing.

Whelan walked over to Bauman and nodded to the little immigrant.

"Not speak English," the man said, apparently wanting Whelan to have as much knowledge of the situation as Bauman.

"It's okay," Whelan said. He patted Bauman on the shoulder and said, "Nice man. Very nice man." The little man nodded and Whelan pointed to Bauman's chest and said, "American general—strong man," and struck a bodybuilder pose. Someone in the crowd, someone with a little more English, snickered, and Bauman scanned the bystanders with blood in his eye.

"I said take a walk, alla you." He made an all-inclusive motion with his finger and the crowd evaporated. "And *you,*" he said to Whelan, "be careful."

Whelan pointed to the little man. "He likes you."

"Go away," Bauman growled, and made shooing motions. The little man finally began backing away, still smiling.

Whelan patted Bauman on the back. "You made his day. He thinks he's met Sergeant York." Bauman half-turned, glaring. "Come on, Bauman. You're just worried you're losing it. You're trying to give the guy the evil eye to take back with him to Transylvania and he smiles. Your feelings are hurt."

"You wanna get hurt?"

"Not me. I saw what you did to that poor youth who got in your way."

Now Bauman smiled. "The future of our country." He hitched up his pants and looked around to reassure himself that the crowd had indeed dispersed. Whelan took a moment to admire the detective's wardrobe. For the occasion, Bauman had poured himself into a dark green sport coat and a knit shirt the color of Bing cherries. Little purple squiggles were woven into the body and the collar. A pair of sky blue slacks and then just the right touch of Bauman: dull brown wing-tip shoes.

"I like your ensemble."

"You called me. Whaddya want?"

"What do I want? Since when do I ask you for anything? Seems to me, you're the one who sponges off me."

"Who what? *Sponges?* I sponge off you? Oh, wait. You're pissed, huh? I told you, you gimme something last night and now you're pissed. Well, tough shit, Whelan. What I got wouldn't help you any. Got nothing to do with you. We're not working on the same case, remember?"

From the corner of his eye, Whelan saw a gray Caprice slide along the curb and come to a stop a few feet behind Bauman.

The driver climbed out and leaned against the roof of the car. He was out of season but stylish, dressed in a purplish pastel knit shirt with a pale lavender stripe coming down diagonally from one shoulder. The man peered out at Whelan from behind wraparound sunglasses. Whelan nodded and Detective Rick Landini returned the greeting, though only one accustomed to the minimalist macho gestures of Landini would know a greeting had been exchanged.

Whelan pointed at him. "His shirt clashes with yours."

Bauman snorted. "He's got colors I never saw in my crayon box, Whelan. So what do you want from me?"

"Tell me what I gave you."

"Nah. Like I said, got nothing to do with you. You're after this guy for this old lady, I'm after a killer. Two completely different things. Now I gotta go before the wind messes up my partner's do."

"Suit yourself. But don't ask me for a thing—about this or anything else."

"Whatever," Bauman said over his shoulder.

Whelan watched the big detective shoehorn himself into the passenger's side of the Caprice. It was moving before Bauman had shut the door. As he watched it pull away, he realized that it was no coincidence that Bauman appeared moments after his conversation with Dutch Sturdevant.

All right, he told himself. At least now I'm in a mood to visit Fritz Pollard again.

Ten

WHELAN drove up Elston, following the river, past the warehouses and factories. If you drove this stretch enough, you began to recognize the products of each factory without necessarily being able to say which building produced which smell. At one point Whelan could smell smoked meat and he knew this was from the big Vienna factory where God's Own Hot Dogs were made. He could smell roasting coffee beans and the darker, harsher smells of the big tannery at Webster and the river. If he drove far enough down Elston, he would eventually pass the yards where, during winter, people rich enough to own boats but not rich enough to own a place for them dry-docked their yachts and sailboats, creating an unlikely forest of masts and rigging.

Fritz Pollard's place of business was visible from a quarter-mile away. It clung to the tag end of a block dominated by two factories.

He pulled up across the street and studied the place before he went in: a small storefront on the ground floor, apartment above it with plywood in a couple of windows. The building looked as if it was beginning to give up its long fight against gravity: the rear of the building had a sag to it, lower on one side than the other. It looked like a fighter going down on one knee.

Just under the roof Whelan could see the remains of the delicate wooden scrollwork that had once gone all the way around. In its day, it had probably been a nice piece of work: a heavy stone foundation, top-quality planks, fine woodworking at the corners and under the eaves— probably built just after the Fire in 1871 and now the last of its kind, the sole building from its time left in the area. To one side, a vacant lot had been hastily walled off with planks and two different sizes of cyclone fence, and inside Whelan could see piles of junk, car parts, cardboard cartons, paint cans and tires. Just beyond it all, he could see the cab of the blue pickup truck.

Something moved just behind the door and Whelan realized he was being watched. He got casually out of the car, took his time lighting a cigarette and crossing Elston. The man behind the door seemed to step back, and Whelan picked up his pace. Just as he put his foot on the curb, an unearthly growl curdled the air around him and the nearest section of plank fence shook with the weight of a big heavy body being hurled against it. Whelan jumped back and nearly fell into the street.

"Shit."

Of course, he'd have a dog. This is a junkyard, there has to be a dog.

He looked at the bulging, sagging fence. From a tiny space between two of the planks a moist, dark, crazed eye stared at him unblinking.

I know you, dog. Without even seeing the rest of you, I know you. You're a mutant German shepherd, two hundred pounds: you've got mange and rotten breath, one eye and a bad attitude and people in the next county can smell you when the wind changes. And you've eaten human flesh.

The dog made one final assault on the wood, the fence held, and Whelan crossed the sidewalk to the door. A hand-lettered sign, a little neater than the one on the truck, read simply F. POLLARD. SALVAGE AND HAULING.

He opened the door and found Fritz Pollard watching him from behind a long low counter as old as the building. Pollard's face was pale with exhaustion but his eyes were clear and alert, and in one hand he held a long pipe wrench.

"Mr. Pollard?"

"Whaddya want?"

"Easy. I just need to talk to you."

"I already told you, I got nothing to tell you about . . . nothing." He hefted the pipe wrench. "So just go on and get out."

"I intend to. Just give me five minutes."

"I'm tired, I don't have five minutes for this shit."

"I know, time is money. You're a businessman." Whelan held up a twenty. "This is for five minutes of your time. Just talk to me for a couple minutes and then I'm out of here and you take my twenty and buy a sandwich and a couple of cold ones."

Pollard refused to look at the bill. His small dark eyes remained fixed on Whelan and for several seconds he said nothing. Then the pipe wrench was lowered to the countertop and the man's posture relaxed faintly.

"Arright. Five minutes, that's all you get. Then you get out or I'll set the goddam dog on you."

"No thanks. I saw this movie."

Whelan moved closer to the counter and tossed the bill on the scarred surface. Fritz Pollard hooked a finger into the pocket of his stained shirt and came up with a pack of Luckies. The cigarette that emerged from the crushed pack had a pinched look like its owner, but Fritz smoothed it out and patted it back into shape and popped it into his mouth. He lit it, blew smoke into the air and said "So?"

"So tell me what you know about Joe Colleran that I don't know."

Pollard shrugged. "He's dead."

"How? When? Where?"

"How? Got killed in a car accident. Some kinda car accident. Years back, this was. Nine, ten years."

Whelan pretended to be straying. He let his gaze move around the cluttered little office: call himself what he wanted, Fritz Pollard was still a ragpicker, what they had called a junkman in Whelan's boyhood. There wasn't a bare surface in the shop, not a shelf or countertop or even a windowsill. Tools, pipe fittings, old toys, crockery, glasses, cheap tableware, clothing, shoes: Pollard had found, piled and stored the leavings of a thousand people's lives in his shop on the outside chance that someone would someday pay him cash for a piece of it.

"Where?"

Pollard watched him, his slightly manic gaze moving across Whelan's face, as though he suspected he was being tricked.

"Whaddya mean, 'where'? Where'd it happen? The hell you think? Here!"

"In Chicago?"

"Yeah. He was livin' here."

"A car accident in Chicago about ten years ago."

"That's all I know."

"*How* do you know?"

"What kinda stupid-ass question is that?"

"I've got a million of 'em. For twenty bucks, humor me."

Pollard snorted and shook his head, then said, "I heard from some-body."

"Who was that? Who do you still talk to from the old days?"

"Shit, I don't know who."

"Your brother?"

"My brother? What do you know about my brother?"

"I know he's dead, but was he around then?"

Pollard wet his lips and looked away. "Nah. I mean, he was around, but it—I don't think it was him that told me."

"Michael Minogue?"

Pollard shrugged and a stubborn look came into his eyes. "Maybe it was him. Minogue."

Whelan nodded. Their short conversation had now gone full circle and had slid into territory as comfortable as old shoes: the source was now lying.

"Were you and Michael Minogue good friends?"

A quick squint, a shrug. "We went way back, you know."

"And what about your brother? When did he die?"

Pollard made a small sideways nod and shrugged, then said, "Christ, he's dead years now."

Whelan looked around the little office. "Let's see, what else did I want to ask you? Oh, yeah. Chick Landis. What can you tell me about Chick Landis?"

"Don't know nothing about him."

"You grew up with him."

"Grew up with a lotta people—don't mean I know anything about 'em now. That's forty, fifty years ago, mister. The hell's wrong with you?"

"I'm just trying to get information, that's all. It's what I do. Ever do any work for Landis?"

"No."

"You know the kind of stuff he was involved in, though."

Pollard thrust his hands into his pockets.

"I'm not saying you had anything to do with . . . you know, with that other stuff. The robbery stuff, I mean. I know he was in trouble with the law and, maybe more important, he was in trouble with somebody else—the kind of people you're not supposed to screw around with. You know about that, don't you?"

Pollard stiffened and for a moment Whelan wondered if Fritz Pollard was holding his breath.

"Were you with Landis that time, Fritz? The German guy?"

"Don't know what you're talkin' about. I don't think you know what you're talkin' about, either."

"Maybe not. I'm confused, Fritz. Seems to me there's a bigger picture here that I'm not getting. And I think it has all you guys in it: Michael Minogue, Joe Colleran, Chick Landis, you"—Fritz Pollard put his hands on his bony hips and sneered—"your brother Casey"—Pollard looked off in the distance and Whelan threw the slider—"Ray Dudek," and Pollard's eyes met his.

After a moment of paralysis, Pollard began to collect himself. "Mister, some of these guys are dead forty years. They got nothing to do with me. Know what I think?"

"What, Fritz?"

"I think you ain't looking for Joe Colleran at all. I think you're trying to find out something about Chick Landis and you think you can scare me into telling you something. You asshole, you got another thing comin'."

He picked up the pipe wrench and moved around in front of the counter. He was faster than Whelan had expected, and now he didn't seem so tired. With a sudden movement, he grabbed Whelan's forearm and raised the pipe wrench with his free hand. Whelan put a stiff-arm into the center of Fritz Pollard's chest and pushed, and the older man's balance left him. He fell back into his counter and slid down onto one knee.

Whelan backed away, took a quick glance around and saw a flashlight on a shelf next to the door. He picked it up and let it hang at his side. "Come at me with that pipe wrench and I'll feed it to you."

Pollard got slowly to his feet. His face was white except for points of high color in his cheekbones. His chest heaved and he moved slightly forward, and for a moment Whelan thought the man would come at him again with the wrench. Then Pollard leaned back against the counter.

"Get your ass outta my shop and don't come back here no more."

"Well now, I might have to come back, Fritz. You know that."

"You come back, you'll get your ass busted, mister."

"Won't be the first time, Fritz."

At the door he paused and looked at Pollard. "You know, you've got eyes just like your dog."

Before Pollard could answer, Whelan pulled the door closed behind him and walked toward his car. Darker color was coming into the sky and the big dog renewed his efforts to come through the fence. Whelan could hear the hard scratch of the animal's claws as he tried to climb up the wood.

"Easy there, Rex. Halloween's coming. You'll get to terrify the children."

THERE was no mail. There was no electricity, either, because Commonwealth Edison was attending to a problem somewhere down the block and the power had been shut off.

He went to the refrigerator for a beer and realized belatedly that the refrigerator was, of course, off.

I have no mail, I have no lights, I have no cold beer. I'm having a bad day. My woman is on the other side of the Atlantic, probably having a dalliance with some guy who talks like Michael Caine. Maybe she's having a dalliance with Michael Caine.

There was no chance that he'd sit in the dark and make a sandwich of room-temperature ham and listen to the Uptown street noises—tonight largely consisting of Uptown residents, old people and immigrants and black people and white people, all cursing out the windows at Com Ed for its inevitable, clockwork screwups.

I need someone to cook me something, I need food that will bite me back, he told himself. That narrowed it down to Thai, Pakistani, Korean, or Mexican. Leaving the actual decision-making process largely to chance, Whelan got into his car and hit the radio buttons till somebody gave him a little jazz. Somebody playing a Hammond B-3, Jimmy Smith or Brother Jack MacDuff.

He hadn't gone more than four blocks before he realized he was being followed. He couldn't see the car clearly but he couldn't shake the feeling. At the corner of Sheridan and Irving, he pulled into the Shell station, drove out again and went up Sheridan going the opposite direction. No one followed him and he couldn't tell which car the tail was. He kept going back in the direction he'd come, then turned west on Montrose, skirted the great dark sprawl of Graceland Cemetery, and this time he was sure no one was behind him.

Time to pick food. Driving up Clark Street, he realized he had almost limitless choices: Filipino food from Filipiniana, spicy Chinese from Little Hunan, Cantonese from Mr. Chop Suey, where the two smiley guys over the woks professed a great admiration for Reagan and Bush. He slowed down at Clark and Belmont and toyed with the idea of Ethiopian food at Mama Desta's but realized that he wanted something with a little more edge and then he knew what he wanted.

Like the bodacious sign the boys had purchased for the House of Zeus, the massive display of bulbs, paint and bravado marking the location of Taquería Las Americas took advertising to a new level. It was almost as big as the restaurant whose existence it announced to all of Belmont Avenue, a solid field of illuminated white surrounded by flickering bulbs. In the middle was a somewhat impressionistic representation of a taco nearly four feet long and overflowing with brown, red, orange and green material. It didn't look so much like a taco as a boat carrying a shipment to the Botanical Gardens. Above it, for reasons unclear to Whelan, was a large American flag. This was clearly advertising that worked: Whelan had first discovered the place because he'd seen the sign from a half-mile away.

The food was good, authentic Mexican done up by authentic Mexicans, three or four of them behind the crowded counter at once: a woman wrapping tamales, a young man greeting customers and taking orders in unaccented English, and The Chef, a big middle-aged man with Emiliano Zapata's mustache and a potbelly that jutted out like the Yucatán. There were several dozen things one could have here, the gamut of standard Mexican fare, and a few things one might not see, such as *orchata,* a sweet drink made with rice, milk and sugar. Yes, there were quite a few things one could have, but Chicago had five hundred good Mexican restaurants; there was only one real reason for coming to Las Americas, unless one was a connoisseur of signs: you came for a burrito.

At Las Americas, they cost almost five bucks with tax but no one had ever complained. A Las Americas burrito weighed a pound and a half and carried its load of skirt steak, avocado, lettuce, onion, tomato, cheese and beans without complaint, all bound up in a tortilla the size of a sombrero. The whole package had the weight and solidity of lead shot, the aftereffects of a grenade. The hot sauce was fiery and green from the pureed tomatillos, and the tables were set with little relish bowls filled with chopped and pickled jalapeños. To eat a burrito here, Whelan felt, was to understand burritos on a profound, even primeval level. He felt that if he ate enough, he'd eventually understand Mexico, and this seemed a worthy pursuit.

Whelan ordered a burrito and a completely unnecessary tamale, then stood at the counter and watched the big Mexican chop and shred a long charbroiled skirt steak. Eventually he would take an improbably thick double handful and drop it onto the layer of beans on the tortilla, then fill in the blanks.

He took his plate over to a little table along the far wall, next to a mirror that created the illusion that this was a big place. A few feet away, a young Mexican family sat at a large table amid enough food for a whole village, and at the far end of the room, a striking young Anglo couple sat and made eyes at each other over a plate of nachos.

Over the years, he'd brought several women here. One had found the burritos "gross" and wanted to eat hers with a knife and fork; she had also found Joe Danno's bar too dingy, so the relationship had died young. He'd brought Sandra McAuliffe here as well, and, as she always did, she'd come in intending to find something to like simply because Paul Whelan liked it. She'd been pleasantly surprised at the food but thought one burrito sufficient to feed the Red army. Watching Whelan polish off a burrito and two tongue tacos, she'd decided that she finally understood the most mysterious of all the sins a Catholic girl learned about: she now knew the meaning of gluttony.

Whelan doused the innards of the burrito with the green hot sauce and bit in. Violence mixed with other sensations and he realized he'd chosen well. He was absently surveying the other diners, in particular the handsome dark-haired Anglo girl beside the jukebox, when a bulky form bisected his field of vision and tossed a dark green sport coat on a chair.

This form was larger even than the Mexican with the cleaver, and it was dressed in red, the red of jungle flowers and strawberry soda, and he had no doubt that it was going to join him for dinner. He put down the burrito and sighed.

"Nice-looking dinner there, Snoopy."

"That was you behind me on Sheridan."

Bauman gave him a little heavy-lidded smile and tipped his head to one side. "Ah, it was just something to do. Hone my rusty detective skills. I was driving around and there was Paul Whelan, well-known investigative genius, so I thought, Hey, I'm bored, let's see what Whelan's up to. And here you are."

He could feel the irritation beginning in his stomach, meeting the hot sauce and creating a presumably combustible mixture that would visit him in the wee small hours of the morning.

"Thought I lost you."

"Awright, to be fair, you did. Then I circled around in the direction you were originally headed and I got lucky. Then when you were within a few blocks of this joint, I knew I was watching one of the famous Whelan food runs and I knew just where a guy with style and taste would go."

Whelan blinked. "You know this place?"

"I don't know 'em all like you do, I don't go to a lot of those places where they serve you sheep's innards and goat on a skewer, but this kinda place I know about. Don't sell me short, Whelan, I'm a sophisticated guy. I know about the burrito here and the pizza at the Bucket of Suds and the fish sandwich at Berghoff's and the greasy burger at Mr. G's."

With that, he walked over to the counter and waved at the big man with the cleaver.

"Hey, Hector. How's tricks?"

The Mexican grinned and waved the cleaver. *"¡Hola, Alberto! ¿Qué pasa?"*

"Ah, nothing new goin' on. Listen, I'll have what my friend over there is having. And a pop."

Whelan watched in surprise as Bauman leaned on the counter and made easy small talk with the big Mexican, his Americanized son and his quiet daughter, who favored Bauman with a luminous smile.

Bauman paid his bill and muttered something Whelan couldn't make out but which left his three acquaintances laughing and shaking their heads. The big detective hitched up his pants, picked up his plate and came back to Whelan's table.

Whelan said nothing as Bauman inserted his heavy frame into a tight barrel chair, spread a napkin on his lap, and paused for a moment to survey his food with satisfaction. A little half smile appeared on Bauman's face as he spooned hot sauce everywhere, and Whelan was reminded of Jackie Gleason.

"You appear to be some kind of prized customer."

Bauman gave him a happy smile and nodded. "I am. I been coming here since they opened. I told 'em what kind of locks they needed and put 'em in touch with an insurance guy I knew, I got 'em a little extra attention from the beat guys when they thought somebody was casing the place. Yeah, I'm a prized customer. Uh, excuse me, Whelan." He picked up the burrito, gazed at it the way new mothers look at red-faced infants, and then bit into it.

Whelan let him eat for a while and then said, "So what are we going to talk about?"

"Mexican food."

"I doubt it."

Bauman looked around at the other diners, took a quick glance over his shoulder. "I usta come around here a lot."

"For what? You never worked up here, did you? This is Town Hall."

"Nah. I had a place I liked. This was a long time ago, even before I was coming to this place. I had a saloon down the street that I liked. Old place, real old, everything inside was dark wood. Oak, inside and out. The Oakwood Inn, that was the name, but nobody ever called it that."

"Mindy's," Whelan said. "Bartender's name was Pete. They served food in the back room, great food."

Bauman smiled. "You're a man of the world, Whelan. You drank there?"

"Sure. And when I was a kid, my ma used to take us there for dinner sometimes."

Mindy's had been easily the most interesting of the little neighborhood places of his youth. The walls, ceiling and back bar sported paintings of happy red-cheeked Germanic types holding huge steins of beer, beneath which were slogans intended to edify the drinker: "If you drink, you'll die. If you don't drink, you'll die. So drink."

"And I still want to know why you're here."

"I thought we'd talk. Have an exchange of ideas."

"Nothing to exchange. That's what you said."

Bauman gave him the heavy-lidded half smile again. "Still pissed off there, Snoopy?"

"Whatever gave you that idea? Got a guilty conscience?"

"I don't have a conscience. That's for sensitive guys like you. But the girls probably like you for it."

"Not lately."

"I thought you had somebody you were seein'."

"We gonna talk about my social life now? How about a little focus here, Bauman?

Bauman gave Whelan a benevolent look. "So what's got your B.V.D.s in a knot?"

"Tell me what I gave you the other night."

"It wasn't any big deal. And it's a police matter, not something for Paul Whelan the international sleuth and bloodhound." He chuckled again.

"Have a good time, Bauman."

"The fishing partner, for one. Couldn't find him at first 'cause he moved his spot."

"What else? I know there was something else."

Bauman shrugged. "The guy in the windbreaker and the baseball cap."

"What did that do for you?"

"Sorted it out, Whelan. That's what. You sorted it out for me. We talked to a lot of people down at the lake, and they gave us what they saw. I had a whole list of people they saw roaming around the rocks there communing with the coho salmon."

"Names?"

"Come on, where would I get names? No, I had descriptions." Bauman leaned back and recited. "Young Hispanic couple, old guy on a bicycle, kid with long hair on a bicycle, your completely uniformed and armed Yuppie type on a bicycle—you know, helmet, goggles, gloves—old man in an overcoat, black guy with fishing gear—*your* fisherman—pair of black kids in Bulls shirts, couple of college guys with a football, old lady who talks to herself, *street guy in a windbreaker.*"

"But nobody saw the killing, or a fight or anything like that?"

"If they did, they aren't sayin'. So you see? You helped me out."

"I feel so fulfilled."

"Hey, lighten up. Here, I got something for you for free. Your guy that you were lookin' for, this Joseph Colleran? No record on him whatsoever. Yeah, I checked. Just for my good friend Paul Whelan. Nothing on him or this Michael Minogue, either. No records here, not wanted in other states, no outstanding federal warrants. See? I did a little work for my old buddy Whelan."

"You made a call and somebody else spent five minutes at a computer."

Bauman gave him a peeved look. "Hey, I ran both of 'em myself, even though it meant spending more time inside the ivied walls of Area Six than I like."

"I can't imagine you on a computer."

Bauman shrugged. "I can dance, too. Anyhow, now I figure you owe me."

"Nothing on either of them—how far back?"

"Birth, Whelan, since birth. Neither of 'em ever did shit anytime in their lives. No juvie stuff, no panty raids, no strong-arm robbery, no ax murders. Nothing. Okay? See, now you got everything I got." Bauman squinted at him and shook his head. "And you're still not grateful." He picked up the last section of his burrito and attacked it.

Whelan watched him for a moment and said nothing. "All right, thanks. I'm grateful. And I still think you're holding things back, and I think they'd make my life easier."

"Nah, you don't get the picture. I get information, it's mine. There's no 'holding it back': It's police information about police business, and in case you suffered memory loss from the hot sauce, you aren't a cop no more."

"Fair enough," Whelan said in a monotone.

"I give you what I had on these other guys." When Whelan said nothing, Bauman forced conversation. "Maybe sometime we'll go have something to eat at that crazy guy's place. What's his name—Raul?"

"Raul. Right, but—"

"There's a guy that missed his calling. Oughta be running a small village somewhere, wearing a white suit and a lotta rings. You been by there lately?"

"It's closed."

Bauman looked genuinely disappointed. "What happened?"

"Went back to Mexico."

"What's he doing there? Same thing, restaurant?"

Whelan found himself smiling. "He's the *alcalde,* Bauman."

"He's what?"

"What you said. He went back to his ancestral village with a suitcase full of money. Now he's the mayor."

Bauman grinned. "Helluva world, ain't it?"

"It sure is. Complicated world."

After they ate, they stood for a moment outside the restaurant, and the gaudy flickering sign had great fun with the colors of Bauman's shirt. They each lit up a smoke and idly watched traffic. Finally Bauman shrugged.

"You feel like a cocktail?"

"Not tonight. I think I'm going to be a good boy and go to bed."

"Arright. See you, Whelan."

Whelan nodded and walked across Belmont to his car. As he drove home, he thought about his crumbling case and the wall he'd run up against.

In his mind's eye, he saw Bauman giving him a smug wink and lighting up one of his cigars, but he didn't think Bauman really knew any more than Paul Whelan. Mrs. O'Mara, it occurred to him, would be able to put a name to the man in the windbreaker. Mrs. O'Mara would know him.

Eleven

WHEN he woke up the next morning, a crisp breeze was having its way with the curtains, so this might be a lovely fall day in Chicago, which would be a fine start. There was electricity, and it might even be on when he came home. There might be good weather, he might get a letter or a card from Sandra, something might turn up so that he wouldn't have to tell Mrs. O'Mara her brother had been dead for a decade.

Over a cup of instant coffee and a couple pieces of toast, he thought about what he'd learned the day before. He had no great confidence in the subconscious as a tool, but he couldn't shake the feeling that somewhere in his conversation with Mrs. O'Mara or Fritz Pollard or the Gaynors, he'd picked up a fact that meant something more than he realized. His brief talk with Betty Henke stood out for its obvious information, and he went over it again, panning for something overlooked.

She'd said that Michael Minogue had taken care of the funeral and had made what few calls he'd been able to make. If only someone could give him the particulars to take back to Mrs. O'Mara. The funeral: a small funeral for an old-country Irishman. An Irish Catholic funeral. Now he recalled his conversation with Minogue's great-nephew in the Empire Hotel, and then he had it.

The old man's wallet. Of course.

He pulled out his own wallet and found the business card, dialed the number, and got a recording. Whelan left his name and number and then hung up.

There was something else in all these conversations, he knew, and he'd have bet the rent that Fritz Pollard could tell him all sorts of interesting things, but for the moment the clue Betty Henke had given him was all he had.

Not much, but more than he'd had. He studied the sun flooding his living room window and listened to the radio on his kitchen counter. It was giving him Maynard Ferguson's exuberant version of "Birdland." A clue, some music, bad coffee, and lunch with his mentor, the great Walter Meehan.

Things were looking up.

AT the office, he threw open the windows to let in the autumn smells and then checked in with his service. No calls.

He was standing at the window watching a couple of young Latino men putting up the letters on the marquee of the Aragon Ballroom, when he sensed rather than heard the noise. He stood motionless for a moment and then heard the scrape of feet. Another footstep against the silence told him it wasn't Nowicki coming to work late.

Silently, Whelan crossed the office. At the door, he paused for a long ten count, and when he'd almost convinced himself he was hearing things, his visitor moved again. Whelan peered through the clouded glass door into the dark hall and silently cursed the building's owner. He held his breath, then grabbed the doorknob and pulled the door open. He was out into the hall in a half-second, in time to see a figure moving fast down the stairs, a small bony shadow disappearing into the darkness. Whelan was conscious of the heavy smells of sweat and tobacco.

The escaping figure was already at the first-floor landing when Whelan began pursuit and Whelan heard him yank open the glass door at street level. He took the stairs two at a time and made it out onto Lawrence in seconds, then got to the corner in time to glimpse someone slipping into a gangway half a block up Winthrop. The gangway ran between two dark brown apartment buildings. A tall young black man leaned against the doorway to the one on the left and watched as Whelan entered the narrow space between the buildings.

Whelan ran through the small courtyard behind the building and then out to the alley. At the gate he stopped and watched for a moment. Nothing moved in any direction. He took several steps into the alley and then stopped.

No, not this time, he told himself. I get into trouble in alleys.

Back on the street, he stopped next to the young man, who watched him with a sardonic expression on his face.

"Did he come out?"

The man shrugged and looked away.

"Just tell me if he came out."

The man gave him a quick look, then glanced up the street toward Lawrence. "Got nothin' to do with me, man."

"What did he look like?"

"Don't ask me. You the one chasin' him."

"I was chasing shadows," Whelan said, walking away.

He decided to put off the calls till later and closed up the office. Time for a ride.

In the car he punched the long-suffering buttons of his radio, looking for something soothing. As he pulled out into traffic on Lawrence, he realized that he didn't need a description of his visitor anyway. He'd seen the cap, he'd seen the dark windbreaker, just as Michael Minogue had.

He went up Clark and as he crossed Foster, the gaily colored neighborhood banners the city of Chicago had recently fallen in love with told him he had entered Andersonville. Once a dense pocket of Swedish settlers, now, like much of the North Side, the neighborhood bore a closer resemblance to a UN meeting. One was just as likely to run into Indians and Pakistanis, Koreans, and Latinos as Swedes. But if most of the Swedes had long since left Andersonville, they'd left their mark: restaurants, delicatessens, gift shops and a little museum. Surrounding the Swedish remnants were antiques stores and coffee-houses and restaurants from other parts of the planet.

Like Chinatown or Argyle Street or Greektown on a good day, the whole neighborhood smelled of food. In a three-block strip, there was Swedish food, Chinese food, Turkish food, Greek food and Persian food. This early, however, it was the Swedes who were announcing their presence. Whelan could smell the fresh meat from a pair of Swedish markets, the big hot breakfasts from Ann Sather's. Peering in the windows of butcher shops and diners, Whelan wanted to eat. The Swedes were not known for their culinary prowess, and this fact mystified him: if there was one unifying fact Whelan had uncovered in his tireless sampling of the city's oddest, finest restaurants, it was that all God's children could cook.

Gerry Costello's apartment proved to be just down the street from Svea, a crowded little eatery with paintings of Swedish scenes on the steamy windows. There was no bell to ring, so he pushed his way into the cramped hall with a high, narrow stairway that smelled of four generations of tenants and all their troubles. A pair of mailboxes set into the wall said that apartment 2A had a tenant named Shah and 2B was home to Costello.

The banister was coming loose, so he put his hand on the cold plaster wall for balance and climbed the stairs to the second floor. Apartment 2A was awash with the sounds of small children and an outnumbered adult short on patience. A high thin male voice shouted threats and warnings, issued commands and probably muttered prayers in a language that could have been Urdu or Gujarati. The low murmur of a television was the only sound issuing from 2B. Whelan waited a moment, then knocked.

He heard the sound of someone padding to the door in slippers, a long pause, then the voice from the phone.

"Who is it?"

"Mr. Costello? My name is Paul Whelan. We spoke on the phone.

The man inside the door hesitated for five or six seconds, then repeated his stance.

"I told you I don't talk to none of those people anymore. I haven't seen nobody. What're you bothering me for?"

"Because you're just about my last possible help."

"I can't *be* no help. Just go 'way."

"Can we talk like this? I don't have to come in. Here, let me slip my card under your door so you know I'm legitimate."

He slid the card in and waited. A moment later, he heard Gerald Costello snort. "So what's this prove? You got a card, so what?"

"Okay, it proves nothing and you're afraid to let me in, fine, we can just talk through the door and—"

"I ain't afraid of *nobody.*"

The door swung open and Whelan found himself facing a pudgy man no more than five six, with a potbelly, a white crew cut, and dark eyes. A pair of high red points stood out on his cheeks and the brown eyes emitted hostility.

"Come on in outta there. I don't need these people to know my business." The little man shot an irascible look in the direction of his neighbors and then surprised Whelan by grabbing hold of the sleeve of Whelan's jacket.

"Easy on the jacket."

"Come on if you're comin' in." Gerry Costello slammed the door behind Whelan and then backed up a couple of steps. Whelan waited for an invitation to come farther into the apartment. He was standing in a small tidy kitchen. On one side was an old-fashioned sink, so clean he could have eaten out of it. A small table covered in yellow oilcloth had been pushed to the window so that Costello could watch Clark Street. On the other wall, Whelan saw a double row of hooks: the upper hook of each pair held a cap or hat, the lower hook a jacket or coat. Whelan saw a Cubs jacket and a baseball cap, a dark gray overcoat with a snap-brim cap, a corduroy coat with a heavy fur cap. No wonder he doesn't invite me in, Whelan thought. He's afraid I'll make a mess.

"Maybe we could talk at your table."

"No," he snapped. "We'll talk in the front room." Without waiting for Whelan, Gerry Costello spun and waddled into his living room.

He dropped himself into an armchair facing the television and shut off the set with a remote. Whelan took a seat on the sofa a few feet away. Costello watched him settle in and then sat for a moment, as though studying him. For just the tail end of a second Whelan had the eerie feeling that the little man could read minds. He shifted uncomfortably on the sofa. Then Costello said, "Joe Colleran, you said you were looking for."

"Yes, although the nature of my investigation has changed a little since I talked to you. Right after we spoke, I talked to a Mrs. Lars Torgeson, who you knew as Betty Henke, and she told me that Joe Colleran died in an automobile accident about ten years ago. Now I'm just trying to get the particulars to give to his sister. I don't have any good news to give her, so I'm hoping at least to be able to give her a clear picture of how he died and whatever else I can find out."

The little man watched him and said nothing for a while. Something had softened in his posture or expression but Whelan couldn't have defined it. Then he nodded. "Betty Henke. She was a great gal. Wasn't stuck-up or anything like some of 'em. I liked her. Too tall for me, though. I never liked 'em tall. Guy like you, you're tall, you can go out with those big gals, but . . ." He shrugged. "Maggie was a nice girl, too. It was too bad about Joe. He was an okay guy. So what do you want from me, since you know Joe's dead?"

"You knew he was dead, then."

"Sure I did," Costello said, with the air of a man discussing common knowledge. "Wouldn't call it a car accident, though. He got *hit* by a car."

"He was a pedestrian?"

"What else would you call it?"

"I guess I assumed he was in a car himself. Do you remember the date?"

"Nope. Long time ago. Like you said, maybe ten years. At least ten years. Maybe more like twelve."

"How did you find out?"

"Saw it in the paper. Wasn't much of a story, couple of lines. Didn't say nothing about arrangements and I didn't see no obituary, so I didn't go to the wake. Woulda gone to the wake, you know."

"It would really help if you could pin down the year and maybe the time of year."

"Like I say, twelve years ago. That's the best I can do."

"All right. You weren't in touch with Joe Colleran, though."

"No. Didn't even know he was back in town. Him and Mike Minogue, they run a saloon down south somewheres. But I wasn't in touch with none of 'em. I kinda keep to myself. That's the kinda guy I am. I don't go out much except to go to a picture, go out to get a bite to eat. I wouldn't even know half of these people if I saw 'em now." He shrugged. "But I woulda gone to the wake."

Whelan wondered whether Costello knew about Michael Minogue but said nothing. He took the photo out of Mrs. O'Mara's weathered envelope and handed it across to Costello. The old man's face drew together in a frown and he shot a suspicious glance at Whelan, but he took the photo in trembling, tobacco-stained fingers and stared at it, turning it slightly to one side to catch the light. He squinted at it and then looked around the room.

"I need my glasses." He spotted them on top of the television and got up to retrieve them. "They're just reading glasses," he said over his shoulder. "I can see fine from far away." When he'd put the glasses on, he sank back into the chair and studied the photo for a long while, occasionally nodding almost imperceptibly. For perhaps five minutes, he said nothing. Then he lowered the picture, took off his glasses, and looked at Whelan.

"This takes me back. You know how long ago this was?"

"Nineteen forty or thereabouts, I guess. Maybe 1941."

He squinted at the picture and shook his head. "No. '40, 'cause Herb Gaynor's in the picture and he joined the navy the summer before the war broke out." He pointed to the tall angular figure of Gaynor. "Summer of

'41, he was already overseas. Lot of guys joined up early, 'cause everybody knew we'd be gettin' into the war. If not with the Japs, then with Hitler. Herb Gaynor was stationed on Midway when the big fight came. You know about Midway?"

"Sure."

"Turning point in the Pacific, that was. Anyway, this picture was 1940."

"There was some trouble around that time, wasn't there? Involving a couple of these guys. A robbery, I heard."

Gerry Costello gave an angry little jerk of his head. "That's got nothing to do with me. Don't ask me nothing about that."

"I didn't say you were involved."

"That's good, 'cause I wasn't."

"And you haven't seen any of these people in a long time."

"No."

"And I know some of them are gone now. Ray Dudek is dead."

"He got killed at Riverview. Somebody knifed 'im for his wallet." He looked at the photo again. "Lotta these guys are dead. Tommy Friesl died in the war, Tommy Moran, too. I know Landis is still alive, but—"

"I've talked to Herb Gaynor and Fritz Pollard. And I know that Casey Pollard is dead."

Costello snorted and glared at Whelan for a moment. "The hell he is. I seen him on the street not two months ago."

"Are you sure?"

"Damn sure. I looked 'im right in the eye and he pretended he didn't recognize me. But he knew me. He was a punk when we were kids, just a punk. I had to slap him around a couple times."

"Where did you see him?"

"Up here on Clark and Wilson. I'm waitin' for a bus and I see him, he's panhandling right there, big as life. Soon as he sees me, he goes up Clark Street in the other direction with that little jerky walk of his."

"What else can you tell me about him?"

"To watch your back. He's got no guts, never had any guts. Always yellow, he was. But he's crazy, that one." Costello made the little circling motion with one finger next to his head, and Whelan wondered what Costello would think if he knew how his old acquaintances viewed him.

"Crazy how?"

"Crazy, that's all. You find him, you just look in his eyes. You'll see."

"What was he wearing?"

Gerry Costello wrinkled his nose. "What the hell kinda question is that?"

"It could tell me something."

"This was summer, it was hot. He was wearin' a T-shirt and some kinda pants. Looked like the bum he was."

"Anything else you can tell me?"

"Nah. Like I said . . ."

Whelan got up to leave. "Well, thanks for your time, and give me a call if you think of anything that might help."

"Okay. Now you see? I ain't afraid."

"I can see that."

The little man fixed him with the dark eyes. "I served my country in the Big War, mister. I saw combat, I was wounded. I was a POW. I'm not afraid of anything." He punctuated this with a little nod and showed Whelan to the door.

"Well, thanks again," Whelan said.

"Don't mention it," Gerry Costello said, and sealed the hatch on his little world.

Out on Clark, he could smell Swedish meatballs cooking somewhere up the street, but today he was getting a home-cooked lunch. He got into his car and pulled out into traffic, thinking about what Gerry Costello had given him. Among other things, it was now a little more important for Whelan to talk with Michael Minogue's nephew.

WALTER Meehan lived far to the north in a redbrick bungalow on a serene block so completely taken over by trees that it seemed to have been built beneath a canopy. One side was lined with sycamores and dark-leaved maples and on the other was Indian Boundary Park, so called because it marked an early dividing line, between settlers and native people, that hadn't lasted long.

Walter's house sat in the shade of a catalpa tree, and several of the long seedpods—"Indian cigars," Whelan had called them in his youth—had dropped onto the front porch. Whelan parked across the street, on the park side. The last time he'd seen the park, it had been overrun with what seemed like ten thousand day campers. Now just a handful of smaller children played in the park, and old people watched them from benches and occasionally called out to them.

Walter Meehan was waiting for Whelan at the top of the stairs, hands in his pockets and a calm smile on his face. As always, his cheeks were red and his thick gray hair defied combs and brushes. He looked like any other short, chubby retired gentleman, and Whelan wondered if any of the neighbors realized that their quiet neighbor had been a brilliant detective. In his days on the police force, Walter Meehan had been adviser, mentor and sounding post to half the detectives in the city, no matter which area office they worked out of. Whelan had gotten to know Walter during Meehan's last two years on the job, and the two had become friends. When he first set up his office, Whelan had gone to Walter on several occasions for advice.

Walter looked from Whelan to the Olds across the street and laugh lines appeared at the corners of his eyes.

"Nice car," Walter said in his slow, careful way. "I didn't like your old one. It had hubcaps."

"Nice seeing you, too, Walter," Whelan said, and came up the stairs with his hand outstretched.

Up close, he could see that Walter hadn't aged much in the three or four years since they'd last seen each other. If anything, he looked healthier, his skin slightly tanned.

"Been out in the sun, Walter? Let me guess—you've taken up golf."

Walter Meehan snorted. "You know what Mark Twain called golf?"

" 'A good walk spoiled.' "

Walter nodded. "My wife told me she'd leave me if I ever took up golf. I think she was serious. I work in my garden with my beloved tomatoes and onions. Well, come in, come in. The neighbors will think you're a salesman if I keep you out on the stairs."

With that and a wave of his arm, Walter Meehan led Whelan into the little redbrick bungalow.

Whelan inhaled the thick perfumed smell of the flowers in the window boxes and followed Meehan inside, where the flower smells were immediately scattered by the aroma from the back of the house.

"Oh, I can tell good things are happening out in that kitchen."

Walter patted his hard little belly. "She has left a permanent mark on me, Paul."

"This is for her," Whelan said, handing Walter a bottle of wine.

"Give it to her yourself."

"Hello, Lily," he called out.

Meehan shook his head. "She's out back picking tomatoes for our lunch. Do you still grow tomatoes?"

"I've given up for a while. I had a few problems with my garden. Bugs, neighborhood kids, and worst of all, a rabbit."

"A rabbit in Uptown? It's a world of wonder, isn't it?"

"I saw one in a prairie just outside Cabrini-Green. I think they can live anywhere, they just pretend to be fragile."

"How about a beer?"

"A beer would be fine."

Walter nodded and padded out to the kitchen for a beer. While he was gone, Whelan wandered around the house. It was a house of partitions, of peaceful coexistence perfected over fifty years of marriage: the living room was Lily's, with perfect furniture and tasteful draperies and cut-glass bowls and polished silver. The dining room was oak and darker colors and one wall showed the initial compromises: a four-tiered shelving unit given over to Walter Meehan's greatest passion in life, the collecting of toy soldiers. Whelan studied the little armies in their unlikely uniforms and bizarre headgear, waves of little lead men in scarlet or forest green or sky blue, with banners and obsolete weapons. Three of the shelves were crammed with figures, but the top shelf held just five, medieval knights on horseback, the warhorses decked in gaudy tournament colors as though about to enter a jousting field.

"You like my knights?" Walter asked. Whelan turned and received a bottle of Samuel Smith pale ale and a glass.

"They're great. I thought you had more."

"Oh, show him the mess in your study, Walter," a new voice said.

"Hello, Lily." Like her husband, Lily Meehan did not appear to have weathered much. She was a small woman with whiter hair than her husband's but younger skin and lively gray eyes. Whelan hugged her and she kissed him on the cheek. He handed her the wine.

"Thank you. Should I serve it with lunch?"

"That's for you. I don't drink wine."

"Now, Paul Whelan, give an accounting of yourself."

"My bills are paid, I'm not drinking any more than usual, I still have the house and my office rent is paid."

She nodded. "Time to take a wife."

"Nobody asked you," Walter said fondly.

"Show him your soldiers and be quiet."

Walter led him into a small room off the dining room, flicked on an overhead light and laughed when Whelan gasped.

There were thousands of toy soldiers in this room, marching bands and cavalry troops and horse artillery units, even a horse-drawn field hospital. They lined shelves and inhabited glass cases and the windowsills, and in the middle of the far wall, a pile of faded, damaged-looking ones awaited Walter's ministrations.

Walter Meehan stood beside him and seemed ready to erupt with joy at the chance to show off his little companions.

"I've never seen anything like this."

"Some of them are more than a hundred years old, Paul. The men who made them, the women who painted them so beautifully—it was almost always the women who did the painting—the little boys who played with them, they're all long dead. I think about the people behind them. I think about the people the figures represent, too."

"Just like when you were a policeman, Walter."

"Perhaps." He lifted a red-coated horseman off a shelf. "This is one of my favorites. He is an officer of the Romanian cavalry, in the era before World War One. Look at him, he thinks he's the whole thing, Paul. The Romanian cavalry! All these countries, they all thought they were the genuine article, Paul, and then the twentieth century came and warfare was serious and brutal and complete, and the men in pretty uniforms were gone. I don't know if these fellows could fight, but I'll bet they made a wonderful parade!"

Whelan smiled and put an arm around him. "Your collection is too big. What would you save if the house burned down?"

Walter Meehan surveyed his troops and nodded. "I'd save Lily. But I'd think about the five knights out in the dining room. They're Courtenays. I paid a thousand dollars for the five of them, and they were a bargain.

"It's true, Paul, he did," Lily called out from her kitchen. "A thousand dollars for the little men. Lucky the children are out of the house."

Walter shot a long-suffering look in the direction of the kitchen, then turned back to Whelan. "Before you faint, come and sit down."

They sat at the big oak dining room table with its rosemaling designs and watched Lily Meehan set her table. She brought out a salad featuring her cherry red tomatoes and a loaf of warm French bread and a tureen of new potatoes, and then she came back one more time with a platter of salmon.

"Here we are," she said unnecessarily.

"Good God, do you eat a lunch like this every day?"

Lily Meehan fixed him with an acidic look probably reserved on normal occasions for Walter and said simply, *"Omidon."*

"My grandmother used to call me an *omidon.* She used to call me all sorts of things in Gaelic. She could swear in it."

"Special lunch for a special guest, Paul," Walter said, and Lily pointed with her fork.

"Take some fish. It doesn't keep."

They talked of old times and current events and common acquaintances from the police force and the Meehan children, and Lily force-fed Whelan and her husband until the salmon was but a fishy memory.

After lunch Whelan helped them clear the table and then went into the living room, where the three of them had coffee.

"So are we ready to cut to the chase, Paul? What was it you wanted to ask about?"

"Sorry about this, Lily. This is an old one, Walter, and I'm not sure you'll be able to dig back far enough."

"He remembers everything," Lily said.

"If he doesn't, nobody does. In the course of another investigation I came across an old crime that is somehow connected to my case." He spent a couple minutes running down what he'd learned about Joe Colleran. Through it all, Walter Meehan watched him with his boyish blue eyes and said nothing. Twice he scribbled a little note to himself on the back of an envelope, and he frequently nodded, but he did not interrupt.

"Here's the first thing I want to try out on you. Raymond Dudek."

Without hesitation, Walter shook his head. "The name by itself means nothing. I knew a fellow named Dudek once, but no Raymond."

"Okay, now try Seaman First Class Raymond Dudek, and Riverview."

A little stunned look came into Walter Meehan's eyes and he nodded slowly. "The boy who was stabbed. By Aladdin's Castle, it happened. I can remember it as clearly as I can see you."

"I know you can."

"Poor boy. Just home from the service—he wasn't even out yet, he was up there at Great Lakes—and he was stabbed. It was very terrible. He was quite a handsome young man, and this was a beautiful summer night. I remember there was a little group of very pretty young women in summer dresses, all standing with their arms around one another and peering back where the body was. I have a feeling Riverview was never the same for any of them after that."

"I'm sure. What else do you remember about it?"

"I remember that his wallet had been removed. We found it a few yards away, no money in it. He had a ring that they had tried to remove, but it stuck on his knuckle so they gave up on it. Sure I recall that one, Paul. A sailor coming home, and a killing at Riverview. I don't remember anything of the kind ever occurring before that at Riverview. We had fights there now and then, boys from different neighborhoods, black boys and white boys, that sort of thing, but never a murder."

"A robbery, then."

Walter Meehan blinked at him and seemed to be distracted. "That was our official assessment."

"And your own?"

A little smile appeared at the corners of his mouth. "What do you think, Paul? Do you think that's how you'd do it if you needed money? In the city's most crowded place? On a hot summer night in Riverview?"

Whelan laughed quietly. "No, I don't think I'd look for such a big audience."

"And if you did, would you pick a young able-bodied serviceman? A fellow who'd just come back from physical training and perhaps had seen action? And this fellow, from what I recall, he was all muscle. Not a weight lifter type, you understand, just a lean young guy with no fat to him. I don't think that's who I'd choose." Walter looked away again and then said absently, "Stabbed from the front, no less. Up close and from the front. Not how I'd do it."

"Nope, I guess not. But I was told that Ray Dudek had a short fuse, that he was quick with his fists. Maybe this was a fight. He got into a fight and the other guy panicked and knifed him."

"No one saw or heard any kind of disturbance. A fight like that has its own sounds. You've seen hundreds of them. You can hear them half a block away and they take time to develop, the noise draws a crowd: loud talking, profanity, shoving, people yelling. No one heard anything. No one saw any kind of fight. Witnesses saw this young man smoking out in front of Aladdin's Castle, and two minutes later he was dead. It doesn't sound like a fight to me."

"No. So what else can you tell me? Do you remember the suspects?"

"Not well enough to be helpful."

"What if I helped you with names. Do you remember the name Landis? Chick Landis?"

Walter smiled. "Of course. What a piece of garbage. And he still is, from what I know. Yes, I suspected him because he was there that night. He was seen talking to the sailor earlier. But—"

"Do we know that for sure?"

"Yes. He denied it at first, but there were witnesses. He was seen going in."

"What do you remember about Landis?"

"He had a sheet. Nothing prodigious, you know, but a sheet nonetheless. Grand theft auto, charges dropped. Gambling—he ran a little book. Known associate, that sort of thing."

"Known associate of who? Whom, I mean," Whelan said, with a quick look at Lily, a former English teacher.

"Low-level dirtballs. No one famous."

"Did Ray Dudek have a record?"

"Not that I recall."

"I keep running into hints that these guys and the ones I've been talking to, that all of them were in some trouble before the war. It had to be something in their neighborhood, it seems to me, and that was your beat. From what I can tell, it had something to do with a robbery. What it was, I don't know, but it was something that would make a bunch of young men run like hell to get into the service."

Walter stared at him for a moment and then a little reddish color came into his fat cheeks. "I don't know about this poor kid at Riverview or these men you're looking into, but there was something involving Landis just before the war. Just before Pearl Harbor, it seems to me."

"A robbery."

"Yes."

"Somebody with a German name."

"You seem to know enough without my help."

"Table scraps, Walter. I need to put it together. I heard it was a German guy."

Walter thought a moment and shook his head. "Not German, Dutch. His name was Hoegstra, I think his first name was Jan or something like that, but he called himself Joe. He was Dutch."

"Who was he and what happened to him?"

"He was a gambler and errand boy for the North Side mob, a small-time fellow who thought he was going to be Chicago's first Dutch gang leader. And what happened to him was that he was robbed. After a card game he ran, in the back room of a saloon over on Clybourn and Damen—Yancey's Shortstop, it was called. Anyway, this card game he ran, which was fixed, had just broken up and the players were slinking off into the bushes to lick their wounds, and our fellow Hoegstra was staggering down the street with his pockets bulging and a bunch of young kids jumped him. There was a fight and Hoegstra was pretty badly beaten up—his head hit the sidewalk, he got a concussion, that sort of thing."

"So they hit a mob guy and took his money."

"They probably didn't know he was connected in any way, and there was some doubt at the time that Hoegstra was actually anything more than the lowest-level functionary. But that's what they did. And Mr. Hoegstra put the word out that these were local kids and he'd recognized at least one of them. Probably Landis, who had done errands for him. Hoegstra let the word out on the street that he was going to kill the ones responsible. That probably explains the sudden onset of patriotism in these fine young men when Pearl Harbor was attacked. There was also some speculation that Hoegstra hadn't been playing with his own money that night—that he'd been out collecting beforehand and thought to make a little off his employers' profits."

"Is it possible that Hoegstra was responsible for the killing of Ray Dudek?"

Walter Meehan gazed at him for several seconds and Whelan realized he was calling up the old memories. "Five years later?" He shrugged. "I don't know whether he was on the street at that time," he said with a slow shake of the head. "Hoegstra also had seen a sudden need to seek out other climes. We found the body of his partner stuffed into the trunk of a green Packard. Their employers apparently tired of their incompetence. This was late 1943, as I recall. A couple of very vivid killings, Paul. I remember both of them well. Not that I saw many that were nondescript, you understand."

"When do you know for certain that Hoegstra came back?"

"Much later. In the fifties. I don't know what sort of hoops his former associates made him jump through to reclaim his good standing in their community," Walter said, chuckling. "But he came back and eventually we busted him for a number of things, all small-time. An irritant to society rather than a menace. He still enjoyed playing the big shot but he was finished. You would have enjoyed Hoegstra, Paul. He looked like a wharf rat and dressed like the chorus in *Guys and Dolls*. But, given his antisocial proclivities, we were forced to send him into exile."

"And he's dead now?"

"I never heard one way or the other. But if he's still alive, he would be in his seventies."

"Was this man capable of murder?"

"Who can say? He was a loudmouth, full of braggadocio, full of hot air. In the course of his business dealings, he was known to have manhandled a few people. I never thought of him as a killer, but this affair was personal for him, so who knows? Have I succeeded in muddying your waters enough?"

"No. I think you've clarified a couple of things. As I hoped you would."

Walter stared off into space for a moment and when he looked at Whelan again, he shook his head. "A good policeman wants . . . *closure* in these things. What always frustrated me most were the ones that seemed solvable but were somehow never closed. This case of yours, Paul—it's possible that you'll be talking to the killer of that boy at Riverview. And I was always troubled by the belief that I talked to the killer as well. I never believed what I was supposed to believe about that boy's murder. Ah, I'm babbling."

"No. I really needed to run some things by you and I think you've helped. And"—he looked at Lily—"I got a lunch out of it."

She nodded toward her husband. "He wouldn't mind so terribly if you were to stop by sometime and talk, even if you weren't working on a case. Nor would I."

Whelan felt himself blushing. "I think about the two of you a couple times a month and tell myself I'm going to come visit. I'm embarrassed. It's not as though I've got a lot of better things to do."

"Are you still unattached, Paul?" she asked.

"Uh, officially, yes."

"But you're seeing someone?"

"Yes."

Walter sighed and gave her a warning look. Lily shot him one back.

"Bring her over sometime when you think she's known you long enough to put up with your boring elderly friends."

He got to his feet. "I don't have any boring friends, Lily, especially not you two."

They said their good-byes and Walter walked him to the door. At the top step, he patted Whelan on the back.

"Come and see us. Bring your ladyfriend or come alone."

"I'll do that."

"Do you see anyone from the job?"

"Al Bauman. Remember him?"

Walter laughed. "Who could forget him? A land mine waiting to go off. Is he well?"

"For Bauman, yes. And he's grown on me."

"Oh, I always liked him. He was the most intelligent of all the detectives I met back then. I just thought he'd ruin his health."

"He's still working on it."

"And you're friends?"

"Yes, I think we are. Came as a surprise to me, Walter."

Walter indicated the park across the street. "Some of those old men on the benches are friends of mine. If you had told me thirty years ago that my sweet Lily and I would retire into a neighborhood full of Russian Jewish grandmas and grandpas, and that we'd like it, I would have laughed in your face."

"Sounds like a good mix, Walter. You'll be learning about Mother Russia and there's no one I'd rather have them learning about us from than Walter Meehan."

Walter Meehan shrugged and Whelan went down the stairs and across the street to his car. Inside, he gunned the engine and sent a cloud of slate gray exhaust into the air.

"I'll call the cops," Walter Meehan shouted, and went inside laughing.

Twelve

"I'M back in the office for a while, Shel. More or less."

"More or less is right. You had a caller actually ask if you really have an office, or just a phone service."

"Who?"

"A Ted Riordan from Riordan Accounting Services."

"That it?"

"Nobody else is interested in detectives today."

"Good. Thanks, Shel."

"Toodles."

He pressed down the button on the phone and dialed Ted Riordan. This time he got a person, not an advertisement.

"Riordan Accounting, Ted speaking."

"Paul Whelan, Mr. Riordan. Thanks for calling back. You mentioned something when we met that just occurred to me now."

"What was that?"

"Your uncle's wallet."

"His wallet? What about it?"

"You said it was full of old lottery tickets and holy cards."

"So? You looking for a new way to pick your numbers?"

"No. I was wondering if you still have the holy cards."

"Uh, yeah, I do. I mean, what do you do with 'em, you know? I never know what to do with them. I just keep 'em."

"Everybody does. You go to a Catholic wake, you get a holy card in honor of the deceased and you're afraid to throw it away because it's religious."

Riordan laughed. "The nuns used to tell us they were blessed and you couldn't throw out anything that was blessed. What do you do with 'em?"

"I toss 'em in a drawer."

"That's what I did with Uncle Mike's. His are in with mine."

"Could you grab them while I've got you on the phone?"

"Well, sure. Hang on."

Riordan returned a moment later and said, "He had a lot of 'em. Probably friends, mostly."

Time to play hunches.

"Read me the one for Joseph Colleran."

"Okay. That's the guy you were asking about, right? Here it is. 'Joseph Owen Colleran. Born January seventh, 1917. Died October nineteenth, 1975." What else do you want, the funeral home?"

"No, I don't need anything else." Then as an afterthought, he asked, "Where was he buried?"

Riordan read from the card. "Uh, St. Joseph's. Guess that figures. More Irishmen there than County Galway. Anything else?"

"No, that's all I needed. You've been very helpful."

Riordan chuckled. "I have, huh? If you say so."

"Well, thanks."

"Uh . . ." He could hear Riordan scrambling for something to keep him on the phone.

"What do you want to know, Mr. Riordan?"

"This has something to do with Mike, right?"

"It might. If I find out anything, I'll call."

"Okay. Thanks."

Whelan thought about calling Bauman and decided he wasn't ready to complicate his day. Instead, he picked up the phone book and in seconds had learned that there was a North Side man listed as J. Hoegstra. The address given was 2624 W. Belmont. Just below was another listing—same address and phone number but the name here was Hoegstra's Lucky Strike.

Sounds like a gin mill to me, Whelan thought.

THE tavern was still there, just across the river and a short stroll to Area Six. The cops probably answered calls at this one on foot. It was a tavern whose days were numbered. A world-weary and much-abused black Cadillac was parked directly in front: a great dark aircraft carrier of a car, a car from the days when it had been a sign of status if your car guzzled gas, a car with fins that suggested an imminent takeoff or perhaps just a designer who drank.

Whelan pulled up behind the Caddy and got out. He paused for a moment to study the old car: rust was having its way with the door panels and the heavy body sagged toward the driver's side, as though the shocks and suspension had given in to the weight of the driver.

The building was a companion piece to the car: a soul mate in brick, it belonged on the same block as the sagging wreck where Fritz Pollard made his living. Whelan looked at the cracks in the masonry, the tape-patched windows, the crumbling wooden stairs leading to the upper floor. A quick glance at the dirt-clouded windows showed that there was no apartment above. If this was Hoegstra's address, he lived in back of the tavern. The sign hanging over the saloon door merely promised Budweiser, but the windows were painted with a pair of dice, a poker hand and the legend LUCKY'S.

"I'll bet," Whelan said.

He pushed his way in and found himself in a cave. What little light there was came from the unpainted tops of the front windows and from the blue lights at each end of the bar mirror. Even without the light, Whelan could see all the signs of rigor mortis setting in on this place. It probably cost the owner as much to pay off the building inspectors and other licensing authorities as it would have to fix the place.

Two men were watching him. The bartender, a little stoop-shouldered man in a wrinkled white shirt, straightened up from washing glasses to squint at Whelan through the gloaming. The second man sat at the far end of the bar. He was taller, quite a bit taller, from what Whelan could make out, and he looked like a man with a buck: coat and tie, white shirt, and a razor slice of a mustache, of a type that had only been worn by guys in black-and-white movies. Whelan nodded at the bartender.

"Not open yet," the bartender said.

"I'm here to see this gentleman." Whelan kept his eyes on the bartender but saw the other man stiffen slightly.

Whelan moved to the far end as the tall man studied him. Up close, Whelan saw a man gone to seed but clinging doggedly to the old-fashioned trappings of prosperity. His dark hair was shot with gray and his face was seamed and jowly. He'd had a rough night, a long, old-time bar owner's night, and the purplish circles under his eyes were probably more or less permanent features of his face. There was a faint edginess to him, as though his existence was a long series of little tremors, an unending battle with the shakes. His skin was sallow, cheeks mottled by dark clusters of burst capillaries. The man's stare dared Whelan to start a conversation, and Whelan decided on the aggressive approach.

"You're Mr. Hoegstra," Whelan said.

"So what," the man challenged. He stared unblinking at Whelan and took a sip from what looked to be a scotch and soda. He set down his glass with an unsteady hand.

"So you're the person I've come to see."

"About what? You a salesman, or what?"

Whelan leaned on the bar. "No, I'm a private detective and I've been looking for a man named Joseph Colleran."

The other man squinted slightly as though trying to place a familiar but dusty name but said nothing. "Name don't ring a bell. So now what?"

"Now I've learned that he's dead."

"I'm supposed to know this guy? He drink here?"

"No. And maybe you don't know him. But now I'm interested in learning the how and why of it all and I've turned up a number of names of people he knew and that I believe you knew as well. At least in the old days."

"What old days?"

"The ones around here."

The man started shaking his head and Whelan kept going.

"When Riverview was up there at the corner of Belmont and Western and there was a saloon over on Clybourn called Yancey's, and a guy looking for a game could find one, and find you there, too." Hoegstra gave him a sharp look. "Those old days," Whelan said.

"That was fucking a hundred years ago. Don't bother me with this shit."

"But you're Joe Hoegstra and you hung out at Yancey's."

"Maybe I did. So what? That against some fucking law I don't know about?"

"You ran a game there."

"Who'd you get that from?"

"A couple people who had occasion to know you in the course of their law-enforcement careers."

Hoegstra stared at him with his yellowed, bloodless eyes and sipped at his drink. "Get your ass—"

Whelan held up a hand. "But I don't want to talk about anything you did in those days, Mr. Hoegstra. I want to run these names by you. Joseph Colleran—"

"I tolja I don't know anybody by that—"

"Ray Dudek, Michael Minogue, Fritz Pollard—"

Hoegstra clambered off his stool and leaned forward, a clenched fist on the bar, and Whelan never took his eyes off the man's face as he dropped the last name.

"Chick Landis."

"You lousy asshole."

"Take it easy, you don't look so good. What can you tell me about Chick Landis."

"He's a piece of shit. He ain't worth my spit."

"I got the impression he was a sort of business hotshot."

"So he's a smart thief, so what?"

"I need to know about Landis. Or about you and Landis, or you and any of the others I just mentioned—I'm not fussy. Give me something I can take back to my client and maybe I won't have to bother you anymore."

"This is all a thousand years ago, I got nothing to do with any of 'em anymore. I don't even know most of these people."

"You know Landis. And I think you knew the people he knew. I think you did business. And I think you know about another guy—Ray Dudek."

A wild unfocused look came into Hoegstra's eyes. "Yeah, I know Landis. And let me tell you something about him: there's one guy with more sense than you got. He wouldn't let his ass get caught in my saloon, not unless he had a gun, that slimy bastard."

"Still have a hard-on about that little misunderstanding after the card game, huh?"

Hoegstra blinked. His long gaunt body seemed to unfold and he craned his neck forward until Whelan could smell his tavern breath. For a second he glared at Whelan, wetting his lips. Then he nodded. "I owe people for a lot of shit. And I got a long memory. I'll bury 'em all, all those bastards that screwed me. And Landis, I'll see him in the fucking sewer where he belongs."

"Well, I paid Landis a visit the other day. And right now I'd have to say he's doing just fine." Whelan pretended to assess the dark little saloon. "He thinks all you guys from the old days are just small-time. That's what he said—'small-time.' "

Hoegstra leaned on his bar, fist clenched. He had big bony hands and the marks of knuckles broken in violence more than once. "You think he's big shit, huh? Maybe he is, maybe he ain't. Talk's fucking cheap, mister. I do things my way, and before I'm through, I'll have him by the balls, him and all them other ones. And you, too, if you're one of them."

"Can't hang that one on me, sir. I wasn't even born when they jumped you."

"Get outta my saloon before I bust your ass."

"I've got all kinds of old men threatening me these days and frankly, sir, it's beginning to piss me off." He nodded to the bartender and left.

He took a last look at the cadaverous tavern building and decided it suited the dead-eyed man in the dark coat who ran it.

LANDIS was wearing a blue suit this time, an almost perfect match to the one his son was wearing. Father-and-son outfits, Whelan thought. Cute.

The streetwise office manager looked at him over her half-glasses and cocked an eyebrow.

"Mr. Whelan, isn't it?"

"It is. I just need to ask him a quick question."

"One moment." She hit a com-line button and announced Whelan. A moment later, she looked up at him. "He says he's busy."

"Me, too. I'm very busy. He wouldn't believe how busy I am," Whelan said as he pushed past her into Landis's office.

Landis frowned and half-rose from his seat. "Hey, what the hell! This is an office, what the hell do you call this—"

Whelan closed the door behind him. "Quit shouting. This should take two minutes, maybe less." A quick glance through the glass wall told Whelan that the kid in the fine blue suit was shooting concerned looks in the direction of his father's office. Whelan shook his head quickly and waved the kid away.

"I just talked to an old acquaintance of yours—Joe Hoegstra."

"I knew you weren't looking for nobody when you came here. You're here to bust my balls, I knew it. . . ."

"I'm not interested in you or Hoegstra. I don't care if he's having your baby. I'm here to find out things to help me locate another man. But there are holes and you've caused some of them. Tell me about you and Hoegstra."

"He's nothing to me. That bullshit was all forty, forty-five years ago."

"You had a problem, the two of you."

"That's right. But it's all in the past. I'm a grown man. I'm a businessman. Hoegstra, he was a common street punk. He was a low-class hood. I don't even know what that old shit is doing now."

"Thinking about you, for one. Your trouble with Hoegstra, that's what sent you guys packing into the big war. But tell me this: is that why Ray Dudek had to be killed? Because of what you guys did with Hoegstra?"

"Dudek got robbed. Somebody robbed him and they stuck 'im."

"What if he wasn't robbed?"

"Then I don't know a thing about it."

Whelan shook his head. "I think you know something about it. You were there."

He watched Landis's face go from confidence to confusion, and he waited.

"I don't know what you're talking about."

"I know you were there."

"Who told you that crock of shit?"

"A police officer who would know. They questioned you. I think you were even a suspect, Chick."

Whelan allowed himself to enjoy the new look on Landis's face, the one that said he was impressed.

"You were there that night when Dudek was killed. When we talked the first time, I didn't know that. I showed you that old picture; you didn't even mention Ray Dudek."

"So I missed him, so what? There's about two dozen people in that shot."

"No. You named every single person in the picture except Ray Dudek."

"Meaning what?"

"Meaning that you know a lot about the night Ray Dudek was killed and you don't want anybody to know. And I think you ought to tell somebody."

"And I think you oughta go back to whoever you been talking to. Get the hell out of my office."

"I'm not finished."

"Yeah, you are. Excuse me." Landis hit the com line and then said, "Send Ronny in." He was staring at Whelan with a little half smile on his face when the office door opened and the younger Landis entered, pocket handkerchief and all.

"Ron? This is Mr. Whelan. He needs to be shown the door, and make sure he don't come back. I'm too busy for this shit."

"Okay, Dad." The kid gave Whelan a belligerent smile and indicated the open door with a nod. "Out."

The younger Landis was a big boy, wide in the shoulders and obviously fond of weights and muscle-building apparatus.

"All right," Whelan said.

As he slid past the younger man, he felt a hard shove in the small of his back and he started to plunge out into the hall. Whelan grabbed a desk to stop himself from falling and turned to face the kid. Young Landis came at him, flushed and smiling and having a fine time.

"Don't put hands on me again, friend."

"*Out!*" the kid said, and took two quick steps toward Whelan. He grabbed Whelan by the back of his arm and half-pushed, half-carried him toward the door. Whelan tried to tug his arm loose and heard the seam of his jacket giving way.

He put a hard shoulder into the other man and when Landis lurched to one side, Whelan grabbed Landis's tie with both hands and yanked hard. The kid was attempting to right himself and Whelan moved behind him, still tugging on the tie as he wrapped it around the kid's throat. Landis's face was red and he swung his big fist at the air around him as he fought to loosen the stricture around his throat. He half-turned and began whacking at Whelan's hand. Whelan gave a final hard pull and then let go suddenly, throwing a quick forearm into the back of the kid's head for good measure. Landis fell back onto a desk, slid down the side and onto the floor, where he sputtered and fought his tie and collar for air.

Whelan looked at him. "Free advice, Champ: don't pick fights with strangers, but if you're determined to be an asshole, never, *ever* pick a fight when you're wearing a tie."

Chick Landis stormed out of his office. "Hey, what the hell! You punk, get your ass out of my office."

Whelan pointed at young Landis, who was getting to his feet. "Your trained monkey put his hands on me. There was a brief scuffle."

The elder Landis took a step in Whelan's direction.

"Oh, come on, Landis. How messy do you guys want to make this? I'm leaving—I'm just not leaving with your kid's oily hands on my jacket." Whelan pretended to study his sleeve. "What is that, acne medication?" He shrugged, turned and made for the door.

"We're gonna call the cops."

"Somehow, I doubt it," Whelan said without looking back.

In his car, he gave Landis Realty a final glance and told himself he'd be back. An idea was beginning to form, and there was a special place in it for Chick Landis.

At five he found himself at a window table in Best Steak House at the corner of Wilson and Broadway, a Greek-run diner that boasted cheap prices and the world's smallest bar. The diner ordered his food cafeteria-style and took his tray to a table. The owner, a dapper man with an Errol Flynn mustache, dispensed mixed drinks and pitchers of beer from his tiny bar off to one side. Whelan sipped at a cup of coffee and watched the other patrons: three construction workers sharing a couple of pitchers and an American Indian family eating chicken.

He scanned the pages of the *Sun-Times,* from time to time glancing out the window at the passersby.

I need a break. I need mail. I need something to cheer me up.

He looked at the pullout section of the Friday paper and put it aside, then suddenly picked it up again. The cover story of the entertainment section was "Chicago's Ethnic Heritage"; the pullout contained stories on ethnic festivals, parades, shops, neighborhoods, and, of course, eateries.

Quickly, he paged through the section, ripping several pages in his haste, and then, in the center, he found what he was looking for, a story with the byline of Kermit Noyes.

"Oh boy," Whelan said.

The story ran for two and a half columns below a grainy picture of Gus and Rashid, both grinning maniacally behind the counter of the House of Zeus and looking like Persian ax murderers. According to the story accompanying the photo, Gus and Rashid had, in the opinion of the reviewer, much in common with ax murderers. The story bore the title "Fear and Loathing at the House of Zeus" and opened with the most memorable first line of journalism Whelan had come across since Grantland

Rice's famed line about Notre Dame football: "Out of the gray November sky, the four horsemen rode again. . . ."

This one began "The vomiting has subsided, but the tube is still in my left arm."

Whelan scanned the review quickly and began laughing, once or twice looking up, embarrassed, to find the other customers staring at him. When they realized he was laughing at the newspaper, they decided it was all right. He went back to the beginning and started over.

> The vomiting has subsided, but the tube is still in my left arm. My fever has gone down and the shakes that were in some ways the worst of it have calmed down. Two days of diarrhea have left me weak and seven pounds lighter, and my stomach aches when I breathe deeply. My appetite has left me, and when it returns—*if* it returns—I have no doubt I will develop a deep craving for white bread and steamed rice, lukewarm tea and saltines. They say I might be able to eat solid food again by next week. Then again, I might not.
>
> I have eaten in a restaurant so bizarre that I thought I was being put on, a place where the gyros wears an iridescent purple sheen, where the souvlaki smells like a hooked rug after a long rain, where the spinach and cheese pie has the consistency of window caulking, where the lettuce looks like the leavings of the first frost, where the hamburger goes from a dark gray as it is slapped, still teeming with microscopic life, onto the grill to a dark green color when "cooked," if I may use so misleading a term. I have eaten in a "Greek" restaurant in Uptown run by a pair of Iranian song-and-dance men without the faintest notion of cleanliness, freshness, or sanitation.
>
> I have eaten at the House of Zeus, and they tell me that I may live.

Rock on, Mr. Noyes, Whelan thought.

And the estimable Mr. Noyes did indeed rock on, admitting that the excellent fries and cold root beer had lured him into a false sense of security, encouraging him to make, to Whelan's mind, the most disastrous of mistakes, a blunder to rival Custer's dramatic charge into the largest Indian village on the planet, Napoleon's decision to invade Russia without mittens and galoshes: Mr. Noyes had ordered the deep-fried shrimp basket.

"Oh, for crying out loud," Whelan said. A couple of the construction workers looked up. Whelan pointed to the review. "He ate the shrimp. He's lucky he's not on the obituary page."

One of the construction workers looked away, unwilling to be drawn into conversation with an eccentric.

Whelan read the rest of the review, including Mr. Noyes's description of the shrimp as "a nightmarish descent into the world of toxic waste," and concluding with his final rating: "I give the House of Zeus a half star for boldness, for its owners' audacity in calling this sewer a restaurant, and for the favor they have done me, for I now know the location of the worst restaurant in Chicago, if not the continent."

Whelan reread the review, finished his coffee and left Best Steak House renewed.

He was parked fifty yards away from Landis Realty, the songs on his radio drowned out at intervals by the guttural urban roar of the Ravenswood El pulling into the station almost directly overhead. The sky had long since gone a rich navy blue and the steady rush-hour flow of people from the El station had exhausted itself, but there was still business being done inside Landis Realty, deals were being cooked, money was being made. If he peered long enough through his side mirror, he could occasionally glimpse Junior Landis strutting through the office, and there were still a couple of women hard at work, but he couldn't see into the inner chamber where Chick Landis was wheeling and dealing. Whelan was glad there was no one to ask him what he was doing.

"Surveillance," he would have said. Any time a detective didn't know what to do next, he began to call all his activities "surveillance." He told himself there was little likelihood that this would be productive, but felt justified by the degree of his dislike.

Whelan saw the young Landis enter his father's office and come out smiling. The kid looked too cheerful to be upset, and Whelan had to admit that meant nothing he had said or done had gotten to Chick Landis.

When it looked as though Landis Realty would continue to sell real estate and make money long into the night, a vehicle pulled up. This was an entrance guaranteed to attract notice, for the car entered the one-way street from the wrong end and proceeded to park backward in front of Landis Realty. The car itself would have engendered comment, for it was the length of the USS *Forrestal.* Whelan nodded appreciatively, for he had seen this car only a few hours earlier, in front of the ramshackle tavern on Belmont that had the nerve to call itself Lucky's.

This is promising, Whelan said to himself.

The driver flung open his door and just missed having it taken off by a Yellow cab coming up the street in the proper direction. The cabbie hit his horn, yelled out the window and gestured at the Cadillac, and Hoegstra yelled obscenities and threatened violence. He pulled his long bony frame out of the front seat with a stiffness born of liquor as well as age, stood for a half-second and then fell back against his car. When he was apparently satisfied that he wasn't going to topple over, he reached down under his seat and came up with a crowbar.

Hoegstra hefted the crowbar, pushed himself off against the roof of his car and slammed the door. Then he staggered toward the door of Landis Realty. At the curb something caught his attention: the blue Buick Park Avenue, and Hoegstra lurched toward it, his dark raincoat flowing and flapping out behind him like gargoyle wings.

Drunk or not, he attacked the Park Avenue with surprising speed, and it was clear to Whelan that Hoegstra had done this before. He started with the side windows, first the driver's side and then the one behind it, then brought the bar down against the doors themselves and left each one bruised. He moved back a couple of drunken paces, spread his feet for balance and seemed to be assessing his workmanship. Then he lurched to the front and brought his bar down on the hood twice, raising sparks and creating a pair of large gashes. The next victim was the windshield, which he turned with a pair of whacks into a concave bubble of shattered glass. Apparently this was more exertion than Hoegstra was used to, for here he paused and leaned against the hood of the Buick, gasping and staring straight ahead.

The door to Landis Realty opened and the kid came out, yelling and gesturing, and when he saw that his opponent was an old man, he broke into his charge, which lasted until he saw Hoegstra turn and raise the crowbar. The kid circled the old man, right fist cocked back and spewing street challenges while Hoegstra cursed in a hoarse screech, banging on the hood of the Buick.

"I'll bust you up, old man," young Landis said, and the old man snarled at him and swung the crowbar.

Chick Landis emerged now, followed by one of the young women from the office and a middle-aged man who looked terrified.

"My fuckin' car!" Landis yelled. When he saw who was ravaging his beloved wheels, he charged onto the street bellowing and screaming. In seconds the two Landises had Hoegstra between them, the young one still circling with his fists up, the older one pointing with his chubby finger.

"You're dead, you bastard, you old fuck, lookit my car!"

"I'll take him out, Dad," the kid said.

Your heart's not in this, kid, Whelan thought.

"You son of a bitch," Landis shouted, and Hoegstra cackled and stared with his bulging yellowed eyes at Landis, then whacked the hood of the Buick again with a gravelly shout.

"I'm gonna kill you, you prick!" Landis screamed, and drew closer.

The younger Landis came in from the other side and threw a looping right hand that caught Hoegstra on the shoulder at exactly the same moment as Hoegstra swung the crowbar at Chick Landis, catching him on the forearm.

Chick yelled, "Ow, goddammit!" and drew back, clutching his arm. Hoegstra lost his balance and fell backward onto the car and the kid was on him in two quick steps. Whelan saw the kid's fist come down twice on Hoegstra and decided it was time to break this one up. He slid out of his car and ran across the street, yelling for the kid to let the old man up. A crowd had gathered near the Buick and one of the women from Landis's office was crying.

Hoegstra was partially hidden by the burly frame of his attacker and Whelan could see the younger man's heavy fist coming up and down, pistonlike. Then Whelan heard Hoegstra growl, and the crowbar reappeared and came down on the crown of the kid's head. The young Landis screamed and sank to the street, holding his head in both hands and rocking back and forth. Chick Landis was holding his injured arm and still screaming that he was going to kill Hoegstra, and then Whelan was between them.

"You!" Hoegstra yelled, and raised the crowbar again.

Whelan faked a punch, then put a shoulder into the old man, knocking him into the car fender. Hoegstra fell to the street and lost his grip on the weapon.

Squad cars appeared from both ends of the street and Whelan took a couple of steps back and folded his arms. The cops from the first car pulled up in front of Hoegstra's car and the second squad rolled in behind the wounded Buick.

Time to blend in with the scenery, Whelan thought. He moved closer to a group of men who'd come from the direction of a tavern on the corner.

All three of the would-be pugilists were down on the pavement. Landis was rocking around theatrically and clutching his arm as though it was no longer fully attached. His kid was seated on the blacktop a few feet away, head in his hands. Only Hoegstra looked as though he hadn't heard the final bell. He struggled up on one knee, fought the tail of his unwieldy coat and made snarling sounds as he reached for his crowbar. One of the two uniforms stepped on the bar and wagged a cautionary finger at him.

"Uh-uh, guy. I think you been bad."

A third squad car came up the street the wrong way, this one carrying only a white-shirted sergeant. He got out, hitching his pants over a tight round stomach and squinting at the scene. Whelan recognized him as Sgt. Michael Shea. Sergeant Shea came forward slowly, shaking his head, and Whelan took a couple more steps back into the shadows and wondered if he could make it to his car without being seen.

Landis was being helped up now by one of the officers, and his son made a fine macho show of shaking a cop's hand off his arm and struggling to one knee. He paused there and shook his head as though to clear it.

Whelan would have bet the rent that Hoegstra would be the one to give the cops trouble, and he was right. The old man righted himself, wobbled a little and then made a sudden lunge for Chick Landis. A young cop jumped into his path, nightstick held chest high, one hand at each end.

"Back off!" the cop said, and Hoegstra went around him. The kid cop was good: with a minimum of movement, he cut off Hoegstra's path and got the nightstick under his chin. He lifted it sharply and moved the old man back, slightly off balance, and then pushed him up against the car. He bent Hoegstra backward onto the hood of the Buick and held the stick under Hoegstra's chin.

Whelan waited a moment until the four uniforms were all occupied with the brawlers and Michael Shea was talking to one of the women from Landis's office, then slipped off toward his car. A few steps later, he chanced a look over his shoulder and Michael Shea was staring at him. Whelan nodded and the old cop crooked his finger at him.

The jig is up.

Sergeant Shea put his hands in his pockets and strolled a few steps to meet him halfway.

"Mr. Whelan, am I right?"

"Yes, Sarge. What can I do for you?"

"Well, for starters, you can talk to a lonely old man surrounded by youngsters," he said, indicating the four young cops. Shea had slipped effortlessly into a County Galway accent. "And you can tell me how it is that yourself keeps turning up wherever there's trouble."

"There's trouble everywhere, Sarge. Have to stay in your house to avoid it."

Shea nodded slowly but squinted, first up at the sky, then down at the ground, then at Whelan.

"What I'd like to know is, how is it that you're here? You seem to turn up in the oddest places. I get a call that some asshole is burning a cross on some colored guy's lawn and I find you there in a donnybrook. Swinging an ax, I recall, and doing damage to a citizen's automobile."

"It was across from my house."

"Then I get a call about a dead body in Lincoln Park and there you are, in the company of my old friend Albert Bauman. And now a call comes in, we got a free-for-all going in front of a real estate office. I show up and there you are, like the bad penny. Tell me, son, do you cause all these things? Our Albert seems to think you're a sharp young fella. Are you really a menace to the community instead?" The old cop wrinkled up his nose and fixed a pair of blue eyes on Whelan.

"I'm dogged wherever I go by bad luck."

The old cop stared till Whelan met his eyes and Whelan smothered the complaints of his conscience. "You can't think I had anything to do with these old clowns fighting over a car. Come on, Sergeant."

"What I think, Mr. Whelan, is, if I answer another call anywhere in this *Urbs in Horto,* this City in a Garden, and find you, I'll arrange accommodations for you over at Six and you can begin your rehabilitation." He turned without waiting for an answer and walked away.

Whelan went to his car, started it up, and pulled away. He hit a button on his radio and it gave him McCoy Tyner and a very large band. He had to admit that he felt a little guilty about his role in old Hoegstra's raging performance, but only a little. He told himself it would justify everything to know what this little piece of street theater really meant.

I'm having a bachelor Friday night: first the fights, then dinner, something traditional. He decided to have one of Fena's lovely pizzas at Joe Danno's tavern.

Thirteen

SATURDAY morning ushered in a cold rain, with low, heavy clouds and a nasty wind from the north that carried the rain slanting down onto the streets. Whelan got up at nine, turned up the heat against the window-rattling wind and drove to the newsstand at Wilson and Broadway, where the happy little man from Pakistan sold him a *Sun-Times*. Whelan drove back home and decided not to fight the weather. This was a day for a four-course breakfast, for college football on TV and lounging in the bathtub with a book.

He cut onions and a green pepper, then chopped the tail end of a piece of ham. While they simmered in a pan in a little pond of melted butter, he broke three eggs into a steel bowl, poured in a little milk, a handful of grated Parmesan cheese, and salt and pepper, then began to beat the eggs to death.

He put three sausages in the toaster oven and when they were almost done, poured the eggs into the frying pan and put a couple pieces of toast into the toaster. He was halfway through the omelette when he saw the story little more than a couple of inches of one column deep into the paper.

SECOND MAN SLAIN ON LAKEFRONT

The body of an unidentified man was found by a jogger in a grassy area near Foster Avenue Beach. The man, described as a white man in his late fifties or sixties, had been shot once in the head, apparently at close range. It was the second murder on the lakefront in less than a month. Earlier this month, the body of a gunshot victim was found on the Montrose Harbor breakwater. Police have no motive in the slaying, and there is no evidence of a connection between the two slayings, according to Detective Albert Bauman of Area Six Violent Crimes Unit.

No evidence of a connection, Whelan thought. Right.

Bauman, of course, wasn't in when Whelan tried him at Area Six, and the detective who answered the phone sounded distracted. In the background Whelan could hear him typing on a computer keyboard.

"What's this in regard to, sir?"

"It's a personal call, actually."

The detective relaxed. "Now why would you expect to find him here with all us normal types? He's never here—he's like the wind!"

"I never thought of him that way. If he calls, tell him Whelan needs to see him."

"Will do, sir."

Whelan read the article again and wished there was a description of the victim. He told himself that there wasn't a thing to connect it logically to his case or to Michael Minogue. Nothing except the leaden feeling in the pit of his stomach that it was connected, and that he would be able to identify the body. He thought of Dutch Sturdevant.

The rain had stopped but the bench in front of the Empire Hotel was empty. He parked at the edge of the bus stop and walked toward the entrance of the building, trying not to acknowledge the heavy pressure in his chest. At the door, he paused and looked around. As he pushed his way into the lobby, he heard someone calling his name.

It took a moment to focus on the direction of the voice. Eventually he saw Dutch Sturdevant, Walkman in place, standing in front of the Burger King across the street. Sturdevant waved like a kid at a ball game and Whelan found himself grinning as he crossed the street.

"Too wet for bench sitting, Dutch?"

"Nah. I don't care if I get my ass a little wet. I just got hungry. I wanted a piece of pie. You should see what we gotta eat over there," he said, nodding in the direction of his home. "They feed us things you can't identify. We play fucking parlor games to figure out what we're eating. The meat's gray, the chicken's gray, the salmon—the salmon's *yellow*. What the hell kinda salmon's yellow? I fed mine to the rat in my room. Now I think his feelings are hurt. So what's up, kiddo?"

"Just dropped by to see how you were," Whelan said.

"I'm great. It's Saturday, my favorite day."

"What happens on Saturday that's so special?"

"Now? Not a thing, kid, but I've had seventy years of 'em and I liked 'em all."

"Cup of coffee?"

"Why not?"

Whelan bought them both coffee and saw Dutch watching a kid across the aisle digging into one of the little individual pies.

"Another pie, Dutch?"

"I'd get sick."

Whelan handed him two dollars. "Go get us each one. Make mine blueberry."

"I been looking for that truck," Dutch said a moment later through a mouthful of pie.

"I appreciate that."

Dutch nodded and bit off enough pie to fill both cheeks. He wiggled his scraggly brows and eyed Whelan's untouched piece. His lips were an unearthly blue, his cheeks still jammed to bursting, his hair stuck up along the back of his head like the crest of a bird caught in the rain. An old man to give the neighbors sleepless nights, Whelan thought.

"You gonna eat that?" Dutch said.

"No. I'm not hungry. Here, you take it," Whelan said, shoving the pie across the table.

"Great." He smiled contentedly at his pie.

"Haven't seen the blue truck, huh?"

"Uh, nope." Dutch shot him a quick look. The old man made a pretense of surveying the room. He sniffed and scratched at his ear and squinted and looked around like a man making a decision. "You ever think maybe you're getting suspicious about things that there's nothing wrong with? In your line of work, I mean?"

"All the time. I think it's one of those side effects that you can't avoid. Like that stare the cops have. Why? Have you noticed something out of the ordinary around here?"

"Not around here, no." Dutch looked embarrassed. "This was over . . . you know. By you, actually. Your office."

"I see."

"I was taking a walk and I decided to see where you have your office, in case I ever gotta go see you there, you know?"

"Right," Whelan said, wondering where this was heading.

"Well, maybe I'm just nuts, which wouldn't surprise me at all, but . . . I saw this guy."

"What guy?"

"He was standing across the street from your building. In a doorway by the corner there."

"On the corner? Dutch, there's always somebody on that corner. There's a bunch of black kids who hang around there all the time, and I see a couple of old white guys there now and then, and . . ."

Dutch shook his head. "This guy was watching your building."

"Are you sure?"

"Yeah. He never took his eyes off it."

Dutch watched his reaction and Whelan realized that the old man was both embarrassed to have been caught peeking around at the office and uneasy about what he'd seen.

"Describe him."

"Ain't much to describe. Small, like me. He was wearin' a kinda wool coat. . . ."

"An overcoat?"

"Yeah. An overcoat. A dark gray overcoat, and a wool cap. You know, with the snap on the brim."

"Sure."

"Mike used to wear one of them. I think all them old micks used to wear them hats. Hell, in the old days I guess we all did, but the Irish guys never give 'em up."

"Did you get a look at his face?"

"Not a good one. Had his collar up and his hat kinda made it hard to see his face. A weird-looking guy, though. Skinny and pale, it looked like."

"When was this, Dutch?"

"Same day you come over and we talked about the truck."

Whelan thought for a moment. "Dutch, remember the guy we talked about, the one who panhandled you and Michael Minogue that time?"

"The one from the old neighborhood? Sure."

"Could it have been him?"

He thought for a moment. "Clothes were different."

"You can change clothes, Dutch. In ten seconds, you can change clothes."

The old man met his eyes and nodded. "Coulda been. Anyway, I guess I screwed this up. I was kinda watching this guy and then I see he's lookin' my way. So I start walkin' in the other direction, and when I look back, this guy's movin' away in the other direction. Toward the lake. It coulda been that other guy, Mr. Whelan."

Whelan remembered what Gerry Costello had told him. "Did he walk with a limp?"

Dutch gave him a surprised look and then grinned. "Yeah, sure he did. And that guy that other time with Mike, he had a bum leg, I could tell that right off. You're pretty good."

"You're pretty good yourself, Dutch. I'd sure be interested if he shows up again."

The old man looked embarrassed. "You probably think I'm an old busybody, walking around by your office."

"No. I put you up to it."

"So what did you come here for today?"

"Oh, just . . . you know . . ."

Dutch fixed his unblinking bad-boy's gaze on him and it was Whelan's turn to be embarrassed. He could feel the color coming into his face.

"Tell you the truth, I was checking to see if you were still alive."

An amused sparkle seemed to come into the old man's face. "No shit? What, I was supposed to croak this week and nobody told me? From dinner last night, maybe. Fish sticks, they give us, like it's Lent. Fish sticks. I coulda beat my pal Koski to death with mine. Fire the fucking things outta guns, you'd bring down buildings. I hate fucking fish sticks."

"They were kind of a childhood nightmare for me, too. But you survived them."

"Yeah. So how come you were worried?"

"Because the cops found a dead man down at the lake. It was an older man and the body wasn't far from where they found Michael Minogue."

"So you thought maybe I was down there sayin' novenas over Mike and somebody killed me. Wait till I tell the other inmates." Dutch grinned and gave him a loopy look, and Whelan laughed in spite of it all. "You think maybe I can't take care of myself?"

"I think you're probably a badass for your age, but this was done with a gun."

"Well, thanks. I just don't want you to think I'm some kinda old fart that can't take care of himself."

"I don't think that. I was just afraid I'd gotten you into something."

An odd look came into the old man's eyes. In a bigger, younger man, Whelan would have said it was intimidation.

"Look at me, kiddo. I always been like this. I was always the runt. In my house, in the old neighborhood, at school. There was always somebody beatin' my ass. Then one day when I was about thirteen, fourteen, this big asshole picks a fight with me over a ball game. Just to be an asshole, really. Wasn't much of a fight: he stayed out there at long range and we boxed, and he landed all his punches and I couldn't do shit. He cut me over my eye and I had a fat lip and my nose was bleedin,' I looked like fuckin' Roland LaStarza when he fought Marciano. Remember him? He was a bleeder, LaStarza."

"I remember."

"Anyhow, this fucker decided he was gonna rub my face in it. He grabbed me in a headlock and pulled me down on the ground and he landed on me with his fat ass and he was gonna pound me till my face was hamburger, and I knew it was just to humiliate me in front of all the kids watching. And I couldn't take it. I went a little bit crazy. I dug my finger in his eye and I clawed at his nose with my nails, got my fingers right up his nostrils. Then he started to choke me, and I knew I couldn't get his hand off my throat. So I bit into it. I don't mean I bit him like kids do, I bit *into* it. I tore off a big piece of skin and he started howlin' and whacking at me, and I grabbed him with both arms around the neck and pulled him to me and I got his ear between my teeth and I bit through it. I bit through it and I tore at it to make sure I got it right. I elbowed him in the head and I got up and kicked him and I was picking shit up off the street and throwin' it at him and then my friends got nervous and grabbed me. They had to sew this fucker's ear back on, and he had blurred vision for a week, and my nail marks on his nose and my teeth marks on his arm. And nobody ever tried to do nothing like that to me again.

"So now I'm an old man and I look like somebody helps me piss in the morning, but if they come for me and they got anything less than a gun, I'm gonna leave marks."

"This one *has* a gun."

"So he shoots me with it. Then I'll stick it up his ass. I give you my word as a gentleman."

Whelan laughed and got to his feet. "You've convinced me. Just do me a favor, don't go bogarting around the neighborhood. If you see the guy in the coat again, or the truck—"

"I'll get on the horn."

"Good enough."

WHELAN was pleased to see that other tenants were at work on a Saturday. There were lights on in several of the first-floor offices and he could hear voices. On his floor, he was surprised to hear Nowicki's voice coming out of A-OK Novelties. Apparently this was a hard day in the novelty business. Nowicki sounded flustered.

He brought in his mail and tossed all of it in the wastebasket and tried Bauman again, without success.

He hung up the phone and thought about what he'd learned from Dutch Sturdevant. On an impulse he crossed to the window and looked out at the street corner. There was no one standing in doorways keeping him under surveillance today. Still, there was something about Dutch's account that nagged at him.

He decided to have a cup of coffee and think on it. He walked out of his office, shutting the door with one hand while he wrestled himself into his jacket. With his back still to the hall, he realized he had company. He froze for a moment, then caught the strong scent of cigar smoke and Right Guard and said "Hello, Bauman."

"Shhhh." He turned and saw Bauman crouched low, his ear to the door of A-OK Novelties, his face red and swollen with his struggle to keep from laughing. He looked up at Whelan, held out a hand for silence, and resumed his eavesdropping.

Inside the office of A-OK Novelties, Mr. Nowicki was engaged in one of his more heartfelt business conversations. Much of it was delivered in the intense, muttered style of speech that indicated the speaker had much to hide, but the texture was peppered with Nowicki's strikingly original use of profanity.

Whelan moved a couple of steps closer so that he could hear Nowicki. The little potbellied man seemed to be talking through gritted teeth to someone named Ross. He and Ross had a problem and, if Nowicki had sized up the matter accurately, the problem was Ross's sad deficiency in the area of personal honor.

"I go to the wall for you, Ross, to the wall, and what do you do? You fucking screw me, Ross. I'll tell you what's wrong with you, Ross: you're a lowlife. You're small-time and you're always gonna be small-time 'cause you screw the people that pulled you up by your fucking bootstraps and made you somebody. And let me—"

Here Ross apparently made a case for himself. There was a ten-second pause and Nowicki exploded with "You small-time prick!" and then seven or eight profanities strung together like bad lights on a Christmas tree.

Bauman's big body shook with suppressed laughter and he looked at Whelan with tears in his eyes. "This guy's an artist," he whispered.

From within, Nowicki interrupted his profanity to do something, and when he resumed his tirade, it was clear that he'd taken time to bite into a sandwich. He listened to Ross for a moment and then spoke through his tuna salad.

"Fine. By Monday, no later. And gimme some shit that I can sell or I'll have your ass." Then Nowicki slammed the phone down with a loud crack and muttered, "Asshole."

Whelan grabbed Bauman by the elbow and half-beckoned, half-dragged him into the office.

"So why don't you just give in to your curiosity and break into his office the way you've broken into mine half a dozen times. Then you'll know what 'novelties' are."

Bauman grinned. "Hey, quit casting whattya call 'ems on your neighbor."

"Aspersions."

"Give the guy a break, Whelan. He's just a small businessman whose suppliers let him down. He's the backbone of the economy. Besides, I got a pretty good idea what this guy means by 'novelties' already."

Bauman helped himself to a cup of water from the cooler and sat on the edge of Whelan's desk. "You keep callin' me, people are gonna think we're having an affair. So what did you want to talk about?"

"The body down at the lake, among other things."

"What about it?"

"You tell me. All I know is what I read in the paper."

Bauman gave him an amused look. "You saying you didn't get an accurate account from your local rag?"

"I just figured I could get a little more from a personal interview with the celebrity cop quoted in the story. Detective Albert Bauman. How about a little help here, Bauman?"

"This don't have a thing to do with you. We got a stiff. Jogger found the body. Probably didn't even stop jogging—they never do. I got this mental picture of a guy running in place while he checks for a pulse."

"And you're certain there's no connection between this killing and the other one?"

"That guy was shot, this guy was shot. That's it. Close range, powder burns on his hair and his neck and his collar. What else you want to know?"

"He saw the killer."

"Maybe he got a look, maybe he was sleeping."

"What did he look like?"

A little smile appeared on Bauman's face. "A ratty-lookin' guy. Not a big guy, kinda bony."

"How old?"

"Hard to say with some of 'em. This guy, I'd make him fifty something, sixty, max. Brown hair with a lotta gray, brown eyes. Funny eyes, real close together."

Whelan watched him for a moment and said, "Wearing?"

Bauman shrugged. "Red baseball cap and a blue windbreaker."

Whelan met his gaze for several moments and tried to show nothing. He bit his tongue to hold back the last question. He could see from the little look of satisfaction that Bauman already had the corpse ID'd, and Whelan doubted he was going to share it.

I refuse to bite, he told himself.

He shrugged. "Okay, you're on top of it." Then after a moment, he added, "Homeless guy maybe?"

"Maybe."

"Have any of his stuff with him?"

"No. Some of 'em don't carry anything."

"Getting colder out at night," Whelan said.

"Some of 'em don't carry anything with 'em, Whelan."

"You're probably right."

Bauman watched him through a squint and then smiled. "I hear you were out monitoring the community again last night."

"I was a bystander."

"Not what Mike Shea thinks. Michaeleen thinks you're some kinda agitator. You show up and there's a beef." Bauman laughed. "Old Michaeleen's got that Irish way with words: he called you 'a catalyst for commotion.' I like that."

"I had nothing to do with it. Couple of old guys who didn't like each other, nothing more."

"A 'donnybrook,' " he called it. Broken windows, damaged cars, punches thrown, crowbars flyin' through the air. It sounded pretty good, Whelan. And no, I don't think you were just standing there."

"What do you want me to say?"

"Who were these guys?"

"I can tell you that one of them, Landis, is a Realtor who knew the guy I was trying to find."

"Was? So you're finished."

"Yeah. He's dead."

Bauman nodded. "Then these guys knew Minogue, right?"

"Well, one of them did. They grew up together."

"So you still got your nose in my business."

"Not from where I'm sitting. Anyhow, the guy I'm looking for was killed about ten years ago." Bauman looked ready to continue the argument and Whelan headed him off. "And I need a little help with that."

"Help? What kinda help?"

"I need you to run something for me on the guy. 'Death Cases' file. Joseph Colleran. Killed in an auto accident, October nineteenth, 1975."

"You got balls, Whelan," Bauman said, but he took out a pencil stub and a small spiral notebook. "If you already got cause of death, what are you looking for?"

"I'm curious."

Bauman fixed him with a dark look and said, "Any of your other work I can do for you, O Great Sleuth?"

"As a matter of fact, you can: the other guy in the fight last night. Hoegstra's his name. Run him."

"They'll already have that done."

"Then it won't be any trouble for you, Bauman."

Bauman muttered, "Shit," and began writing in his notebook. "Spell it," he said.

Whelan gave him the spelling. "This guy did time. Find out when he came back and if he's been involved in anything. Mostly I'm interested in knowing what years he was out on the street."

Bauman gave him an irritated look and Whelan said, "I'll buy you lunch." The detective gave him an almost imperceptible nod and got up.

"Anything you find out that's even remotely connected with police business, you give it up, hear?"

"Absolutely."

"Don't say 'absolutely' like you just sold me a zircon ring. And don't call me no more, arright?"

"Deal."

After Bauman had left, Whelan sat at his desk and thought about their conversation. Bauman was having a good time with his little secrets but by the end of it, he'd reverted to form, he was Bauman being irritated. Not Bauman about to make a nice collar or Bauman with all the answers. He hadn't cracked this one yet, and Whelan had a feeling each of them was holding information vital to the other.

He went over the previous day's rocky itinerary and the people he'd questioned.

Hoegstra, Landis, and Fritz Pollard: I got the bum's rush in three different places, he thought.

He toyed with the idea of calling Mrs. O'Mara and convinced himself that he'd be in a better position to discuss things if he knew more. Besides, he reasoned that he was not going to charge her for anything past yesterday.

Outside, the rain seemed to have let up for a while and he decided to go out for a walk. If he wasn't near the phone, he couldn't call her.

He'd gotten a block and a half when the sky opened up again. His nearest sanctuary was the House of Zeus, and they were waiting for him.

Three customers sat at window tables and stared out at the street, and Whelan would have bet all three had gotten caught in the rain and now believed themselves to be trapped like the denizens of an old Rod Serling screenplay, stuck in the House of Zeus till time wore itself out.

"Mr. Detective Whelan!" Rashid yelled out, and Gus emerged from the dark kitchen carrying a piece of what appeared to be raw skirt steak. He tossed it on a table, wiped his hands on his apron and produced a newspaper clipping.

"You see?" Gus waved the clipping at him. "We are in the newspaper, with picture!"

Rashid flashed four dozen teeth in a grin and opened his arms wide. "We are famous. Everyone will know our restaurant."

"There are two ways of looking at that, Rashid. The reviewer seems to have had a few problems."

Rashid shrugged. "Everybody gets sick. I'm kinda sick today."

"The flu, this one had," Gus added.

Rashid gave Whelan a benign smile. "I am owner of restaurant, I know about these things. All publicity is good, even bad publicity. Bad publicity announces restaurant to public. And it is free, this one."

"Yes," Gus agreed, "free." He spoke the word as though it had talismanic properties.

"You ought to put it up in the window."

"Yes, we gonna do that. I maybe scratch out couple sentences, some not nice words, upset customers."

"Nice to see you don't hold a grudge."

Rashid shrugged magnanimously. Gus broke into a rare smile. "And we talked to our cousin."

"Reza, huh? Calling out the big guns again."

"Sure. He is number-one lawyer. Maybe we gonna sue this guy, huh?"

"It's the American way, guys. May the best man win."

IT was still raining when he got home, and it appeared that the rain would last till the end of time, but there was mail waiting, one piece of mail. It was a letter in a tiny envelope, and two-thirds of it seemed to be covered by postage, odd postage of queens and alien vistas, and he tore the envelope apart like a dog falling on raw meat. Inside he found a short note on beige paper.

Dear Paul,

    I hope you get this before I come home. I'm having a wonderful time, at least during the day. You'd love the castles, you'd love the pubs, you'd talk to old English guys on all the corners. At night I don't have such a good time. I feel like I'm the only person in the world.

I believe this means I'm in love. We must talk.
See you soon.

Love, S.

He stared at it for a moment and then found himself taking a quick, stealthy sniff at the stationery, seeking a trace of her perfume. He thought he could just make it out, faintly, like background music.

She says she's in love, he told himself.

THE rain never did let up for the rest of that day. It ran off the awnings in sheets, came out of gutters in little waterspouts, collected in deep wide puddles. The first windfall of leaves had already blocked the sewers so that sidestreets all over the North Side turned into wading ponds. Whelan went out once for groceries, soaked his clothes and his shoes and didn't mind at all. Several times he caught himself in the act of humming.

In bed that night, he listened to a jazz program in which a disc jockey interviewed a woman who'd been a vocalist with the Dorseys and Artie Shaw and Tex Beneke. He tried to concentrate on the little anecdotes that the woman told about the great times with the big horn players, but he found himself remembering Dutch Sturdevant's account of the man watching the office. There was something about Dutch's story that bothered him, something that stuck out like a frayed end. But if he was right, that man wouldn't be watching anything anymore: that man was on a gurney in the morgue.

The singer was talking about being caught in the rain with an avuncular bandleader who gallantly took off his coat to protect her. He decided to go to sleep. As he drifted off, he was thinking about that last anecdote, about the bandleader and the young singer being caught in the rain in Omaha.

Fourteen

ON Sunday he woke up with the conviction that the world was once more a fine place. His good humor was tempered by a darker image that had crept into his mind just as sleep stole in, Dutch Sturdevant's image of a man in an overcoat watching his office.

He's not watching anyone anymore, he told himself, but he wasn't sold.

He had breakfast at the Subway Donut Shop—eggs over easy, hash browns, bacon and toast. He sat in the window and wiped the steam from the glass with the sleeve of his shirt. He paged idly through the *Sun-Times,* half-noticing the news stories until the paper caught his attention for the second time in as many days. This time, it told him that the dead man from the lakefront had been identified.

He had to read it twice to verify what he was seeing. The paper told him that the man was Raymond Dudek, aged sixty. No address was given.

"No," he said aloud. "No, it's not Ray Dudek."

He returned to his house and made a fast call. After three rings, Walter Meehan intoned "Hello" into the phone.

"Good morning, Mr. Meehan."

"Paul Whelan? Three times in one week I get to talk to Paul Whelan. Oh, what a good boy am I!"

"The pleasure is mine, Walter, but I'm sorry to be calling on a Sunday."

"It's fine, Paul. I'm retired, all my days feel like Sundays. What can I do for you?"

"A man was found shot to death down at the lakefront on Friday night. According to the paper, he has now been identified as Raymond Dudek."

Whelan waited through Walter's long, judicious pause. "And coming just after the death of a boyhood friend of the other Raymond Dudek, you aren't willing to accept coincidence as an explanation—fate having a little fun with you."

"No. Tell me, Walter, was there any question about the identity of that dead sailor in Riverview?"

"None. Someone from his family identified him, an uncle or cousin or someone like that. I never heard any question about the boy's identity. The funeral was open casket, so there was no doubt at all. It wouldn't attract much notice now, but it was a fairly big story then, Paul. Someone would have said something if the man in the casket hadn't been who we thought he was."

Whelan was silent for a moment. "What would Walter Meehan, homicide detective of the old Chicago Police Department, do about this?"

"I don't know. He would be puzzled, as he was almost every time he investigated a murder. He was a stubborn, singularly untalented man, so he would ask questions, over and over, of the same people and write down what he learned and sit staring at it in his room. Until he got something. Nowadays, Paul, you have another problem."

"What's that?"

He could almost see Walter deliberating, choosing the perfect word. "A terrible *randomness* that we didn't have. In my day, if we found a body, we knew there was a killer somewhere in the vicinity. But you don't know that. Your dead men on the lakefront might be the victims of total strangers, people passing through in stolen cars, madmen. Your killer might be heading west on the interstate."

"Yes. But I'm pretty sure this one isn't random, it's got roots that go way down. And I don't think my guy is leaving town."

Walter took a long, deep breath. "Then there are only the two possibilities: that you have talked to the killer already, or that you'll probably talk to him eventually. Am I making your situation more confusing?"

"No. You're saying what I already thought. I just wanted to be able to rule out the possibility that the man back there outside Aladdin's Castle was a ringer. Thank you, Walter."

"Good luck, Paul."

He spent the afternoon doing exactly what Walter Meehan had said—

176

jotting down what he knew and staring at it, looking for patterns and finding none.

WHELAN shaded his eyes and peered in through the dirty window. Inside the Alley Cat, time appeared to have come to a halt. A drunk was sleeping in the window, the same drunk who always seemed to be sleeping there. At the far end, the bartender was wearing the same rumpled white shirt he always wore and sitting on a stool, craning his head back up to stare at the TV. The picture on the set was so faint that the barman could have been watching a blank screen. Detective Albert Bauman was sitting in the exact center of the long, dark bar and staring straight ahead of him. Spread out before him were all his toys: a half-empty shot glass, a bottle of Beck's, a tin ashtray piled high with the bent ends of Bauman's vile little cigars and emitting a little column of dark smoke.

No one turned when Whelan entered the bar.

Maybe they're all dead, he thought.

He pulled out a stool next to Bauman and slid onto it. He tossed a ten on the bar and lit a cigarette, then looked at Bauman.

"Living in that fast lane again, huh, Albert?"

"Hey, sometimes it gets exciting: a guy died in here once."

"Last time I was here, there was a fight in progress and a guy on the floor. I think it was that guy in the window."

"Gibby. Yeah, he don't even drink much, he just has a couple and he passes out for the hell of it." He turned and called to the bartender. "Hey, Ralph. When you get off your break, we got a thirsty guy here."

Ralph appeared startled, and he tripped climbing down from the stool.

"He'll have what I'm having, Ralph." He turned to Whelan. "Gotta make it simple for old Ralph. He gets a little exercised now and then." Bauman waited as Ralph filled both shot glasses and set up a Beck's in front of Whelan.

"Take it outta here," Bauman said, indicating his money on the bar. When Ralph had taken a couple of bills, Bauman saluted Whelan with his shot. *"Salud."*

"Slainte," Whelan said, and drank half the shot off.

"Enough exchanging pleasantries. You're here to bug me about that stuff you asked for."

"If you've got anything for me."

Bauman gave him a long sleepy look, then recited, "Your guy Joseph Colleran died as the result of injuries in a hit-and-run."

Whelan looked at him for a second and then nodded slowly.

"You knew that already? And you had me spinnin' my—"

"No, I didn't know it. I just suspected it."

Bauman picked up his beer, took a long pull, and set it down again. "This guy Hoegstra, he's a hood—small-time hood, but genuine. He did time in Statesville, twice. You want his sheet?"

"No. The times, if you've got 'em."

"Come on, Whelan."

"Nineteen forty-six. I need to know if he was on the street or inside in 1946."

"We sent him away in '49. Again in '55."

"Thanks. Well, one good turn deserves another. Got something for you. About Raymond Dudek."

Bauman's eyes narrowed and he said nothing.

"By the way, I think you had the name when we talked yesterday."

"So what? What do you want to give me about Raymond Dudek?"

"The scoop. The skinny. That he was a boyhood friend of Michael Minogue and of the guy I've been looking for, Joseph Colleran. Oh, and that he's been dead for about forty years. How's that for starters?"

Bauman gave him an unblinking stare, and Whelan thought that this was probably how Bauman looked just before he decked somebody.

"Talk to me," Bauman said, and it wasn't a request.

"The body of Raymond Dudek was found on a hot summer night in Riverview, in June of 1946." Something changed in Bauman's eyes, but he waited. "He had been stabbed to death in an apparent robbery attempt. They found the body behind Aladdin's Castle."

"Who says?"

"Just about everybody who knew him. And one of the investigating officers."

Bauman lit up a little cigar and raised his eyebrows.

"Walter Meehan," Whelan said.

Bauman looked at his cigar. "The great Walter Meehan. When he was still a uniform."

"He was a sergeant at the time."

Bauman blew acrid smoke into the air. "Could be two guys with the same name. Probably half a million Dudeks in Warsaw. Probably half a million Polacks along Milwaukee Avenue named Dudek."

"Right. Ray Dudek was a boyhood friend of Michael Minogue, and now you find this corpse—what, five hundred yards from where Michael Minogue was killed, and it's supposed to be coincidence?"

Bauman studied his cigar ash and waited.

"What identification did the body have?" Whelan asked.

"Same kind a lot of these old guys have. Lot of 'em that served in World War Two, they still carry their discharge papers. That's what this guy had on him. His discharge papers."

"Nothing else?"

"ID you mean? Nah, that's it."

"Autopsy?"

"*Autopsy?* Whaddya think, they're miracle workers?"

"I think it's a homicide that might be connected to another open case, and I think the ME got the body Friday night. Unless a cruise ship sank and flooded the morgue with dead people, I think there's been an autopsy."

"What do you care, Whelan? No, don't answer. You'll tell me about your case for the old lady and her lost brother. Okay, we got an autopsy and it told me what I knew already: the guy's dead."

"Cause of death?"

"Like I told you yesterday. Gunshot at close range. One shot."

"What kind of gun?"

Bauman gave him a sardonic smile. "Artillery. We got us a serious shooter here, Whelan, wanted to make sure: used a forty-five automatic."

Whelan thought of what Gerry Costello had said. He took a sip of his beer and said casually, "Was there anything in the report?"

"You got an idea who this is, don't you?"

"No, actually I was hoping you could tell me."

Bauman watched him for a moment, then shrugged. "Hey, look at the bright side: we can eliminate Raymond Dudek, one way or the other."

"And not much else. What else did the autopsy say about this guy?"

"Nothing that would help with what you're doing. Nothing recent. Looked like he'd got himself shot up once. One leg was kinda, I don't know, twisted. Had a buncha scars. Old war wound, I guess. 'Consistent with shrapnel,' is how this guy in the ME's office puts it. He's got a poetic streak, this guy. So, this do anything for you?"

"No."

"So you saw Walter. How's he doing?"

"He's great. He likes being retired."

"Good. He was the best I ever saw."

"Helped me out a lot when I was trying to get started," Whelan said.

Bauman gave him an odd smile. Two strange pupils, Whelan thought, from one great teacher.

They made small talk over another round of drinks and Whelan got up to leave.

"What's your hurry, Snoopy?"

"I just stopped for a quick one, Bauman. Another time we can do old war stories all night. We'll have one of our little adventures where I take you to a restaurant and we have a few pops and you get me into a brawl or some other form of street entertainment."

"Hey, that happened *once*. Wasn't my fault."

"I gotta go."

Bauman nodded and then added, "So Walter's okay?"

"As far as I can tell. And he asked about you."

"He did, huh?"

"Yeah. I think he liked you."

"To know me is to love me, Whelan," Bauman said, and Whelan left.

He sat for a moment in his car and thought about the autopsy information and what it told him about the dead man. He thought about why the dead man would be carrying Ray Dudek's discharge papers, and he soon realized there was only one possible reason.

And I don't think this guy was homeless, Bauman. I've got his name, his history, I think I even know where he lived.

FRITZ Pollard's truck was parked up against the weathered siding of the building, and Whelan could see one light from somewhere behind the shop. He drove by and parked halfway up the block, then made his way back to Pollard's storefront.

Whelan walked behind the truck and peered into the side windows of the building but could see nothing. The light seemed to be coming from a hall. Coming around to the front, he saw that the storefront was also empty. He shot an uneasy look at the warped planks of the wood fence but saw no sign of the Hound from Hell. He paused a moment, then gave the heavy door a shove.

Just inside the door, he stood motionless for several seconds to let his eyes adjust to the dark. The shop smelled of fire, old fire, burnt paper perhaps, and the air inside was close. There was another odor present, masked by the burning smell, and he couldn't quite place it.

A narrow door opened onto a long hall behind the shop and Whelan stared into it for a moment. It was here that the single light shone. He crossed the room in silence and stood listening at the doorway. There was no sound but the creaking of the old frame building fighting the wind. He stepped into the narrow hall, smelling the pungent odor of damp, ancient plaster and rotting wood, and the burnt smell became stronger. The other smell was heavy now, calling attention to itself, and it slowly dawned on him what it was.

A door at the far end probably led to the back or basement. Four rooms seemed to line the hall, and the doors to all four were open, but Whelan knew the odors were coming from the one nearest. He paused at the doorway and felt inside for the light switch, then flicked it on. A faint plume of smoke from a small table told him where the burning smell had come from: a lighted cigarette had fallen out of an ashtray and set fire to the edges of a small spiral notebook, and the fire had blackened one corner of the book before burning itself out.

The table was set up close to a single bed, and a man sat on the floor with his back against the bed, still clothed, his head tilted to one side. He was dead, and the blood that soaked his hair and clothing and the bedclothes was the source of the other smell that Whelan had noticed.

Whelan studied the mess on the bedsheets, the blanket that sagged down to the floor, the blood that showed what had happened. Fritz Pollard had been shot while lying on the bed, shot perhaps from the doorway, and the shooter wasn't much good at it because the shot had gotten Pollard in the right side of the chest, and he'd sat up and the shooter had probably come in and squeezed off at least three more rounds. One had caught Pollard just below the throat and another had hit him in the side of the head, and there was one in the wall just above the headboard.

Fritz Pollard had slid off the bed onto the floor and bled everywhere, especially from the throat wound. It looked as though he'd gotten up and fallen again. His bloody handprint was on the bedclothes. On the edge of the door was a partial handprint, smeared on the old paint.

Whelan went into the room, holding his breath against the blood smell, and knelt down close to Fritz Pollard. He felt the cold skin for a pulse but knew he was just going through the motions. Then he looked at the bullet holes. They were big holes, .45-caliber holes, each with its own exit hole on the other side. He stood and looked around the room. No drawers pulled hastily from their runners, no rifled papers. On the top of Fritz Pollard's crudely painted dresser lay a small pile of cash and some keys.

He stepped out of the room to suck in less tainted air and calm his raging stomach. When he felt better, he stood at the door to the next room till he was certain he was alone. Then he found a light switch and entered and found what he'd come for. Like Fritz Pollard's room, this room was a bedroom, a sparely furnished room where one man had slept. His outlines could still be seen on the dirty and wrinkled bedsheets. The ashtray beside this bed was as full as the one beside Fritz's, and an empty beer bottle stood beside it. The room smelled of dirty cotton and cigarette smoke and sweat—a far cry from the terrible odors of the other room. Whelan looked around the room for something to identify the man who had slept here but didn't really expect to find anything.

He believed he already knew who had slept here, and that the man had just been found shot to death at the lakefront. This had been Casey Pollard's room, and he would have bet his house that the short, skinny man with the bad leg found dead at the lake was Casey Pollard.

Now he rummaged through the small closet and the little musty pile of clothes on a chair for something else, something he hoped he'd find but did not. There was no overcoat, no snap-brim cap. He sighed.

Nothing is ever simple, he told himself.

He remembered the dark thought that had stolen into his consciousness just before he'd gone to sleep the previous night, a man in a dark coat, and something else. He shook his head.

What I don't know would fill a book.

He was about to leave when he heard movement at the back of the house. He stood perfectly still, held his breath and listened, and stared at the door down the hall. For a long moment he remained motionless, waiting for the door to open, and then he moved toward it. He guessed that it led either into the basement or out onto the back stairs. The sound came again, a heavy padding sound, as though someone in stocking feet moved behind the door. He thought of the bloodbath in Fritz Pollard's room and wondered if somebody was out there waiting for him with a large-caliber gun.

No, he thought. The shooter would have panicked, would have opened fire already. He would have taken me out as soon as I came in.

He sighed and moved toward the door. For several seconds he waited with his ear to the door, listening, and when it sounded as though the person on the other side was moving away from the door, Whelan yanked it open.

He saw the eyes before he could make out anything else, eyes like none he'd ever seen in his life, and they'd been expecting him. Seen in its entirety, it was a dog out of fantasy, a creature out of nightmare, part German shepherd, probably part werewolf, a huge animal, with the most enormous head he'd ever seen.

"Shit," he heard himself say. Whelan heard the beast growl from deep in its great shaggy chest and then the dog was at the bottom step in a heartbeat. Whelan could see the mangy patches in the dog's hide, he could smell its filthy yard smell. The dog filled the back stairway and covered the stairs in two bounds, snarling and dripping spittle and foam, and Whelan thought he would choke on his own heart.

The dog lost its footing at the top stair and thudded down several steps, its claws scratching at the wood, and then it righted itself and regained the top. Whelan slammed the door in its face and ran as the animal threw its body repeatedly at the door, as though this were a personal matter.

"Jesus *Christ*," Whelan said through his teeth, and it did not surprise him at all to hear the doorjamb splintering and bursting open and the animal bounding toward him. There was no time even to turn around. He raced the beast through the hall to the shop in front. He moved behind the big oak desk and grabbed hold of the first heavy object he found, a cast-iron ashtray overflowing with Fritz Pollard's spent smokes. Whelan swung round with the ashtray and brought it down just as the dog left its feet in a leap. The metal caught the dog on its snout and the animal fell on its side, yelping. Then it was up again, and Whelan hurled a table lamp at its head. The dog growled and bared huge yellow fangs, then came at him again, and this time Whelan grabbed the desk chair. Gasping for breath, he swung the chair in a high arc and brought it down on the animal's skull, and the dog hit the floor with a crash that shook the room.

Whelan raised the chair again and stared at the animal, which lay spent on the floor, panting. Blood showed along the side of the dog's head. Whelan stepped back, still brandishing the chair and watching the dog. The animal followed his movements with one crazed black eye and began to get up.

"I'll kill you, dog," Whelan said, and hoped he sounded more convincing than he felt. He backed toward the street entrance.

The dog got up on its forelegs, then slowly raised its haunches and growled, watching him with its moist mad eyes.

Holding the chair in front of him, Whelan opened the door carefully. He took a last glance at the dog. It was up on all fours and showing fangs, and Whelan wondered if this was how Cerberus looked. He tossed the chair, slipped out through the door and slammed it behind him.

He made the call from a pay phone, told the detective who answered that Bauman would want to know about it. He declined the detective's invitation to leave his name.

"He'll know who it's from."

"All right, sir."

"And they'll need something from Animal Control."

"Whaddya got there, rats or something? Rats at the body?"

"No, there's a dog in the apartment. You'd have to see the dog. It doesn't even look real, it looks like special effects from a movie. I think it's the Hound of the Baskervilles."

"This dog's never met Bauman, sir."

"This dog is special," Whelan said.

The cop chuckled. "We gonna need those darts, tranquilizer darts like they use on *Wild Kingdom*?"

"No darts. Call in an air strike."

HE took a bottle of Gosser's out of the refrigerator and drank it in the dark with the radio on low. He had all kinds of pieces now—the discharge papers and the man in the overcoat, and what all the players had told him, and he had the feeling it was all coming together, but he couldn't quite see it yet.

Before he went to bed, he peered out onto the street and then went to the back of the house and looked out onto the yard and the gangway. He wondered if a figure in an overcoat had stood in the shadows and watched his house.

THE small windup clock beside the bed said 6:41 A.M. and he already knew who was calling.

"Yeah?"

" 'Yeah'—that's how you answer your phone now? Wake up, Whelan, and put your party manners on. So you found us another stiff."

"Yeah."

"I'm listening."

"I had a hunch the guy at the lakefront was the brother of a junk dealer named Fritz Pollard. It made sense to me that he was staying with his brother, so I went out hunting, and what I found, you know about."

"You touch anything? Take anything? Have a snack from the guy's fridge?"

"What do you think?"

"What other hunches you got, Whelan? How much of this shit you think I'm gonna let you get away with?"

"You know what I'm doing."

"Oh yeah, I know what you're doing. You're looking for a guy that's been dead for ten years and you knew that days ago, so you're playing with yourself."

"One of these people—either the guy you found down at the lake or the person who murdered him—killed the man I've been looking for."

"It was a hit-and-run. You're seeing conspiracies where there's just the same shit that happens every week, every day even."

"Right, it's all a coincidence. This guy died and his best friend went underground. Yeah, it's all coincidence, like the guys who died after opening King Tut's tomb. But I'm like you, Bauman: I don't buy coincidence."

"You're gonna *be* in King Tut's tomb, Sherlock, you keep gumming up this other thing."

"What have you got that I'm 'gumming up'? Just tell me that."

He could hear Bauman sucking at one of the baby cigars, he could hear the wheels turning, there were always wheels turning in Bauman's head. He knew what was coming next and it gave him enjoyment.

"This is mine, Whelan."

"Absolutely. But it's mine, too."

"Nothin' is yours. It's all mine."

"All right."

"Anything you get, anything, it's mine. It's nobody else's, not anybody. It's all mine or you're gonna wish you died of King Tut's curse."

"Deal."

"I don't make deals."

"Figure of speech. I owe you."

"Just don't make a mess, Whelan."

HE went back to sleep for a while, and it was almost nine when he pulled himself together and made his circuitous way to the office. A dark blue Mercury was parked in front of the building when he went in. The driver was a burly man in his sixties with eyebrows like drugstore cotton. The man glared at Whelan through the windshield and looked away when Whelan paused at the door to the office.

The staircase smelled of perfume, a flowery, older woman's perfume. The perfume trail led him to his own office, where he found a tall woman in an old-fashioned blue woolen coat standing in the hall. The woman held her purse in front of her with both hands and watched him warily as he ascended the stairs.

To put her at ease, he nodded and said, "Morning." She stepped back from his door, and when he took out his keys and approached, she straightened.

"Mr. Paul Whelan?"

He recognized the voice, he'd heard it before, a cool, confident voice with musical notes. It went with the lively brown eyes and youthful complexion, but he had never seen this face before.

"Yes. Are you waiting to see me?"

"Uh, yes. If you're not too busy." And now he guessed her name, even as she was saying it. "I'm Betty Torgeson. We spoke on the phone. . . ."

"Betty Henke," Whelan said.

She gave him a polite half smile and nodded. "Once upon a time."

He stared at her for a moment. And now I've met all the survivors, he thought.

"Come on in, Mrs. Torgeson. Hope you haven't been waiting long."

"Just a couple of minutes. I should have called first anyway."

"Why? Nobody else does." He showed her into the room, pulled out a guest chair for her and opened a window to chase the stale air.

"We can split this," he said, holding up his coffee. "I've got another cup somewhere. I can also offer you tea. I have tea bags, and my cooler makes hot water."

"Thanks, but I don't need anything."

"Okay." He settled himself in, flipped the top of his coffee and took a sip as he studied her. She perched at the edge of the chair as though ready to flee if this all proved to be a bad idea. Betty Henke wore her silver hair short and used very little makeup other than a light lipstick. It was a long face and she was a big-boned woman, not as delicately featured as Ellen Gillette Gaynor and not as feminine as Maggie O'Mara, but it was a lively face, attractive in other ways. Whelan suspected that they'd been quite a trio back in the halcyon days when they'd posed for pictures on the beach.

Whelan held up his cigarettes. "Cigarette?"

"No thank you, but you can. My husband smokes: I'm used to it."

He lit a cigarette and raised his eyebrows. "And the vigilant-looking gentleman sitting out front in the Mercury would be the estimable Lars Torgeson?"

"You're observant and you're good with names."

"He's hard to miss—he's right out there glaring at everybody who passes by. Looks like an old prize fighter."

"He's worried about me. He didn't want me to come here. He wanted to come see you himself, but I'm a big girl and this is my problem."

"What problem?"

She seemed hesitant, as though what she had to say embarrassed her. "You. Who are you, Mr. Whelan?"

"I'm who I said I was. Here, this is my card. You can check me out, call the cops. Area Six, Violent Crimes, they know me there. Or check on my license with the secretary of state."

She shook her head. "That's not what I mean. I want to know why these things we talked about are of interest to you."

"I told you that. I'm working for Mrs. Margaret O'Mara."

"Yes, to find Joe. Joe is dead, Mr. Whelan. I told you that. I think you were looking for something else. And then, over the weekend, I read in the paper that they found a body. . . ."

"Ray Dudek. You read about them finding the body of Ray Dudek, and the dead man was about the same age Dudek would be if he were still alive."

She glared at him for a moment, her eyes reflecting a mix of fear and anger. "Yes. I read that story and I haven't been able to sleep since. I can still see his face, I can see Ray Dudek's face on the night he was killed. He's dead, Mr. Whelan, that man they found is somebody else. . . ."

"He had Ray Dudek's discharge papers on his body."

"I don't know anything about that. I just know Ray is dead, has been dead for forty years almost. . . ." Something in Whelan's face seemed to bother her. She made an exasperated noise and leaned forward in the chair. "I *know* Ray is dead, Mr. Whelan."

"You were there."

"Yes. I mean, we were all there, all of us."

Whelan pulled out the photo from his top drawer. "All of you—from this picture?"

She seemed to soften as she took the photo from his hands. She studied it for a long time, shaking her head softly and several times saying something to herself that Whelan couldn't quite make out.

Eventually she let it rest on her lap and met his eyes. "So many of them are dead. More than you'd think. We aren't that old."

He decided he wouldn't tell her about the Pollard brothers. It would serve no purpose. He wanted to take her back to that other night.

"Who was at Riverview that night, Mrs. Torgeson?"

"Just about everybody. We used it as a meeting place, Mr. Whelan. There were a couple of big halls attached to taverns that we went to to dance, but during the summer if the weather was nice, we went to Riverview. It only cost a nickel to get in," she said. "It cost a nickel and there was a beer garden, and the rides and the freak show and the arcades. Rides and music and kind of a haze in the air from all the cigarette smoke, and you could smell the gasoline smell from some of the small rides." Her voice had taken on a dreamy quality and she seemed to be watching a point somewhere off to the side of his office. "We didn't even go together, we just met there, all of us."

"Who? Who was there that night? Chick Landis?"

"Yes," she said slowly.

"Either of the Pollards?"

She thought for a moment. "Fritz. I remember seeing Fritz. I . . . he wanted me to go out with him, but I was seeing a boy from work. But Fritz was there, he—we said hello, I think."

"Casey?"

"He showed up later, after we heard about the—about Ray."

"Who else was there? I think this is important, as unpleasant as it may seem."

She gave him a sardonic look. " '*Seem*'? Oh, it doesn't 'seem' unpleasant, Mr. Whelan, it is. I was there while a friend of mine was murdered. I'll never forget it—what would it say about me if I could?" Betty Henke looked around his office, visibly organizing her thoughts, and Whelan said nothing. Then she sighed and flashed a sad smile. "I never went there after that. Riverview. It was such a wonderful place, but . . . I never went there again."

"That's what Mrs.—that's what Maggie O'Mara told me, Mrs. Torgeson."

She gave him a long look and then straightened slightly. "Let's see . . . who else was there? Michael Minogue. He was there because he was supposed to meet Ray. Joe Colleran was there, of course, because he and Michael were inseparable. They were all going out later, to look for girls." She raised her eyebrows significantly but Whelan didn't understand the emphasis. "Gerry Costello was there."

"Herb Gaynor?"

"No. I mean, he was there but he wasn't with us, he was working."

"He was at the gate?"

"Yes. And . . . and the three of us, Mr. Whelan"—she tapped the picture of the three laughing girls on the beach—"we were all there, all talking about man trouble."

Whelan straightened. "Man trouble?"

"Yes. I was trying to get rid of Fritz Pollard, and Ellen was having difficulties with Herb, who was a jerk even then."

"And Maggie Colleran?" Whelan asked.

Betty hesitated for a moment, her brown eyes clearly showing a moment of panic, and Whelan realized she didn't want to answer. Then she sighed. "She was trying to break it off with Ray Dudek, Mr. Whelan."

Whelan looked at her and let her words hang there for a moment, played with his cigarette as he let them sink in.

"You didn't know," she said.

"No." A dark weight settled on his chest and he strained to keep his voice neutral when he spoke. "Do you know why she was trying to get out of it?"

"Of course. Ray was trouble, he was just trouble for any woman unlucky enough to fall for him. He didn't deserve to die that way, Mr. Whelan, but he was no good." She shifted uneasily in her seat.

"I got the impression that he was a hard case. I've heard that he was quick to use his fists, for one thing."

"Oh, he had a terrible temper, and he was fearless. Some of the boys like that, the war took it out of them. But it didn't do a thing to change Ray, except maybe to make him more violent. The first week he was back, he was still in uniform, and he got into a big fight at a nightclub down on Wells Street. But that wasn't all, Mr. Whelan. Ray was very manipulative, he was . . . we used to call it 'on the make'; he was always on the make. For a way to make a buck, for a new girl."

She looked down at the picture. "He was such a handsome boy, Mr. Whelan. And it wasn't just his looks, there was something about him, something that suggested a wild, lost little boy, an angry little boy, and women just wanted to take him in hand and calm him down. He had to beat the girls off with sticks. I think we all had a crush on him at one time or another. I know I did, and Maggie. Even Ellen, before she was paired off with Herb. Ray Dudek always had a girl, but if you were his girl, you couldn't count on being that for more than a few weeks."

"Mrs. O'Mara didn't actually tell me this, but I gathered that she liked a fellow who didn't come back from the war."

"Tommy Friesl. There were two boys in that group who didn't come back, the two Tommys—Tommy Friesl and Tommy Moran—and she was in love with Tommy Friesl. And he was great, he was just right for her. A good guy, Mr. Whelan, a real good guy. That's who she should have wound up with. They were a fun couple, she was a witty, charming girl." She looked away. "I hope she was happy while her husband was alive."

"I got the impression that she was pretty . . . content, and he left her comfortable."

"I don't know how much that counts for, Mr. Whelan. Wouldn't count for much with me." She leaned forward with a look of urgency. "Now I want to *know* about this, Mr. Whelan. I've answered all your questions, now answer mine."

"I wish I could tell you something to make it sound less harsh. But I believe that the person who killed Ray Dudek is still around. Still here.

I think he killed . . . the man on the lakefront, the one the cops thought was Ray Dudek, and I think he probably killed . . . other people." For a moment he couldn't meet her eyes. He fumbled with the cigarette pack for another smoke and looked at her when he heard her sigh.

"How horrible. Oh my God, how horrible. After all these years."

"Yes. I think so, too. One more thing I need to know—in those days, did you know a man named Hoegstra?"

"I don't think so but I know that name. Oh. Was he the man they—" She stopped and waved one helpless hand for him to finish.

"Yes, he's the guy they robbed back in 1941. But you didn't know him?"

"No. Is that what you've really been investigating?"

"No. I was really trying to figure out what happened to Joe Colleran."

"Will you tell me how this turns out?"

"Yes. You've been very helpful, and I appreciate your coming here."

She got up and frowned slightly. "Are you working with the police investigation now?"

He laughed. "Not exactly 'with' them. But I'm working on a case that happens to be connected to theirs. They don't exactly like it, but I'm giving them what I find."

"You have a strange line of work, Mr. Whelan."

"I wouldn't have it any other way."

She nodded as though he'd given the correct answer, then extended her hand. He shook it and showed her to the door. In the hall, she turned and gave him a small smile that seemed to show relief. He nodded and closed his door.

I'm glad if I made you feel better, Mrs. Torgeson. You sure didn't make me feel better.

Whelan sat down and finished the cigarette he'd started and looked for the silver lining in Betty Henke's new cloud. When he decided there wasn't any, he took out the phone book, looked up a number and called St. Joseph's Cemetery. It took the office staff at St. Joseph's a few minutes to find a name for him and when they did, he felt worse than he'd felt since the beginning. He depressed the receiver button, then made another call, to Mrs. Margaret O'Mara.

Fifteen

SHE met him at the door with a wary look and said, "Come in, Mr. Whelan."

"Thanks. I hope I'm not keeping you from the shop. We could have met there."

"Antique dealers usually close on Mondays." She led him into a small, intensely cluttered living room bathed at the moment in bright sunlight. Mrs. O'Mara's home was a crowded treasure trove of Victorian furniture, knickknacks, pictures in ornate frames, standing lamps. In one corner she had a Victrola. Whelan pointed to it.

"Is that walnut? I've never seen a walnut one."

She nodded in approval. "Sit down, Mr. Whelan. Anywhere you like." She ushered him into an overstuffed armchair.

"Would you like a cup of coffee?"

"Sure."

He listened to the rhythmic ticking of her wall clock and the kitchen noises of Mrs. O'Mara trying to forestall the inevitable, and he tried to find another answer to it all. A moment later, she bustled in with a tray holding cups and the paraphernalia of coffee. In the center she'd placed a little plate of butter cookies. She set the tray down on a small inlaid table, handed him a cup and sat down.

"Good coffee," he said. Then he took a quick look around the room. "Your living room reminds me of my grandmother's house. She had big fat chairs like these and a sofa like yours and a Victrola that you cranked up. You have a few nice things she didn't have, but then she had wax fruit. Bowls and bowls of wax fruit."

"I had wax fruit in my home when I was a young woman. It's very pretty, but it melts and gets scratched and discolored."

"Doesn't taste good, either."

She paused in midsip. "You ate your grandmother's wax fruit?"

"Only the grapes. I was four. And a slow learner."

She smiled and made a little befuddled shake of her head. He watched as she set down her cup with a shaking hand, and he was on the verge of making more soothing small talk when he decided to get it over with.

"Mrs. O'Mara, I'm very sorry to tell you that Joseph is dead. He died as the result of a hit-and-run accident on October nineteenth, 1975. I believe he probably died instantly, he suffered no pain."

She made the tiniest of nods and sat stiffly with her cup and saucer poised on her lap, waiting for more. Whelan looked down at his cup.

"He had a wake and a decent funeral, and all the arrangements were taken care of by Michael Minogue, his lifelong friend. A very good friend, it seems to me."

"Oh, Mike was a good friend to him, always. They were the best of friends, ever since they were just babies."

"Joseph was buried in St. Joseph's Cemetery. His grave is well tended. But you knew that—because you take care of it, as you have done for years."

A stricken look flashed in her pale eyes and then she looked quickly away.

I have no stomach for this, he told himself. He took a deep breath and went on.

"You took over the care of your brother's grave from Mike Minogue, I don't exactly know when, but you did. You know when he died and I suspect you know how he died, and you've been watching me jump through hoops for reasons that you probably don't want seen in the light of day."

She shook her head and kept shaking it for several seconds, refusing to meet his eyes.

"Mrs. O'Mara . . ."

She turned her face farther away and he could see that her cheeks were wet, and he decided to get it all out.

"Did you kill Michael Minogue?"

She swung her head abruptly to face him, eyes staring and mouth agape, and for several seconds he thought she'd faint. She had gone pale and he could hear her raspy breathing, and he told himself this was not the time to be solicitous of an old woman's feelings.

"Well?"

"What kind of man are you?" she said in a harsh voice.

"Just answer the question. You've lied to me about everything else. This one, you answer. If I don't like your answer, I'm walking. Not far, just up Belmont to Area Six Police Headquarters. You know, right up there where Riverview used to be."

"*Bejesus,* you're an awful man."

"Consider the kind of people I work for."

She set her cup and saucer down on a table and glared. "I don't know how you expect me to pay you. . . ."

"You haven't given me a dime yet, so don't let the money worry you."

"I have the money, sir. I don't need you to be telling me whether to be worried about money. And money for what, that's what I want to know. You call yourself a detective, running around for days, and all you can come up with is, 'Did I kill Michael Minogue,' as if a daft thing like that even makes sense. Get out of my house, sir."

He nodded. "And that completes the circle, lady. I've been running around talking to your old cronies from the bad old days and they've all given me the gate. Only fitting that you should."

"What cronies? Who did you talk to?" Her face softened, as though she'd momentarily forgotten her righteous anger.

"All of them. I've talked to Ellen Gillette and Herb Gaynor, to Betty Henke, to Gerry Costello, to Fritz Pollard, to the delightful Mr. Chick Landis, even to an old hood named Hoegstra."

She gave him a disoriented look. "I don't know any Hoegstra." She looked down, frowning and shaking her head, and he thought he could see her lips moving.

He started to explain. "Hoegstra was a gambler from—Mrs. O'Mara, I just hit you with a bunch of names from your past, but you still haven't answered my question."

"Oh, for God's *sake,* Mr. Whelan, are you a mooncalf? Do you think I'm the kind of woman who could . . ." She waved her hand helplessly and just said, "Poor Michael Minogue, of all people."

Whelan said nothing for a moment, assessing her performance. He pictured himself in Fritz Pollard's room with its slaughterhouse smell and ravaged walls and could not imagine this old woman there.

"No, I don't. Not really. I'm not certain exactly *what* you are, Mrs.

O'Mara, but I don't think you're a murderer. What I think is that you're a liar—and maybe an actress. A very good one, but that doesn't make it better."

"I wanted someone to be my investigator, I wanted to find the truth. I wanted to know who killed Michael."

"So this was never about your brother."

"Yes, it was, but I knew he was dead. I found Michael Minogue when I came back to Chicago. The people at the Veterans hospital—Hines—gave me an address. Both Michael and Joe had been out at Hines Hospital. Michael told me about poor Joe. He told me how he'd given him a nice funeral and all of that. He was a great friend."

She sighed and looked at Whelan. "I called the police when I read about Michael, Mr. Whelan. But the policeman I talked to just said they had no leads. He talked to me that same way *you* do sometimes, like I'm an old ninny without the sense God gave her. I thought maybe a man like you, an independent man, would be able to find something out."

"So you fed me information and hoped I'd come up with Michael Minogue's killer."

"And Joseph's," she said after a long silence. "Michael told me he thought they were trying to kill him when they ran poor Joe over in the street. What a terrible thing."

"Who, Mrs. O'Mara?"

She shook her head. "It doesn't do any good now. You investigated and you couldn't find a thing. I'm not going to make a fool of myself naming names."

He sighed. "Mrs. O'Mara, it's about Ray Dudek, isn't it?"

She gave him a quick look. "Yes."

"Let me try something out on you. Michael knew who killed Ray Dudek. He was supposed to meet Ray that night at Riverview. And Michael was killed—your brother was killed—because they knew the killer."

She blinked several times and studied him, and he was beginning to see the faintest glimmer of approval in her eyes.

He leaned forward and spoke quietly. "You hoped I'd find the killer, and I think I know the name you hoped I'd come up with. Chick Landis."

Her eyes took on a glittery look, as though she was suppressing something. "He was there. To meet Ray."

"Why?"

"Money. He said Chick owed him money, a lot of money, and he was going to get it. It was over money."

He thought for a moment, then shook his head. "That's what I thought. But it wasn't about money. I'm just not sure what it was about. And it wasn't Landis. It was Casey Pollard, Mrs. O'Mara."

She frowned. "What? Casey Pollard? He was just a boy."

"He was old enough to do this. Maybe not on his own, but I think it was him."

"Why Casey?"

"I don't know why. I was hoping you'd tell me. Casey took Ray's discharge papers from his body. He had them on him when he was found."

"Found?"

"He's dead, too."

"Oh, dear Lord."

"The police found a body down at the lake over the weekend, and I'm pretty sure it will turn out to be Casey. I think he killed Ray Dudek, and now he's dead because someone murdered him. And his brother. And I know Fritz is dead because I found him."

She shuddered and seemed dumbfounded.

"Are you going to be all right?"

"Yes. What a terrible thing. All these men dead . . ."

She let the thought trail off. For a second she tried to busy herself with her cup and then she flashed him a sudden look. "It's him, then, Mr. Whelan. Him that put Casey up to it, and him that killed them."

Whelan was already shaking his head before she finished.

"No, it wasn't Landis. He's a creep, but I can't see him as a killer."

"No, I'm not talking about him. *Herb.* Herb Gaynor. He was there that night."

"I know. He was working the main gate. But why? Why would he?"

"Because of Ellen. Because of *Miss Ellen Gillette.*"

"I don't understand."

"I never liked him, I always felt like he was watching everybody, and he was, when it came to Ellen. Looked like a hawk, he did, with his long nose and his dark eyes. I never trusted him. I never knew what Ellen saw in him, but she didn't have much sense about boys, Miss Ellen Gillette. He was a little older than everybody else, Mr. Whelan, he had pocket money and a car before anybody else did, and she was impressed. But she had eyes for Ray."

"Well, Betty Henke told me Ellen once had a crush on Ray . . . before her relationship with Herb Gaynor."

"Ah, that's just like Betty, always looking for the good in people. Ellen had a crush on Ray Dudek before, during and after. But . . . but he never really took her seriously."

"How do you know?"

Mrs. O'Mara fixed him with a proud look. "He wanted me, Mr. Whelan." Embarrassed now, she looked away. "She looked like a movie star—you should have seen her—and she had such lovely clothes. Men used to stop and watch her walk by. You didn't see her then, and you can't tell from that old picture—something happens in pictures, you can't see what's really there. She was a beautiful girl, but he didn't want her." She paused for a second. "He wanted me."

"And you were there to meet him that night. To tell him you couldn't see him anymore."

She looked embarrassed. "Who knows what I would have told him? But that's what I planned. And then he was dead."

He thought over what she'd revealed and sank back into the chair. He wrestled with all of it, the limping killer, the dark figure in the overcoat outside his office, and the story about the girl singer caught in the rain with the courtly bandleader. He put it together with something that had bothered him from the beginning and knew he had one final stop to make.

He set down his cup and got up from the big chair. "I'm going to finish this, and I'll give what I have to the police. When I'm done, I'll call you."

"Yes, please. And don't worry about your money."

"I never do. I never worry about it at all. A defect in my character."

AS he drove, he was hearing Bauman's voice reciting the list of people seen on the beach the evening of Michael Minogue's murder. "Old man in an overcoat," he could hear Bauman saying, just before he got to the man in the windbreaker and hat.

Old man in an overcoat.

He drove the short distance to the Gaynor house and pulled up across the street. At first there was no sign that anyone was home, but a light was on in the back of the house and another in the living room. For several minutes he sat in his car and listened to music, trying to decide how to handle this final conversation. He thought about giving it all to Bauman and reading about it in the papers, but he had his own questions to be answered, and he thought he had a right to the answers.

When he noticed the furtive movement of a drape, he knew it was time to finish this.

Ellen Gillette Gaynor opened the door for him as he'd expected. She smiled, but there was a tension in her eyes. She leaned halfway out through the opened door as though greeting a salesman.

"Mr. Whelan. You've got more questions for us?"

"A few. May I come in?"

"Oh, of course. But my husband is lying down. Do you need me to get him up?"

"No, ma'am. I can just ask you, and then I'll be going."

She relaxed a little and moved back to open the door for him, then led him into the living room.

Whelan sat down, declined her offer of a cup of coffee and waited as she lowered herself into a chair. She shifted her weight awkwardly, trying to find a comfortable position, and then leaned expectantly toward him.

"Is the gun here?"

She wet her lips and went wide-eyed, an aging Kewpie doll.

"The gun? You mean Herb's gun? Well, I hope so, unless somebody got hold—"

"Nobody got hold of it, Mrs. Gaynor. Heavy weapon, though, for someone your size."

"You're talking crazy, Mr. Whelan. My lord, what are you saying?"

"Maybe I'm wrong. Maybe that man lying down in there is a killer."

"My husband is no killer, Mr. Whelan. He's got his faults but he's no killer, unless somebody threatens his family. Then you better watch out."

"That's exactly how I've come to think about you, Mrs. Gaynor. I think if somebody threatens your family, they'd better watch out. What I'm not sure about is why these old men had to be killed—Michael Minogue and Joe Colleran, after all this time. They seem to have been just a couple of simple guys, harmless people. A couple of old guys in rented rooms—why would anybody kill them?"

"Why ask me? It was terrible, but . . . Anyhow, Joe was killed in an accident. I think we talked about that. I'm almost sure we did. Car accident."

"Nope. No accident. Somebody ran him down in the street. It could have been a drunk, a panicky stranger, but I doubt it. I don't know if that was you, but I know you're responsible for the death of Ray Dudek and I know why."

"This is just craziness!" She held up both palms in a helpless gesture."

"You were having his child."

She blinked and made a sudden sharp intake of breath and her mouth stretched wide in a rictus of shock. She began shaking her head, and he leaned forward.

"He went into the service late, after the older guys, and after Herb: I think you started seeing him then. When he came back from the service, you started seeing each other again—but it didn't last long. Herb was back and working, and you were supposed to be his, but you were having Ray Dudek's child and Ray wasn't . . . he didn't feel the same way you did. He was breaking things off with you. I know he was."

She smiled and shut her eyes and shook her head like an elderly teacher with a slow pupil, and he started over.

"He just wasn't interested. He was interested in other women, Maggie O'Mara, for one, and from what I hear, probably the next girl to come around the corner. Maybe he was interested in half a dozen other girls, who knows? But he was through with you and he made it clear. And there you were with a jealous boyfriend or fiancé or whatever Herb was, and another man's baby. But most importantly, you wanted Ray Dudek and he didn't care. So you killed him."

She stared at him and gripped the arms of her chair till her knuckles went white, but she held on to that smile for dear life.

"Mr. Whelan, I was with the other girls, with Maggie and Betty, when they found Ray. I was never out of their company all night. That terrible night."

Whelan nodded. "I guess not. So you had Casey Pollard do it. He made it look like a robbery, and he also lifted Ray's discharge papers—probably so he could pass for an older guy. The discharge papers were all he had on him when the cops found his body. But I think you hired Casey to do it and that's probably where your troubles began."

She looked away finally, toward the hall, and her eyes seemed to focus on some invisible scene. When she faced him again, she had composed her features once more.

"Mr. Whelan, I think you had better leave. I don't have to listen to this *filth* in my own home, with my husband on his sickbed. . . ."

"I have more. You married Herb Gaynor and had Ray Dudek's baby, and he grew into a fine son who is the most important thing in your life." Whelan shook his head. "That face, Mrs. Gaynor. I noticed that face the first time I saw him, I just couldn't put the two together. But put your son with that fair hair and pug nose next to a picture of Ray Dudek and I think anybody could see the resemblance."

Mrs. Gaynor stared at him, her large eyes suddenly looking very confused, very puzzled. A stiffness seemed to take over her body and he could almost see her caving in.

"What I wonder about is how Herb never saw it."

She shrugged. "You don't notice what you don't want to see. If your wife or girlfriend had a baby, would you be watching to see if the baby looked like one of your friends? Herb never saw anything except what he wanted to see and what I told him. I told him our son had his mouth and his eyes, and that was enough for Herb."

"Will you tell me why these other men had to be killed?" When she refused to answer, he added, "I know you hated them."

She looked away again and when she spoke, her voice was a tired voice, strangely younger-sounding.

"They knew. They all knew. I could see it in their eyes, especially Michael Minogue. He hated *me*—always had, you know. Thought I was stuck-up. He never said anything, he didn't have to. I knew what he thought, and I wanted to kill him. I knew he'd cause me trouble someday." She looked sullenly around her crowded living room, and Whelan followed her gaze till it fell on the picture of her son. A cherished son to protect from the truth.

"Why now?"

"I didn't know. I had lost track of Michael Minogue. He came back and I—someone told me about him."

"Casey Pollard." She looked away.

Whelan thought for a moment. "You had something going with both of them, Ray and Casey, while Herb was in the service."

She grimaced. "Oh, don't be ridiculous. Casey was a boy. You saw that picture, he was a little boy at the time. During the war, he was just a teenager. He was too young to get into the war. I had no interest in him whatsoever."

"But he was pretty interested in you. Now if I have this figured right, you were seeing Ray whenever he came in from Great Lakes and then you found out you were pregnant. You went to Ray, he wasn't interested."

She was silent for a moment. "He didn't believe me."

"So you had Casey kill him for you that night."

"I didn't do a thing."

"Maybe not, but you had it done. You convinced Casey to kill him for you."

Mrs. Gaynor stared at him for a moment and Whelan could see her collecting herself, changing gears. Changing directions. "I didn't convince him of anything. He would have done anything for me. He would have jumped off a building for me. Besides, he hated Ray, he was terribly jealous of Ray."

"And you always kept in touch with Casey, all these years?"

She stared at him with pure distaste. "Casey was *trash*. He followed me home, I think he followed me home a number of times. He wanted money, he always wanted money, all his life. And then he told me about Minogue. He told me he'd seen Minogue. I had thought . . . I'd heard he was gone again. And I don't know anything about what Casey did after that."

"Oh, I think you do. He followed Minogue for you and you took it from there. You had already tried to kill Minogue once before, the night you ran Joe Colleran down."

"You're being ridiculous."

"That's what Michael Minogue told people—that he thought someone was trying to kill him. I think that was you, Mrs. Gaynor. Maybe it was just an impulse, I don't know. Maybe you would have gotten it right the next time, but I guess Minogue knew it was time to lie low."

She looked across her living room as though she heard nothing.

"And I know Casey didn't kill Minogue. Someone using a forty-five automatic did that. The same person killed Casey, probably because he couldn't possibly be trusted with all of this. And probably for the same reason, that same person went to Fritz Pollard's place and blew holes in the wall and in Fritz and left him lying in his own blood on the floor."

She shuddered slightly but refused to look at him. Whelan leaned forward and spoke in a harsh whisper.

"It smelled like a slaughterhouse, Mrs. Gaynor. You're a dog-shit shot. Hard to handle a gun with that much of a kick, isn't it? There was blood everywhere on the floor, I stepped in it, I slipped in it. You probably got it on yourself, and you left part of a bloody handprint on the wall, a very small handprint. There was probably blood on your clothes. It would still be on your clothes, maybe on your shoes, at least in traces. I think he died looking at you. He tried to get up out of bed and you popped him another one and then he tried to get up off the floor, before you finally got it right.

"You did all that, Mrs. Gaynor. You planned it; you set it up. Before that, you followed Michael Minogue for weeks, watching for an opportunity to kill him. You were seen. He saw you himself."

"That's absolutely crazy. No one saw me anywhere. Good Lord, this is crazy."

"A number of people saw you. They saw you following Michael Minogue, they saw you following me, Mrs. Gaynor. It was you that watched my office—someone saw you in a doorway, wearing your husband's hat and coat. The walk had me fooled—I knew about Casey Pollard's limp and his size, so I thought it was Casey everybody was seeing. And it was you, in men's clothing. You have a limp, too, from your arthritis. The clothes faked me out. I didn't put it together till one night I heard a 1940s singer talking about her bandleader throwing his overcoat over her in the rain. She talked about walking around in a strange town wearing a man's overcoat that made her feel like a kid playing dress-up." Whelan sat back in the chair and watched her, then dropped the last of it on her.

"And you were seen that night. You waited for the right moment, maybe just after sunset, and you walked out there and shot Michael Minogue at point-blank range. And you were seen. People will be able to identify you from your little costume."

"You should leave, Mr. Whelan."

"I'm going to. Just tell me—I just want to know who else you were going to kill."

She stared at him and a look of satisfaction came into her eyes. A slight curl took hold of her lip and she pointed one elegant finger at him.

"You." The finger wavered slightly and her voice came in a harsh rasp. "You."

He looked into her chilling eyes and nodded. "Well, sorry to disappoint you. But we'll see each other again, I'm sure." He got up to leave and she shot a quick look at the hall again.

"Forget it, Mrs. Gaynor. By the time you made it to the hall closet with that bad hip, I'd be long gone. Besides, how many rounds do you think you have left? Ever put a fresh clip in it?"

She blinked and looked confused, and he shrugged.

"A clip, Mrs. Gaynor, is the little metal container with all the bullets. The gun doesn't keep firing unless you feed it."

Whelan turned and walked to the door, listening for any sudden movement behind him. He had his hand reaching for the doorknob when it opened and revealed Dan Gaynor. He gave Whelan a slight frown, looked past him to his mother, and was about to ask something when she screamed.

"He's crazy! Don't let him out, call the police!"

The young Gaynor looked from Whelan to his mother and then threw his weight into Whelan, clutching Whelan's jacket and moving forward into the hall. Whelan could feel Gaynor's nails digging in through the material of his jacket, and he went slamming backward into a wall with the other man's full weight pressing into him. When he felt the other man move slightly, he sidestepped, grabbed Gaynor by the lapels of his coat, and threw him shoulder-first into the wall. When Gaynor bounced back and came at him, Whelan put a shoulder into him and threw one quick jab, catching Gaynor in the mouth. The younger man went down heavily onto his hip. He was feeling his lip as he climbed to his feet, and Whelan backed toward the door.

In the background Mrs. Gaynor wailed and screamed for help, and now Whelan could hear Herb Gaynor shouting in his hoarse voice from the distant bedroom, and over them both, their son began to yell.

"*Ma,* what the hell's going *on?* Ma, you all right?" He pointed at Whelan. "You son of a bitch, you stay there," he shouted. "Ma?"

"He's crazy," Mrs. Gaynor wailed, and she made for the hall closet. "He's trying to kill us all!"

Dan Gaynor looked away for a moment and then threw a sucker punch as he came at Whelan once more. The punch caught Whelan on the cheekbone but he was turning his head so it did little damage. He threw one of his own, felt his knuckles on bone, and then threw a combination as he moved to his left. Both punches landed, but Gaynor was still swinging. A right missed Whelan's head and a left caught him just under the eye. He thought he could feel the other man's ring dig into his skin. Whelan grabbed him by the hair and butted his head into the wall. They grappled and Gaynor tried to get his fingers into Whelan's face. In the background he could hear Herb Gaynor cursing and coughing, and Mrs. Gaynor sobbing, and he could hear her coming closer, almost to the closet.

And then she had the gun.

Whelan held up his hand and yelled, "Don't do it!" just as the small window in the door exploded and sprayed shards into the back of his head. He backed away and she pulled the trigger again and the explosion seemed to be next to his ear. Gaynor gave up his grip on Whelan and screamed, "Ma!" and Whelan moved to the door.

Eight feet away, Ellen Gaynor held the automatic with both unsteady hands and turned her head slightly away as she squeezed the trigger. The hammer fell on an empty chamber. She squeezed again and nothing happened.

Conscious of Gaynor's labored breathing and his own gasping for air, Whelan moved backward till he could feel the doorjamb.

"I told you, Mrs. Gaynor," he said, panting. "Gotta feed the sucker or it won't work." He looked at her son. "You call the cops like your ma said. I'll wait in my car."

Three units showed up, all uniforms, then a Tac Unit car. Whelan was leaning on his car with his license in hand, and when the officers approached, he just told them he thought Bauman should be notified as soon as possible.

A hard-looking cop with WITOWSKI on his nameplate took him over to a squad car and told him to climb in back. Whelan had to take a second look at him: pale blond hair and high cheekbones and a fighter's flat, swollen nose. He looked enough like Ray Dudek to be a blood relative. Whelan slid across the backseat of the squad car and that was where he was when Bauman and Landini rolled up the wrong end of the one-way street.

Bauman came out hitching up his pants, green pants with a mustard-colored shirt and a sport coat that was a nightmare of orange and beige and colors yet to be named. A moment later Landini came up beside him, tugging at the sleeve of a formfitting cashmere sweater. Landini's face looked a little pale, and he seemed to be squinting as though he'd just been exposed to bright lights. They spoke to a pair of the cops on the front lawn of the Gaynor house and Whelan winced when both detectives took a long slow look in his direction. He could almost hear Landini snort. After a brief conversation, Landini went inside and Bauman strolled up to the squad car with the air of a man who has nothing but time. At the car, he paused for a moment, hands on his hips, and stared at Whelan. Then he leaned in through the window and his heavy red face seemed to fill the entire front seat.

"The notorious Paul Whelan, the scourge of the North Side, brought to justice at last."

"Ha-ha."

"Whaddya call this shit, Whelan?"

"It's not as bad as it looks."

"That would be hard." Bauman glared for a moment and then seemed to relax. "And you got boo-boos, too. Lookit your face—you wake up tomorrow, you're gonna look like ground chuck." Bauman waved a thick admonishing finger at him. "See? What did I tell you? You nose around in my business and bad things happen to you. Now look at yourself. You're in the shitter, Whelan."

"Talk to your troops. Get me the hell out of here. I have things to tell you."

"Oh, *now* you got things to tell me. How 'bout our deal, you know, where you gimme what you got and I don't have to wait till it's in the paper before I find out about it?"

"I didn't have anything to give you that made sense until—I had to check some things out. Then I put it together. That was less than an hour ago. I wanted to ask some questions for myself."

"Look how it all turned out. See that guy over there, the rook?" Bauman half-turned and nodded in the direction of a shiny-faced young cop who was watching the traffic go by.

"He thinks this was a home invasion. You broke into this nice old couple's house, Whelan?" Bauman's eyes glittered with suppressed mirth. He tried to give Whelan his best badass stare and then had to look away.

"Have a nice time, Bauman. The 'nice old lady' in there killed at least three people. When I go to sleep tonight, I'm going to dream about her face, and in my dream she'll be emptying an automatic in my direction."

"Yeah, Witowski told me. If this wasn't so weird, I'd be pissed off about this. But we got all kinda stories here, Whelan, gonna be hard to sort 'em all out. The son thinks you were shaking down his folks. The old lady says you're some kinda madman, she was just defending herself. The old man don't say shit."

"But when you get the nice old lady's gun back from Ballistics, as I know you will, you'll find out all kinds of interesting things about it."

"Yeah, well, I don't need you to tell me what I'm gonna find out. If you were so smart, you wouldn't be sittin' here beatin' your meat in the backseat of Witowski's car."

Whelan turned away in irritation. In the doorway of the Gaynor house, he could see Landini in conversation with someone he couldn't quite make out.

"I think I need to file charges."

Bauman nodded and said, "First we talk, Shamus, and I need the whole thing. Then we can do other kindsa business." He squinted into the distance past Whelan and Whelan turned to see what he was looking at. Another squad car made the turn on the street, this one driven by a sergeant.

"Oh shit," Whelan said.

Bauman grinned again. "It's your great personal friend Sgt. Michaeleen Shea."

Whelan slunk down in the backseat and leaned his head against the panel of the door.

"You know what he's gonna say, Whelan? He's gonna say you're a menace to the entire community. What was that he called you? A catalyst? Some kinda catalyst."

"Commotion," Whelan muttered. "A catalyst for commotion."

Sixteen

BY the time he'd given everything to Bauman and the cops were through with him at Area Six, the sun had made its exit. He stopped at the Vienna stand on Clybourn and had a couple of hot dogs. He was less than three blocks from Mrs. O'Mara's house but he couldn't bring himself to see anybody else.

It was dark when he got home. He picked up the mail on the way in, a bill, a couple pieces of junk mail, and what appeared to be a check from G. Kenneth Laflin. He tore open the envelope and examined the check. It was for less than half of what Laflin owed him. Attached was a Day-Glo orange self-stick note that told Whelan someone had misplaced some of his expense receipts. The remainder of Whelan's fee would be "forth-coming."

"Forthcoming. A prison sentence is forthcoming. Your death is forth-coming, Laflin."

He pushed open his door and stopped to admire his face in the hall mirror. Bauman was right: by morning, his face would look like fresh sausage. Where Gaynor's ring had caught him, the skin was a mass of bruise and abrasion, with a darker red oval in the center, like the Great Red Spot on Jupiter. The other eye was swelling along the side, and a faint bluish tinge to the skin showed where he'd have purple tomorrow.

He took four or five steps in and stopped completely. He couldn't have said exactly how he knew, but there was someone in his house—in the back of the house. He took a step back. In the hall closet behind him, he had a bat, an ax, and a snow shovel. Moving quietly he back-tracked to the closet and grabbed the bat. Then he went forward. It oc-curred to him that the simplest thing would be to get the hell out of the house and make the call, but it was his house. And he didn't think he could face another blue uniform again.

Heart pounding, he got a sweaty grip on the bat and moved toward the back. He was midway through the dining room when a new idea struck him and his heart began to do a little dance. By the time he reached the closed door to his bedroom, it was obvious—he could sense it, he could feel it.

He could smell her perfume.

Whelan placed the bat on his mother's great oak dining room table, then took hold of the doorknob and threw the door open with a bang.

Sandra McAuliffe gave a startled yell, put both hands to her mouth and jumped up from the edge of the bed, where she'd been sitting waiting for him. She blinked and gave him the startled green-eyed stare that made her look ten years younger.

"Jesus, Paul, you scared the hell out of me!"

"We're even. Come here." The room seemed to be full of her perfume. He kissed her and then grabbed her, and they held each other close in silence for more than a minute, and then she leaned back to look at his face.

"Oh, *look* at you. What happened to your face? Honest to God, Paul . . ."

"I had a complicated case."

"A complicated case. I'm gone ten days and I come back to Paul Whelan looking like . . ."

"Ground chuck is what I've been told. Anyhow, it's a long, unpleasant story."

"Are you all right?"

"Sure." He looked at her and realized that he was grinning. "Right now, I'm fine. But we have to talk."

"Uh-huh," she said, and a wary look came into her eyes. She sat back down on the bed and Whelan settled in beside her and took her hand.

"It's about your note."

"I . . . I thought so." She wet her lips and composed herself, and he could almost hear her telling herself it might be time to tough things out. She looked forty again, forty and a little bit tired.

He took her hand. "I'm not exactly sure where to start."

She looked at him calmly and said, "Start with the first thing that comes to mind."

"The first thing that comes to mind is that I missed everything about you that I could think of. Everything. And as soon as you were gone. I missed you as soon as you were gone. I missed you before the plane left."

She blinked and looked away for a moment, then looked back at him with a shy smile. "This is a very good start."

She leaned forward to kiss him and he held up one hand.

"Did you ever meet Michael Caine?"

"Think I'd be back if I did?"

"Exactly what I thought."

IN the morning, Whelan phoned Mrs. O'Mara and arranged to meet her at her shop. The CLOSED sign was still in the window, but she was there, her back to the door, dusting and arranging a table full of porcelain figures and china. Whelan pushed open the door, and she gave him a little look over her shoulder and said she'd be right with him.

She served him instant coffee. Hills Brothers instant, Whelan thought, and weak—light brown, like rainwater in a barrel, but at least it was hot. Outside, a low gray bank of clouds had darkened the day. The wind had picked up and there was just the faintest wet hint that snow would be coming soon. He sipped his coffee and waited as she bustled around the little shop, and when she was finally sitting nervously across from him, he told her everything he knew. She listened without interruption.

When Whelan finished, Mrs. O'Mara set her cup and saucer down on the little oak side table and gazed at him.

"Will she go to prison?"

"Who knows? My hunch is that she'll spend the rest of her time in a mental hospital. She's crazy, Mrs. O'Mara. It sounds like she's been crazy all her life. I'm no doctor, but I think a sharp lawyer could make a case for her being out of her mind."

"She was never happy when we were young. She was a moody girl. She was never satisfied, she would go on and on about how she'd be living someday in a fine house, she'd marry a man with money. The boys in the neighborhood weren't good enough, you know. She'd be moving out and leaving it all behind. That's why we were all amazed when she settled on Herb Gaynor. She broke off with him more than once, carried on with a lot of other boys while Herb was in the navy, and then she ups and marries him after the war. And now after all these years, I understand why." After a moment's silence she added, "If I was a good Christian woman, I'd feel sorry for her."

She shrugged and gave Whelan a helpless look. "We were just like anybody else. I try not to think about the old days, Mr. Whelan, because it hurts me and because it puzzles me. I don't understand. We were just like anybody else, a bunch of boys and girls like anybody else. We got older—we went to dances at the Aragon and over at Johnny Weigeldt's, we went to the ball games and to the show. Like anybody else. But maybe we weren't."

"Most of you were. One of you was a psychopath. And from what I've been told, the Pollards would have been trouble anywhere."

"They came from a bad home, those boys. The mother died young. I always felt sorry for them. Their father was like a madman when he had the drink in him."

Whelan tried to think of something to say that would end the conversation painlessly. He set down his cup and was about to say he had to run when Mrs. O'Mara spoke again.

"Nothing ever turned out quite the way I expected. After the war, that is. Nothing turned out like I thought it would."

"I know you lost someone in the war. Your life might have been different."

She surprised him by smiling. "Was I that obvious? Like a giddy schoolgirl?"

"There's not much about you that's giddy."

She looked at her hands. "Tommy was a wonderful boy. A popular boy, too. All the girls liked Tommy Friesl, all of them." Mrs. O'Mara flashed him a quick look: he could have had his pick of them, she was saying. "We were going to be married when he came home, but like a lot of boys, he didn't come home. It was four or five years before I could even take another man seriously, and I had my share calling on me. I've never forgotten him, or the way it felt to be in love for the very first time. But that was a long time ago. A long time ago."

"Betty Henke asked about you. She wants to know that you're all right."

"That's Betty. I am all right. John O'Mara was a good man, I was lucky. And now I'm a businesswoman." She seemed to shake off her facial expression along with her mood, and her checkbook appeared in her lap without Whelan actually seeing her take it out.

"I asked Mr. Hill, that nice man, about your fees, Mr. Whelan."

"Why did you do that?"

"Because I didn't think you would tell me. You weren't taking me seriously, you aren't taking me completely seriously now."

"Oh, sure I am. I—"

"Nonsense. You think I'm a batty old Irishwoman at the mercy of the cold hard world. You think I live on canned soup and go through the garbage cans in the alley for my clothes."

"I do not."

"Mr. Hill said your fees are high but fair, considering the quality of your work."

"Hill said *I'm* high?"

"He did. Two hundred fifty dollars a day, he said."

"Uh, that's right."

"Well, that's high, isn't it? But then you don't work regularly, do you?"

"Not in the sense that . . . Not every week. I can go for a while without a case."

"Well then, that explains why you're so high, doesn't it?"

"Uh, I'm about in the middle, when you compare me with other detectives and agencies."

"I wouldn't know anything about that, Mr. Whelan. Now, about your expenses . . ."

"I don't have any."

She gave him a squint to see if he was mocking her.

"I don't," he repeated.

"How many days did you actually investigate? We spoke first on Wednesday."

"Right. So four days, Mrs. O'Mara."

She cocked an eyebrow. "You did no work on Saturday or Sunday?"

He shrugged. Nothing special, he thought: I spent two days unraveling your lies and figuring out who killed your brother, I wasted favors with Bauman, I found a dead man in a slaughterhouse, I fought off the Hound of Hell, I got the shit kicked out of me by a guy while his mother blasted away at me with a Navy .45. I had a very nice time.

"It was just a weekend, Mrs. O'Mara. I don't do much on the weekends."

"You must have done something, Mr. Whelan. You're not much of a businessman, are you?"

"No, ma'am."

She sighed and then wrote out a check with the rapid, assured movements of one who does it a great deal. She tore the check out of the book and handed it to him.

"You ought to find yourself a nice girl."

"I think I have one. And she's Irish."

Mrs. O'Mara nodded slowly. "Well, isn't *that* nice."

Whelan looked at the check. There was an extra day's fee in the total. "You're no accountant, Mrs. O'Mara."

"O'Mara was the accountant, Mr. Whelan, not me. I guess I owe you for not being entirely truthful with you. I just didn't think anyone would pay attention to me."

"Maybe you're right." He got up to leave. It took her a moment to move the cups and saucers out of the way, and he busied himself by looking around the shop. In one corner was a tiny rolltop desk that looked as though it had been made for a child. Whelan looked up and found her watching him.

"A sea captain's desk, Mr. Whelan. It's small because they had no room on board ship."

"It's wonderful. I'll have to come by with my friend. She loves old things."

He noticed a small figure on a shelf of ceramics. It was a toy soldier, a knight with a lance, once brightly painted but now battered and tormented by a child's play and the world's rough handling. It was priced twenty dollars. Whelan picked it up.

"I know an old cop who collects toy knights."

"Ah, you can take that little man. My gift."

"That's very nice of you, Mrs. O'Mara."

She bustled behind her tiny counter and came out with tissue paper and a small bag. When she'd wrapped the little knight, she handed it to him and they walked to the door. As he pulled it open, his gaze fell on a pressed wood chair very much like one that Sandra McAuliffe had in her living room. It was seventy-five dollars.

"Would you take sixty for the chair?"

"Sure. But then I'd have to charge you twenty for the little knight." She smiled and she had a new look in her eye, the one that said he was no match for her.

"I'll be back."

"I'll look forward to it, Mr. Whelan. Thank you for everything."

He waved and stepped out onto Belmont. The sky was no lighter, the air no warmer. And he was hungry. But he had money in his pocket and his girl had come back, and it wasn't turning out to be such a bad day.

He decided to take the long way home, up Western. His route took him past the modern police headquarters of Area Six, past the twin shopping malls, all of it built atop the bones and dead earth of Riverview Park. All that remained from that time were the cottonwoods that still lined the river, but Whelan could smell the smoke and oil of the old park and hear the thrilled screaming of the people on the roller coasters. And he had no trouble seeing the ghosts of a time when ten thousand people a night roamed the Midway and lined up for the rides at a nickel apiece and, for the briefest moment in time, convinced themselves that there was no Depression, no war, no tomorrow.